The Lucky Catch

The Cricket Club
Book 4

Margaux Thorne

ARE YOU SIGNED UP FOR DRAGONBLADE'S BLOG?

You'll get the latest news and information on exclusive giveaways, exclusive excerpts, coming releases, sales, free books, cover reveals and more.

Check out our complete list of authors, too!

No spam, no junk. That's a promise!

Sign Up Here

www.dragonbladepublishing.com

Dearest Reader;

Thank you for your support of a small press. At Dragonblade Publishing, we strive to bring you the highest quality Historical Romance from some of the best authors in the business. Without your support, there is no 'us', so we sincerely hope you adore these stories and find some new favorite authors along the way.

Happy Reading!

CEO, Dragonblade Publishing

Chapter One

Manchester, England, July 1849

BLOOD. SO MUCH blood.

Lady Maggie swayed on her feet, a flash of heat spiking up her neck. She zeroed in on the pathetic, damaged creature as he hung limp and beaten in Samuel Everett's fierce hold.

"Don't look, Maggie," her aunt ordered her sharply, waving a wide fan furiously at her pale neck. "This brutish behavior is not fit for a young woman's eyes… not even yours."

Too entranced by the dramatic scene that had just played out, Maggie let the barb slide. She couldn't respond anyway. Her throat felt dry and permanently locked as she followed the dastardly man—Vine, she'd heard somebody scream—gain consciousness and struggle in her cricket coach's arms.

Samuel, who was never one to temper his colorful words even in the presence of ladies, launched a tirade of curses and dragged Vine out of the chapel, with the remainder of the wedding guests following close behind.

Maggie began to follow, but Aunt Alice stopped her, placing a strict hand on her arm, forcing her to stay in her pew.

"Oh, no you don't. Stay and catch your breath," Alice barked. "Your parents asked me to watch over you and that's exactly what I'm going to do. What will they think when they hear that you've been at the scene of murder… at a wedding ceremony, no less?"

Maggie spun to the altar. Her friend, Ruthie Waitrose, stood strong with her husband, Mr. Harry Holmes, leaning heavily against her side. Ruthie was remarkably composed despite the gory situation. Hers and Harry's heads were together as they whispered back and forth. Blood stained Harry's jacket, though he appeared in much better shape than Vine. As the couple limped down the aisle toward the exit, Maggie's great sigh of relief bounced off the stone ceiling.

Ruthie met her eyes as she passed and nodded to Maggie, seemingly telling her she was fine. Or as fine as someone could be after having their husband shot at and almost killed during their wedding vows.

Maggie turned to her friend. "This wasn't the scene of a murder," she replied off-hand. "No one died."

Alice *humphed*. "Well, no one yet. Things don't look good for the assassin. Did you see the look on Mr. Everett's face when he knocked the gun out of that horrible man's hand?" The billowing wind from her fan caused Maggie to shiver. "I don't think I've ever seen him that angry before."

Maggie stifled a smirk. Clearly, Alice did not play for their cricket club. Samuel, the club's coach, was usually *that* angry whenever Maggie dropped a ball in the field.

She scanned the chapel. Poor Ruthie. It wasn't the wedding Maggie had wished for her friend. Granted, Ruthie had already married Harry weeks before, but he'd planned to give her another, more special memory. Last week, after the London Ladies Cricket Club had played in their exhibition game against the local team in Bath, Harry had gathered his wife's teammates and invited them to the ceremony, saying that he'd wanted it to be a surprise. Rather bashfully, he'd explained that the first time they exchanged vows hadn't been terribly romantic. He'd hoped to rectify the situation and give Ruthie the wedding she deserved.

Maggie wondered if Harry would try again. Or maybe he'd just cut his losses. It was true, having a man try to shoot you dead in the middle of the ceremony wasn't the stuff of dreams;

however, it *was* memorable. Frankly, it would be hard to top.

Footsteps faded into the cobblestone floor as the final guests left. "We should go," Maggie said absent-mindedly, realizing that everyone had exited their pews. For some reason, she didn't want to be the last person in the chapel; something felt oddly morbid about it.

"Not yet," Alice insisted. She flipped her wrist, directing the fan on Maggie's face. "You look entirely too pale, my dear. You've had a fright. We've *all* had a fright... but you look positively dreadful."

Maggie frowned, batting the fan away from her nose. "I'm perfectly fine."

"I doubt that."

"Well, I am."

"No, you're not. You look—"

Maggie snapped, "Stop telling me I look dreadful."

Alice's lips thinned, smoothing out the wrinkles gathering around her nose. She was a handsome woman with bright-green eyes and alabaster skin she tirelessly worked to keep the sun from reaching. Her fan stalled. "Fine," she replied stiffly. "If you insist." She led the way into the aisle, her high forehead pinching. "Do you think they'll still host a wedding dinner for all of us? I am awfully hungry."

Maggie shook her head. The next time she saw her parents, she would give them a piece of her mind. Why on earth they thought that Aunt Alice would be a respectable chaperone was beyond her. The woman was absurdly out of touch, but since she'd been the daughter of an earl, most just considered her eccentric.

"How can you be hungry?" Maggie exclaimed. "You were just present at the scene of a murder, remember?"

Alice raised a regal eyebrow, shrugging a dainty shoulder with the elegance of decades of good breeding. "You're the one who said no one was murdered. I'm sure a real murder would have taken my hunger away, but an attempted one only seems to have enhanced it." She placed a hand over her cinched abdomen. "There's something so visceral about almost seeing one's life taken, don't you think? It's quite thrilling. I feel so alive, like I could climb the highest mountain or eat an entire lamb."

Maggie massaged her temple with her fingers, trying to remember how long her parents said they would be gone this time. Was it eight weeks or twelve? She should have paid more attention, but her parents were always running off to some foreign place with their friends, seeking adventures all over the Continent. Maggie had forced herself to stop caring years ago, but that was when she used to stay with her grandmother, the dowager countess, when she was still alive. Those days had been filled with excitement and learning, a veritable feast of education and animation. She hadn't had time to miss her parents or ponder why they had so little time and energy for their children.

Now that Maggie was stuck with her aunt, the abandonment of her parents stung even deeper.

People had whispered at the time that the dowager countess hadn't been a good influence on the young lady. The old woman had let Maggie run wild, applauding and encouraging her tomboy ways. But Maggie had never felt wild with her grandmother, only free. And for some mysterious reason, people couldn't fathom the difference.

Maggie closed her eyes while her aunt's rambling words continued to dance in her periphery.

"I do hope they have eels. Yes, eels sound wonderful right now." Alice smacked her lips. "And roasted capon… and sour plums! And I hope they have more than one pudding. I'm craving something and I don't know what. I need options. What do you think?"

Maggie ignored the nonsense spouting from her aunt's mouth.

"Maggie? I asked you a question. Honestly, dear, I considered that you were hard of hearing, but now I believe that you *choose* not to answer me."

Maggie sank her fingers into her forehead even further, coaxing away an incoming headache. "Um... I don't know. I'm sure whatever they serve will be good."

Aunt Alice sniffed. "*Good* is hardly good enough for a wedding dinner."

"I'm sure it will be better than good, then. You don't have to worry—Oof!"

Her eyes still closed, Maggie failed to notice the reticule in the aisle, no doubt forgotten by one of her teammates in the drama. She tripped forward, throwing her arms out to latch on to her aunt's shoulders. But Alice dodged at the last moment, leaving Maggie's hands clutching air. Her body tensed as she readied to smack face-first into the cobblestone... and then two arms swept into her sight, catching her waist at the last second.

Maggie blinked, releasing a grateful exhale before straightening her spine. "Thank you so—" The words stalled in her mouth.

Lord Michael. In the flesh, with a lazy smile on his handsome—and so very annoying—face.

Alice finished Maggie's sentence for her, crowding into the viscount's side. Her eyelashes batted like a hummingbird's wings. "Much," she said sweetly, forgetting or maybe just choosing not to remember that she was old enough to be the man's mother. "Thank you so much for saving my niece. You're our hero! Lord knows what would have happened if Maggie had fallen. Her face! Oh dear, could you imagine her face!"

"I would have been fine," Maggie grumbled, straightening her skirts a little aggressively.

"Oh no," Alice went on. "You might have got a cut on your cheeks, or maybe even a black eye." She tutted. "Then you wouldn't have been able to come to dinner. No one wants to stare at a Cyclops when they eat, my dear."

Lord Michael chuckled, dragging Maggie's gaze back to his face despite her best efforts. Speaking of black eyes... he was sporting one, though it appeared old and faded, almost healed. Naturally, it made him seem more dashing.

Shame at her weakness swarmed inside Maggie's chest. Lord Michael was so used to fawning and attention that she hated giving him any ounce of it.

"It was my pleasure," he stated, his words sliding through the air like a knife through warm butter. Maggie's chagrin deepened because she couldn't help but notice the fullness of his mouth, the strong cleft in his chin, the way his wide shoulders broadened at the easy praise from her aunt. Everything was always so easy for Viscount Burlington, the Earl of Waverly's only son.

"And you're quite right, madam," Michael said, bowing lightly to Alice. "Cyclopses don't make the best dinner guests."

Maggie's eyes narrowed. "Because they might turn your stomach? I had no idea you had such a weak constitution, my lord."

Michael chuckled, cocking his head. His thick, dark hair didn't move once, staying perfectly in place, swept off his forehead. "Hardly," he replied as if Maggie was a child who'd given the wrong answer. "Because everyone knows when you have dinner with a Cyclops, *you* are the dinner."

Alice burst into giggles, swatting the center of Michael's chest with her fan. "So true, so true," she fawned, her high cheekbones glowing a dark pink. "I had no idea you were such a wit, my lord. Isn't he a wit, Maggie? Tell him! Tell him!"

Maggie's lips soldered shut as Michael watched her, a teasing tilt to his mouth, waiting, just waiting for her to succumb to her aunt's dictate.

"He's..." Maggie searched her brain for the mildest compliment. "He's truly quite something."

Alice nodded like a crazed chicken. "Yes. Yes, he is. Quite something, indeed."

"Quite something," Michael repeated, trying out the words like foreign food, tentatively and warily. "I've never been called that before. A magnanimous compliment indeed from little Peggy."

Maggie saw red. Instant and scalding. "Don't call me that."

And there. There was the glint in his sparkling blue eyes. The games had begun. Though, Maggie had to admit, she'd known Lord Michael for most of her nineteen years and the games had never really stopped. Like fashion, they just evolved. And just like fashion, never for her benefit.

"Oh, come now," he said, feigning surprise. "We're old friends. Surely intimacy is allowed."

"Of course it is," Alice replied instantly, shooting Maggie with a look of warning. *Behave,* it said.

Michael shrugged. "I've called you that since we were children."

"No," Maggie said. "You called me that *once* when we were children. Peggy Piggy, remember? And then all your friends have called me it ever since."

"Is that true?" Alice asked him, going on without waiting for a response. "Well, that's what friends do, don't they? And I'm sure they don't say it to your face."

Maggie studied Michael, enjoying the wave of uncertainty nipping at his conscience. "No, you're right, Aunt. They stopped saying it to my face years ago. They only say it behind my back now."

"Oh, well that's a relief," Alice said, fanning her face again. "No harm in that."

Michael's countenance turned stony. He was a man clearly not accustomed to having his actions called into question. Maggie made a mental note to do it as much as possible from now on.

"I can't be blamed for the sins of others," he replied stiffly.

"I suppose men never are."

"Quite right. Quite right," Alice said.

"And I'm not the one who told you to play in the mud," Michael added.

Maggie threw her hands up. "I wasn't playing in the mud, and you know that! I *fell* in the mud. Very different."

Michael's lips curled up at the sides.

Maggie had had enough. "What are you doing here?"

The viscount frowned and ducked his head before bending over and snatching something from the ground. He raised a reticule in front of her triumphantly. "Lady… um… Lady"—he snapped his fingers—"Ella. Lady Ella said she'd left her bag and asked that I fetch it for her."

"Like a dog," Maggie quipped.

Alice squeezed further into his side. "Like the most loyal and wonderful dog, she means. Maggie adores dogs. Such a compliment."

Michael squinted wryly. "Yes, I remember Maggie's fondness for dogs. Being likened to a dog is just as moving as 'quite something.' I'm afraid if your niece doesn't stop, I might get a bigger head."

Maggie huffed. "If that's possible."

"Niece!" Alice hissed, offsetting the admonishment with a nervous chuckle.

Michael waved a casual hand in the air. "Oh, you don't have to worry about me, Lady Alice. I'm quite familiar with Maggie's brand of humor. From all the time we've spent together, I've gotten used to it."

Maggie crossed her arms. "We have not spent that much time together." She hated the churlish note in her voice, but it was difficult to stay placid when Michael used that patronizing tone with her.

"We're practically family," he countered.

"We are *not* family," Maggie argued. "Now are you going to tell me why you're here or not?"

Why was his smile getting wider? It practically took up his entire, chiseled face! Damn him for being so attractive! Nay, beautiful. Oh, all right, gorgeous! Maggie could still hate the man *and* admit he was dazzling. During one of her summers with her grandmother, she'd taught herself to juggle. It still came in handy from time to time.

Michael wiggled the gold, beaded pelisse in front of her nose. "You know why I'm here. I already told you."

Maggie rolled her eyes, swatting it out of her face. "Not *here* here." She waved her arms. "Here."

Michael lowered his chin, the smile fading into a confused smirk. "I don't understand."

"Yes, you do! Stop teasing me!"

"Niece," Alice scolded her. "You have to excuse her, my lord. As you can imagine, she's had such a shock today." She patted Maggie's shoulder. "My sister's daughter has such a gentle constitution. I think it was all a bit too much for her."

Maggie gritted her teeth; she could tell Michael was holding back laughter. Why couldn't her aunt see it too?

Michael scrutinized her from head to toe, stopping for a long moment on the hands clenched at her sides. "Yes," he replied slowly, arching one brow. "Your niece has always been a delicate flower, hasn't she?"

"Oh, yes," Alice agreed, gaining momentum. "Just gaze upon her face. Do you see how pale she is… how drawn and deathly her skin looks? Usually, she has a ruddy complexion—all those hours spent in the sun playing that silly game, cricket—but now look at her!"

"You're right. So right," Michael said, holding a hand up to his chin, regarding Maggie like she was the bearded lady in a circus act. "Thank you for pointing it out. She's as white as a ghost."

"I am *not* as white as a ghost," she seethed. "If I'm pale it's only because I wear a hat morning, noon, and night." *And I can't possibly be pale because I'm fuming, and my cheeks feel like they're on fire!*

Alice continued, adopting the same hand-on-chin gesture as Michael. "Yes, ghostly is the perfect word. You're so astute, Lord Michael. Unhealthy is another word, don't you think?"

"Horribly unhealthy," Michael concurred, failing to hide the chuckle in his voice that time. Again, it appeared that Maggie was the only one who noticed it.

Alice's face fell and she turned a dismal eye on the viscount.

"I'd hate for her to miss the wedding dinner." She tilted her head. "Do you know if they're having one still?"

"Indeed, I hear eels are on the menu."

Alice clapped her hands. "Marvelous! Anything else?"

"I think Cornish hen."

"Ah, well, I'm sure that will be fine. I did so hope for capon."

"I did hear mention of a lovely sauce to go with it."

"Mint?"

"Cherry."

Alice clapped once more. "Excellent." Maggie cleared her throat and Alice blinked, as if remembering that her niece was a part of the conversation. She *tsked*. "I don't think you'll be able to handle the excitement, niece. It's all been too much to you. I think it best you go back to your room and rest. I'll make sure something is brought up in time."

Maggie opened her mouth for a rebuke, but Michael beat her to it. "Yes, it's obvious you're not well enough for company."

"It's the complexion," Alice said. "Ghostly."

"So wraithlike," Michael added.

Maggie couldn't take it anymore. She was seconds away from pulling out all her hair, but she calmed herself, knowing it would just make her seem more "wraithlike." "Will you two stop? I am fine. Yes, the shooting was terrible, and I was… *alarmed* by the ordeal, but no more than anyone else in the chapel." She lifted her chin and stared over Michael's shoulder toward the door. She had to get out of that room; she feared for her sanity. "Now, if you'll excuse me, I need to go join my friends—"

"I think you should carry her to her room," Alice cut in, disregarding every word from her niece's obstinate mouth. "Please, dear boy, I don't think she can make it on her own. If she fell, I'd never forgive myself."

Michael nodded instantly, taking a step toward Maggie.

"Don't you dare!" Maggie pushed against his chest. The man wouldn't move. He barely flinched. She had assumed that Michael, like most aristocratic men, was doughy and soft underneath his expensive clothing. However, the steeliness beneath her fingers painted a different story.

Michael glanced down at her hand before slowly meeting her eyes, one brow arched. Maggie retracted her arm. The chapel was sweltering. When had the room become so blisteringly hot?

Her lashes fluttered. "I mean… I don't need… I'm fine… just fine."

Alice's brow wrinkled in concern. She covered her mouth with her hand. "The poor child. Do you see, my lord? Her brain is positively addled by the horrible event. She can't even speak!" She released a sob, and Maggie regarded her in dismay. Her aunt couldn't be serious. She had to be acting for Michael's benefit. Maggie had once bumped against one of her aunt's precious teapots, and Alice had spent the following hour checking *it* for bruises.

"A doctor is needed," Michael stated, his voice hard and distinctly *viscounty*. "I will carry the lady to her room. You have nothing to worry about, Lady Alice. I'm here now. I will take care of everything. You can rely on me."

Alice retreated just in time for Michael to close in on Maggie, sweeping his hands under her and lifting her in his arms like a baby. Maggie squirmed, fighting his embrace, but the viscount only became more adamant, locking his arms around her until she stopped.

Maggie simmered, recounting the last time she'd been so humiliated. It didn't surprise her that *that* appalling event had also involved Michael. Ten years before.

With long, unhurried steps, he strode down the aisle, leaving Alice and her breathless clapping behind.

When Michael reached the thick oak door that was no doubt as old as England itself, he jostled Maggie with little effort, using one hand to hold her while he pushed open the slab. He flashed an arrogant grin before carrying her across the threshold.

"Admit it," he said as they entered the garden leading back to the main house. The sun was beginning to set, and shadows cast by the sycamore trees flitted over him, highlighting the sharp angles of his face. "You're impressed."

Simultaneously, Maggie huffed, rolled her eyes, *and* shook her head. "Because you opened the door with one hand? Hardly."

"Not the door."

"Then what?"

Michael snorted before throwing that toothy, dazzling—and infuriating—grin down on her once more. "That I got through that entire conversation without laughing once." He hefted Maggie higher upon his chest. "It's good to see you, Peggy. Believe it or not, I think I might even have missed you."

Chapter Two

THE HOYDEN FLAILED in his arms. "I told you not to call me that," Maggie seethed.

Michael smiled to himself. He hadn't meant to use that name again. It was just too easy getting her riled up, and he had to admit, he liked easy. It was so much better than hard.

He tightened his grip, holding her closer to his chest as he traveled the gravel path back to the house, angling his right ear so that he wouldn't miss her furious griping. "I told you I don't need any help... I'm perfectly capable of walking... You just can't help embarrassing me... and I don't believe for one second that you missed me."

"But I did!" Michael said.

Maggie turned her nose up to him, regarding him with vicious slits for eyes. He was glad she did. It made admiring the vibrant green more difficult. Maggie had always had beautiful eyes, he remembered—especially when she was yelling at him... which was for most of their childhood. "Then why do you sound so shocked when you say it?" she demanded. "Are you *surprised* that you missed me?"

Michael trained his gaze forward. "Of course not," he responded archly. "Why do you always have to read into things? We're old friends and I told you that I missed you. That's all.

Why can't you accept the compliment and move on—"

"Oh, it was a compliment, was it?" Maggie crushed her arms across her chest. It was either that or wind them around his neck, and Michael was certain she wasn't about to do that. Pity. He would love to tease her about it... *and* see what it felt like.

He shook his head. What an outrageous thought! This was Lady Margaret he was thinking about! Peggy Piggy. The little girl who'd made it her childhood mission to best the boys at every game, every race, every riddle. She was a menace of the first order. And yet... *and yet*... she didn't feel like a menace now. She felt soft... and surprisingly delicate.

Michael couldn't have that. He couldn't have that at all. At an early age, he'd deduced that the world was so much more palatable when you knew its number. He didn't appreciate surprises, nor did he value anomalies. He found comfort in things nice and convenient, predictable—especially his women.

He stretched his fingers away from her body, trying not to notice how lithe and curvy it had become since he'd last seen her. How long had it been? Two years? Five?

"Of course it's a compliment," Michael said. *Wouldn't any normal woman think so?* He forced a nonchalant chuckle. "It's been a long time. I'd hate for you to think that I'd forgotten you."

Maggie responded with a glower that would have forced a lesser man to his knees. "I saw you two weeks ago at the Chapman ball."

"I wasn't at the Chapman ball."

Maggie sucked in an irritated breath. "Yes, you were. You didn't stay, just long enough to steal the first waltz from Lady Wendy."

Michael searched his memory. "Lady Wendy, huh?"

Maggie rolled her eyes. "Stop baiting me! You know you danced with her. I daresay she isn't the kind of woman that men forget."

Wasn't she? Because for the life of Michael, he couldn't re-member dancing with the vapid redhead. If Maggie said he had, then it must be true, but he couldn't dig up any sort of pertinent detail, although that was most likely because most of his social calendar seemed to blend together as of late. One ball felt the exact same as the other… and the same could be said for his dance partners. He only went to those damnable things to please his mother and because it was expected for an earl's heir to attend. Pleasure was rarely—if ever—received in the undertaking.

"What are you more upset about," he replied, "that I danced with Lady Wendy or that I didn't notice you?"

"Upset? Who said anything about being upset?"

Michael shrugged, causing Maggie to latch on to his lapels. "You sound awfully upset. You don't have to deny it."

"I'm not upset!"

"It's fine."

"Do you always have to tease?" she asked. "I'm not upset; I'm just worried. I've heard men your age begin to lose their memory, I've just never actually encountered it before."

Michael laughed. "Men my age? I'm not much older than you. If I'm getting long in the tooth then so are you, my dear."

"Don't call me that."

Michael sighed. *Such a bossy woman!* "I can't call you Peggy, now I can't call you dear. Pray tell, what am I supposed to call you… goddess… my love?"

Maggie might have turned into a statue for how stiff she became. *Dammit.* He'd gone too far. A rush of crimson stained her cheeks, and she hastened to look anywhere but at him. Michael told himself that it was for the best. He didn't need Maggie staring at him, not with those emerald eyes and rosy cheeks. He couldn't decipher why she wasn't married yet. Yes, her personality was positively frightening, but she was an attractive woman… a *very* attractive one. Maybe not in the way that Lady Wendy was—all sweet dimples and shy glances, long lashes and stately bearing—but in a more visceral, earthly way. Less Botticelli's *Birth of Venus*, more Rubens's *Battle of the Amazons*.

The more Maggie tried to push him away, the more Michael admired the flow of her lips, the way they formed an adorable bow whenever she frowned. The more she tossed her errant caramel locks off her face, the more he imagined them draping long and wild along her shoulders. She didn't have to bat her lashes to gain attention—she commanded it the second she spoke.

But Maggie wasn't speaking to him anymore, and Michael desperately wanted to change that. Only his time was up.

He jutted his chin toward the house coming into view. "Most of the wedding guests are ahead. I suppose my fun has ended." He started to lower Maggie to her feet when she threw her arms around his neck.

"What are you doing?" she exclaimed. "You can't put me down now!"

Michael attempted to read the panic in her voice but came up short. He lowered her once more, but Maggie's grip was too strong. "I thought you *wanted* me to put you down."

"But they've seen me!" she yelped, throwing a hand at the group who were openly staring at the couple. "If you put me down now then they'll wonder why you were holding me at all when I didn't need you to. They'll think we were"—she ducked her head—"you know."

Michael absolutely loved it when Maggie was out of her element. She was delightfully awkward. "Enjoying each other's company too much?" he teased.

"Exactly," she groaned. "So now you must keep carrying me… up to my room. We'll tell them I sprained my ankle. It will be fine." Maggie cocked her head, her lips pinching together. "Actually, I shouldn't worry so much. My friends would never believe that I would be silly enough to enter a compromising situation with the likes of you. They know me better than that, and I'd like to believe they don't think so little of me." She tugged at her skirts nervously, making their scene as innocent as possible. "Why aren't you walking?" she asked. "Please, hurry up and get this over with. I'm embarrassed enough as it is."

Embarrassed? To be seen with *him?* Didn't the silly woman know that others would kill to be in her position?

Michael bottled his hurt pride and gathered his steps. He let the matter drop, lengthening his stride toward the group with as sanguine an expression as he could muster.

Lady Everly stepped away from the group as Michael got closer. True to form, she was the first to speak up. He had very little experience with the attractive widow, but her reputation was enough to keep Michael at a distance at Society events. "Maggie, what happened?" she asked, hurrying to her teammate's side. With a gimlet eye, she searched Maggie's entire body before centering an accusing glare at Michael. "What happened to her, *my lord?*"

Michael didn't appreciate what the woman was implying, even if he wasn't quite sure what it was. But before he could put his indignation into words, Maggie spoke up. "Oh, I was just being foolish. In all the commotion I tripped on a root outside the chapel. I wasn't paying attention, and Lord Michael was there to help—"

"Rescue. I was there to rescue her," Michael cut in, enjoying the gasp that Maggie let out before she could stifle it. "I had no idea you were so clumsy, my lady. But you're incredibly lucky I was there." He bounced her higher in his arms, grunting from the strain. "Not many men are as strong as I am, you know."

Michael watched her carefully as she swallowed the fury building in her throat. She wanted to unleash on him—no, she wanted to murder him in front of all her friends. But she couldn't, and they both knew it.

The words gritted out from between her teeth. "Oh, I don't know about that. I'm sure any man here could have done the job."

Michael bobbled her once more. "Probably not, but let's agree to disagree, shall we?"

Maggie shut her eyes. "Please just take me to my room. *My lord.*"

"Gladly." Michael bowed to the group with a pained, reluctant expression, as if the endeavor was almost too much. "Duty calls."

They were halfway up the stairs before Maggie found the will to speak. Her voice was calm now, deadly calm.

"I didn't deserve that," she said. She flipped a clump of curls off her shoulder, whipping him in the nose.

Michael chuckled. "Oh, yes you did."

Following Maggie's curt directions, Michael found her room on the third floor and breezed in, dropping all pretense that carrying her was a hardship. Despite what he'd insinuated to her nosy friends, holding her hadn't been difficult. Lady Maggie was lighter than she looked—not that she looked big. Rather, her razor-sharp quips and elevated opinion of herself made her appear that way. Maybe that was why Michael's memories of her made her seem like a giant in petticoats: the woman loomed large in his mind.

Michael didn't value that reminder.

He sailed toward the bed, plopping her unceremoniously in the middle of the mattress.

"Oof," Maggie cried. She scurried to sit against the headboard, desperately attempting to claim a semblance of higher ground. She pierced him with a burning poker of a scowl. "I don't believe for one second that I hurt your feelings back there."

Michael crossed his arms. He yearned to tear off his fine kid gloves; his palms were unusually sweaty. "I just didn't know you had such a low opinion of me, that being seen with me would be so... *challenging* to your faultless reputation."

"Are you mad?" she exclaimed. "Says the man who teased me for all those years, called me wretched names. What kind of opinion did you think I'd have?"

"I told you, I only called you a name once! *Peggy Piggy* isn't the end of the world!"

Maggie punched her fists into the bed, raising herself taller in her seat. "And everyone else did it for the next ten years. You are their leader, the jewel of the *ton*. You know they follow your every move. Just look at Lord Mason."

Michael jerked back as if her words had been a whip, fast and liable to rip open his skin with a single lash. "Why are you talking about Lord Mason? I spoke to him yesterday. He's actually doing quite well, working with Mr. Holmes's horses, forging a new path for himself, a better one. Or something along those lines."

Maggie snorted. "No thanks to you."

"What the hell does that mean?" Michael was alarmed by the force in his voice. People had stopped having the power to rankle him years ago; why was he allowing this foul-tempered woman to do it now?

"It means," Maggie began slowly, as if addressing a dim-witted child, "that Lord Mason has been a good-for-nothing drunkard for years, spending money he didn't have, embarrassing his family. Don't try to argue with me; Lady Ruthie told me all about it. And you were a constant by his side, drinking with him, encouraging his silly antics, oblivious to the hardships you were causing."

Resentment flared inside him, threatening to boil over. Michael locked his jaw. "I never forced the liquor down his throat. You have a prejudice toward me, believing me to be some devil on his shoulder."

Maggie chuckled, and it annoyed him more than the know-it-all smirk on her round face. "No, you weren't a devil. I wouldn't dare call you one; it might inflate your ego even more." She placed a small silk pillow on her lap and smoothed her hands over it in a gentle, hypnotic manner that made the harshness of her next words cut even sharper. "But you certainly were no angel. You encouraged his debauched antics; his foolishness was entertainment for you and all your ridiculous friends."

"What the… How could you?" Michael blustered, his composure completely forgotten. He paced around the room, afraid if he stared at the woman any longer, she would vaporize from his fury. Lady Maggie didn't know the first thing about him, and yet her opinions were so vehement and obscene. How dare she hold him in such gross regard!

And how dare she accuse him of delighting in his friend's misfortune. All the men in his sphere were young, drunken fools from time to time. They took turns. It was the way of things in his group—although, now that he thought about it, he rarely let himself get out of control, and Mason *had* borne the brunt of most of the laughter.

Still... that was in the past. Mason was rebuilding his character, his fortune, and his self-respect. And Michael was damn proud of his friend. In fact, that was why he'd come to the wedding after Mason wrote him about it—to the wilds of Manchester, no less! Mason's letter had been filled with such excitement and verve and... hope. And when Michael came upon his friend, Mason was just as fresh-faced, clear-eyed, and optimistic in the flesh. Michael had been glad for him, and happy that he'd made the journey to see him, despite losing valuable time training for his next fight.

"You should go." Maggie's words sliced through his thoughts.

Michael's gaze snapped back to her. She sat on her bed, all prim and superior, the unruly, wavy locks that had tickled his nose now safely tucked away behind her ears. Her chin was angled up imperiously, as if Michael were just another servant being sent on his way.

He wouldn't let her get rid of him so easily. "I'll wait," he said, gaining hold of the poise she'd knocked out of him. Michael locked his hands behind his back, directing a casual, lackadaisical smile over her figure.

He reevaluated the situation. Despite his memory of her, Maggie was a small thing. Just an unattached woman, advancing in years, with no marriage prospects on the horizon. She wasn't one to be argued with; she was one to be pitied. It didn't matter that her hair reminded him of melted butterscotch or that her face was so perfectly round that Leonardo da Vinci would find no fault in the symmetry. It didn't matter that the force of her voice and the candor of her words woke something inside of him that had been dormant for as long as he could remember.

Michael was a realist. Their world saw ladies like Maggie in one way, and that was the only one that mattered. But then, why wouldn't his feet move? Why couldn't he leave? It wasn't all about spite.

Michael wanted to be there. For a man who preferred sparring in the ring, he found that he liked it well enough when Lady Maggie did it here.

"I'll wait until your aunt comes," he heard himself say, then rolled his eyes at her incredulous expression. "Don't be nervous. As you remarked, no one would expect anything between us."

"Of course not," she scoffed, though Michael could sense her confidence waning. "It's only..." Maggie inhaled deeply, shaking her head. "My aunt—knowing her, she might be a while."

Michael wandered around the room, surveying her environment. "She's playing matchmaker, eh? Giving us all the time in the world to realize we are hopelessly in love with each other?" He chuckled while picking up a silver comb from the bureau, running the sharp prongs against the pad of his thumb. He could hear the embarrassment in her voice.

"You know she is. She says it's her main priority while I stay with her," Maggie replied helplessly. "Why else would she ask you to carry me? She knew I had no issue that I couldn't handle myself."

"Maybe that was the problem," Michael replied, returning the comb to rest next to its matching hand mirror. "Anyway, she should have known it would be a losing battle with us." He finally turned to the bed, flashing her a rakish smile. "We know each other too well for that."

Maggie continued to fiddle with her pillow, twining loose thread around her long fingers. "I don't know you at all," she replied with a shrug.

"Oh, come now. You've known me since we were young, which probably means you know me better than most. Our parents were constantly together"—he pursed his lips—"for a time."

Maggie lifted her gaze from the pillow, settling it on him with a comfortable yet sympathetic air that made Michael regret opening his mouth.

"How… how is your family?"

"Fine," he answered quickly in his routine, perfunctory way. "And yours?"

"Fine."

Michael meandered to the bed. "I was sorry to hear that your grandmother died last year. I couldn't make it to the funeral. As you are with Lady Alice now, I take it your parents are on the Continent again."

"Where else?" She laughed in an attempt at levity, but bitterness was evident in the two words. Apparently, Michael wasn't the only person who harbored disappointment in his parents.

"They are a lively couple, are they not?"

"The liveliest." Maggie smoothed the rancor from her face and angled her head at him. "I see your mother often enough in town but haven't spoken to your father in ages."

Michael's entire body went rigid. He searched her for guile, or a hidden joke, but when he couldn't find any, he said, "Father prefers the country."

She nodded as if already knowing what he'd say. "Do you see him?"

"Not much. Hardy ever, actually."

"I'm sorry."

"It's the way of things. We're both busy people. I'm actually set to meet him after this. Apparently, he wishes to speak to me about 'something very important.'"

"Ooh." Maggie clucked her tongue with a delightful laugh. "That sounds ominous."

"No doubt it's about marriage, so yes, it probably will be ominous."

She narrowed her eyes playfully. "Not ready for the marital

yoke? What will the *ton* say, Lord Michael?"

"You shouldn't talk," he quipped, jerking his chin toward her bare hand. "There is no ring on your finger."

Maggie inspected that finger, as if she wanted to make sure no one had tossed one on her while she wasn't looking. "And you won't find one there anytime soon."

Michael crossed his arms. "And why is that?"

It was her turn to be defensive. "You know why," she said cagily.

"Afraid a husband won't let you play cricket?" he teased.

She snorted. So unladylike, but also… almost adorable. What the hell was he thinking? "Among other things," she said.

"And what if he did?" Michael asked. "What if you were allowed to be married and play cricket?"

He watched as she held the pillow at both ends like she was ready to strangle it. This woman was vicious, not adorable, Michael reminded himself. But that statement felt entirely wrong; it lacked confidence.

"I'm not in the mood for games of *what if*," Maggie said. Michael had only been joking with her aunt in the chapel, but maybe the events of the afternoon had been too much for her. On closer inspection, Maggie had circles under her eyes and her skin *was* a little pale.

Michael sidled up to the edge of the bed, leaning the front of his legs against the frame. He bent over the mattress until he was inches away from Maggie. It was meant as a lighthearted gesture, nothing to it, but as he came closer, the air became thicker. Maggie's eyes grew larger. Michael studied the color of her eyelashes. They were a deep-chestnut brown, not butterscotch like her hair. It gave her the appearance of a Frenchwoman, painted and sultry.

When she blinked, Michael remembered himself. "What games *are* you in the mood for?"

Had he meant to say that? And had he meant to say it so… suggestively?

Christ. Yes.

Maggie studied him for a long minute. He could feel her attempt to read between his words, gauge the seriousness of his question. Michael knew she hadn't come up with an answer when she replied, "With you? Are you so desperate to lose?"

"I never lose."

She laughed in his face. "Not when you play others, that's true, but always when you played me. You could never seem to concentrate."

And just like that, the atmosphere morphed into something less friendly, more carnal. It was an effort to breathe. Michael bent away from her, standing straight once more. "I was a young boy then—being around any girl was enough to take my concentration away."

"And now?"

"Now I'm a man."

"And now that you're a man, you have more control?"

Michael arched a dark brow, pinning her with an arresting stare that, from experience, made most women weak in the knees. But Maggie wasn't most women. *And* she was already sitting. But who knew? Maybe her knees were trembling under her skirts; he just couldn't see them. Just as Michael's response was a lie, he would make sure she never knew it.

"Absolutely."

Chapter Three

"CHECK." MAGGIE LOOKED up from the chessboard with a self-satisfied smile. *Finally.* After three miserable games where she appallingly ended up on the losing end, she'd managed to get the better of her annoying opponent.

Perhaps she had spoken too soon when she arrogantly asserted that Michael would lose to her, as he'd always done when they were younger. She had to admit, his concentration had gotten better over the years… or maybe it was hers that had worsened.

Because she *was* having a rather difficult time keeping her attention on the board, especially with Michael sitting cross-legged across from her on the bed. It hadn't been her idea! She'd demanded that he sit in the chair *next* to the bed, but he'd been obstinate—something about evening the playing fields and meeting in the middle. Maggie was beginning to believe it had all been a ruse to throw her off her game, and unfortunately, it had worked.

Her cheeks hurt; however, she would keep smiling until he glanced at her. However long it took. She needed to see the realization float across his face when he came to terms with his defeat.

But the obstinate man kept his focus on the board, his tan face frowning at the pieces in single-minded absorption.

"It's your turn," she said sweetly through her saccharine smile.

"I'm well aware," Michael returned, pinching his fingers over his last remaining bishop. "I'm just deciding if I want to beat you in four moves or six."

Maggie's mouth dropped, roping her mind back to the board. He couldn't possibly… could he? She ran through the possible maneuvers. There was no way. She had him. She had—

Maggie fixed on a black rook in the corner of the board that Michael had kept deceptively innocent and quiet thus far.

His laughter was like nails on a chalkboard. "Do you finally see it? I was wondering when you were going to catch on. A little slow today, aren't you?"

Maggie sat back against the headboard, shaking her head at her blindness. She was a good chess player—maybe even great— and playing Michael made her feel like she was learning the game for the first time. Now, it was Maggie who wouldn't raise her chin, wouldn't acknowledge the smug smile shining across her doomed white pieces.

"Oh, don't be a sore loser. Finish the game," he chided her, finally moving his rook out from the corner.

Four moves, Maggie surmised. He'd chosen to claim his victory in four. She had to respect that. Why string her along?

Grudgingly, she sat up, intent on playing out the game. Lord Michael might believe her the loser, but she'd never let him call her a quitter.

Just when she was about to make her move, a knock sounded on the door.

"My lady?" a timid voice called out.

Maggie flew out of her seat, fluidly managing to throw Michael off the bed while not upsetting the game. "Hide!" she spat, pushing him to the adjacent space next to the door, where he shot her a disbelieving glare. Just as Maggie had hoped, when the door opened, it pinned him to the wall, blanketing Michael from the maid's view.

"Lady Maggie!" The maid came to a halt, nearly dropping the long black dog she carried. "Your aunt said you weren't feeling well, but she didn't say you had a fever. Your face is flushed; do you want me to call for a doctor?" She spun toward the hallway. "Maybe I should have your aunt come up—"

"No!" Maggie cried out, snatching the dog away from the maid. The muscular dachshund licked her face in appreciation. "I'm fine, truly, Jane. It's just a little hot in this room, that's all. I'll open a window."

"I'll do it for you," Jane said, marching to the far side of the room. Within seconds, the efficient woman had a nice breeze sailing through. "There. Now, your aunt wanted me to let you know that she'll be up to see you after dinner is over. Did you want me to bring you up a plate? No? All right, then. Well, George has eaten and had his walk, but I'll be by to take him outside once more before bedtime. Is there anything else—" Her words broke off as her gaze settled on the bed where the chess game was still in session.

"I was bored," Maggie explained before the maid could jump to logical conclusions. She would never question Maggie, but that didn't mean she wouldn't gossip the moment she left the room.

The poor woman couldn't hide her confusion. "You're playing… yourself, my lady?"

"Yes," Maggie answered, puffing out her chest with confidence. No longer able to control George's wiggling, she placed him on the ground, only to realize too late that it was a terrible decision. The dog made a beeline for the door, barking voraciously at the wall behind it.

Maggie raised her voice. "I've heard playing oneself is… the only way to get better," she explained lamely. "George, come! George!"

The little dog cast her a doleful expression, thinking long and hard before eventually retreating from the door. Maggie shrugged her shoulders at the maid. "Silly dog. Always barking at ghosts." She tried to pick him up again, but the badly behaved rascal evaded her, instead keeping a watchful eye on the door, growling from afar.

The maid nodded slowly, no doubt wondering if the lady was ill or insane. "All right, then," she began. "Do you want me to help you undress—"

"That will be all, Jane," Maggie replied swiftly.

The maid gave her one last look before bobbing. Maggie followed her to the exit, shutting the door quickly before Michael's laughter could be heard.

"You should have let her undress you." He chortled, straightening his jacket. "I daresay that would have made the night more interesting. Oh Christ, what the hell is that?"

Maggie frowned, not understanding why he was scowling at her beloved dog. George unleashed another round of high-pitched barks. The animal's little legs hopped off the ground as it made circles around the intruder.

"What do you mean?" she asked. "That's George. I don't think he likes you."

Michael meandered back toward the center of the room, keeping a wary eye on the dachshund. "I think you're mistaken, but that's a long-haired rat."

Maggie's hand flew to her chest. "George is a king among princes."

"George is a rat," he replied matter-of-factly.

Maggie couldn't take the barking anymore—nor Michael's harsh words. She scooped up her dog, shushing him into an uneasy quiet. "Don't tell me you haven't seen a dachshund before?"

Michael bent over and peered closer, grimacing at the oddly shaped animal. "I've seen them in pictures, which was bad enough. It's… it's…"

Maggie smiled broadly. "Lovely." She kissed George's smooth black head. "He's lovely and perfect."

"Your dog is missing legs. Do you know that?"

Maggie waved George's front paws. "They're here. They're

the perfect size for hunting."

"Hunting?" Michael scoffed. "His body is too long."

"It's the perfect size for chasing badgers in their holes."

Michael flinched as George let out a low, menacing snarl. "He doesn't like me."

"He is a perfect judge of character. And," Maggie continued, giving the dog a quick squeeze, "George will be a champion sire and his children will demand a lot of money."

Michael surveyed the animal more, no doubt searching for his potential greatness. He tried to raise a hand to pet it, but George's growl forced it back down. "You're going to breed this ill-tempered mongrel? You actually believe others will want something so… misshapen?"

Maggie regarded him stonily. "I hear women like *you* just fine. Anyway, for a man at the center of the *ton*, you know little about its goings-on, don't you? The queen and Prince Albert just acquired a dachshund from the prince's homeland. They're mad for them over there, and they will soon be mad for them here. Everyone emulates the royal family."

"If you say so," Michael replied dismissively, reclaiming his space on the bed. He studied the board for a moment before snapping his fingers. "So, *this* is your little plan. This is how you think you'll stay unmarried. You're going to start a business, breeding these loud toys."

"They're hunters."

He shrugged. "My father loves his hunting dogs, and I doubt he would look at these things twice. Sell them as lap dogs."

His words stung more than Maggie was willing to admit. "Well, he's not the only man in England. And I wouldn't call it a business, more like a passion," she said. "I love dogs, always have. And I like the idea of my dogs finding their perfect companions."

Michael cocked his head, shooting her a lopsided smile. "You and I both know there is no such thing as the perfect companion. For our set, anyway."

Maggie heard rancor in his voice, and it confused her.

No longer sensing Michael as a risk, George urged to be placed on the bed. He hopped in Michael's lap, sniffing every inch he could. "Not when it comes to people, you're right," Maggie replied, "but I most assuredly believe that there's a right dog for every person. And I intend to help others find it."

Michael laughed, though it had nothing to do with what she had said. George was now standing on his little back legs with his paws on Michael's rumbling chest. His tail wagged ecstatically as he licked Michael's face. "Maybe you're right," Michael said, attempting to keep the dog at bay.

"I'm sorry," Maggie said, sitting next to him. "He's still young. He can get rather excited."

"Don't worry," he replied dryly. "I'm quite used to this behavior from others."

She rolled her eyes. "Naturally. Here, let me take him."

"That might be a good idea—Ah, ouch!" Michael inhaled deeply through his teeth. In his overzealousness, George had accidentally knocked his head against the purple bruise covering Michael's eye.

"I'm so sorry!" Maggie cried. "Down, George. Down. Go to your bed," she ordered the dog, putting the chastened animal on the ground. She pointed to the corner where a blanket sat with a couple of plump blue satin pillows. "He's still not completely trained."

"It's all right. No harm done," Michael said easily. He took off his gloves and shoved them in his jacket pocket before wiping his hands on the tops of his thighs. Maggie couldn't help but stare at them. They were large, so much bigger than she'd remembered—and covered in cuts and bruises.

Maggie knew she shouldn't say anything. It wasn't proper. But nothing about this day had been. "Michael," she began tentatively, "what are you doing?"

He reminded her of a stone. He froze at her words, flicking a furtive glance at his knuckles. When he began to breathe again, she heard the tight, fast pulls of air, and they made her chest ache.

"Michael?"

"It's nothing."

Maggie reached out, surprising herself—surprising him. He flinched when she traced the cuts along his knuckles with the tips of her fingers. In so many instances throughout this night, Michael had reminded her of the boy he'd once been—his quick laugh, the taunting sparkle in his blue eyes, the easygoing expression he wore as a mask for his sadness and confusion—but this was different. These marks of anger and violence introduced her to a stranger.

"Whom did you fight?" she asked gently.

"No one. You don't know him."

Maggie chewed on the inside of her cheek. If the man wanted her to pull it out of him, she would. She picked up one of his hands, balancing it on top of her own, his fingers pointing toward her wrist. "Was it over money," she asked, gathering her courage to add, "or a woman?"

"For Christ's sake," he growled, pushing her hand down so he sandwiched it against his thigh. "Don't be dramatic. I was in a fight, but it wasn't a *fight*." He squinted at the ceiling as if looking for the words. "What I mean is it isn't a fight as you know it. It wasn't over something, I mean."

Maggie couldn't understand what he was trying to tell her or if he was being elusive on purpose. What she did know for certain was that he was uncomfortable, which meant she was on the right track.

She took her time, scrutinizing him, from his bruised hands to the bluish-green contusion surrounding his eye. There were other signs too, ones that shamed her because she'd been conversing with the man most of the night and hadn't noticed them. But they'd been there, right in front of her—the way he'd grimaced when he sat on the bed, his limp when he'd carried her from the chapel, the small scratch at his temple that his brown curls mostly hid. However, those were only the negative signs. There were positive ones as well, from the way his suit jacket clung a little too snugly to his upper arms to be fashionable, or the way he navigated his body in space, graceful and determined, like each movement was premeditated to his advantage.

When the answer came to Maggie, it came all at once, slamming into her like a blunt force to the stomach. She grabbed Michael's chin, urging him to meet her. "You're a boxer?" she asked with frank astonishment.

His head dropped from her grasp, but not before she caught his sheepish smile. He pressed harder into the hand he still held prisoner on his thigh as if warning her not to flee from him. The thought had never crossed her mind.

"I've dabbled in it."

"Dabbled?"

He bobbed his wide shoulders. "More than dabbled, then."

"How? Why?" Maggie couldn't envision the Lord Michael she'd grown up with—the beautiful, proud, arrogant boy— putting his toe on the line with common men, inviting them to bust his patrician nose and cut into his blue blood. In what world did that make sense?

"It started when I was younger," he explained, using his thumb to draw little circles on the top of her hand. His touch was light, sinfully sweet, and it brought out goose pimples all over her body. Maggie didn't know why she allowed him to do it—maybe because she wanted to believe that he didn't even know he was doing it. What was the harm in that?

"I found I was good at it." He grinned ruefully. "Or maybe I just had the right amount of anger. Anyway, a man named Tommy Jones saw me a little while back and agreed to help me train. I've been with him ever since."

"How long ago was that?"

"Five years."

"Five years!" Maggie gasped. On reflex, she tried to pull her hand away, but Michael's grasp only strengthened. She thought it would frighten her, but it was the opposite. For a woman who was used to being alone—who reveled in her independence—his hold made her feel *wanted*.

"At first it was only something to do, a way to clear my mind and beat out my frustrations," he continued calmly. "It's only in the last few years that I've taken it seriously."

"Do people know?"

"I'm not hiding it."

"What about your father?"

His glower made her shiver. "He's not particularly happy, and nor is my mother."

"I would say so," Maggie cried. "You're his heir, his only son! You can't gad about having men beat in your skull!"

True pride lit his countenance, and Maggie's stomach lurched. *There* was the beautiful boy. "Not many get the chance. I'm awfully fast," he said.

Finally, Maggie managed to win her hand away and settle it primly in her lap. "If you're inviting me to come and witness it, you'll be disappointed."

Michael leaned back, playfully gifting her with a discerning eye. "You surprise me, lady. I thought for sure you would have jumped at the chance to watch someone make me bleed."

Maggie laughed, dragging her legs up from the floor, hugging them to her chest. "You're right. On second thought, I probably wouldn't mind it so much."

She liked the way his eyes flashed when she made him laugh, and the way his Adam's apple bobbed up and over his necktie. She also liked that she hadn't worried once about what she should say in his company. She just said what she felt like saying. Now, Maggie tended to say what was on her mind—however, she usually worried about the other person's response. But not Michael's. She had a feeling that he would accept anything that came from her lips, giving it the same respect he allowed his male friends.

Friends? Was that what they were now? The idea provoked something deep and odd within her. It was like trying to find the perfect word for something and only coming up with something that was close, but not exactly right.

But before she could find another word, Michael surprised her. He reached in between them and caught a few locks of her hair. With painstaking precision, he slid them off her face behind her ear.

Maggie's laughter stuck in her throat.

Michael licked his lower lip, staring at the offending bit of hair, his brow puckered. "You used to have longer hair."

Maggie blinked. He spoke softly and slowly, yet she felt like she was in the middle of a storm, being pushed this way and that. She longed to put her feet back on the ground but didn't want to let go of her legs. They provided a shield that, for some reason, she thought she needed.

"It used to be curlier," Michael continued before clearing his throat. Why did he look even more surprised than her by his action?

Instinctively, Maggie reached behind her ear, stroking the tendril he'd rearranged.

"It still is… when it's wet," she replied. "My mother let me cut some of it off because it gave me headaches. Have you met Lady Anna, the new Viscountess of Newton? I'd love to cut my hair as short as hers. It seems like it would be so freeing."

"Don't."

She froze at his blunt words. "Why not?"

"Just don't."

Maggie yearned to pick a fight, yearned to tell him that he had no decision in the matter, but when she reached for anger, she couldn't find any. The jibe stalled on her tongue. The fire inside of her had no oxygen. Michael was too close; his body, his presence, stifled it before it had a chance to grow.

So, she said the only words she could think of, the words that Society had bred into her from the time she could speak. "You should go."

Maggie leaned away, but she wasn't quick enough.

"Wait." Michael swept a hand out and hooked the back of her

neck, halting her retreat. The room fell back from them. They stared at one another, both more than a little shocked by his burst of emotion.

A boyish smile crept on Michael's face. His forehead dipped, and he drew them together, so close that Maggie could see all the colors of his bruise, the greens and yellows that melded with the harsher jewel tones along the hollow of his eye. His palm was insistent yet gentle on her neck, warm, his expression even warmer. Maggie was a moth to a flame, attracted to the promise of his light.

And that was when the devastation hit her.

Just as Maggie knew that this man would always be beautiful, always be the rock that his friends broke themselves upon, the cover that they hid under, she also knew that he was the sad boy she'd always be in love with.

Sitting there with him, entranced by his body, his familiarity, Maggie attempted to keep the shame at bay. Because she prided herself on being different, and loving Michael made her like every other girl in the *ton*. Like them, she'd fallen under his spell from the very beginning. But unlike them, she would never wait around for him to *hopefully* direct his rays of light upon her. One didn't need to read fairytales to know that men like him didn't marry women like her. So, long ago, she'd decided to salvage her pride and reject him first.

Maggie knew firsthand the havoc that savage love could wreak, and she'd determined that she would guard against it— guard against him.

But how quickly all that self-care went to waste! The joke was on Maggie, because here she was in her room, on her bed, in the arms of the very man she'd sworn would never get the better of her.

And she was doing nothing to stop it. Because she wanted it. Wanted him. So badly. Just once. This one time. Because why not? She would never have a chance again. Nor would she want it.

When his hand tightened and he pulled her across the divide, Maggie obeyed willingly. She placed her hands on his thighs, curling her fingertips into the taut, rolling muscles. She melted in his embrace, molding herself to his torso, folding her body into the space he created, just for her.

Shyness overcame Maggie. When his nose grazed hers, she ducked her head, embarrassed by the intimacy. Michael followed. He nudged her to face him. Eye to eye they watched one another as he cradled her cheek with his other hand. She was entirely surrounded by him, contained by him, and lacked the power to leave or move forward. Maggie waited for him to kiss her, waited to know what it would taste like if Michael claimed her as he did the other girls that she'd secretly envied from across ballrooms and garden parties.

His breath mixed with hers. She opened her mouth to take in more, holding him inside her lungs, making him a part of her forever.

That fanciful thought made her smile. There was no forever with Michael. Only now.

"Maggie, I…"

"Yes?"

She could see tiny flecks of silver in his blue eyes, an uncharted land, a solar system for her discovery.

"Maggie…"

"Yes?"

His lips were on the precipice. One jump, one tiny step, was left.

"I…"

But one step proved to be too far.

Maggie didn't know what the thought was, but she saw the change sweep over Michael's face when he landed on her smile. Like a man waking from a dream, he blinked and slowly, so very slowly, dropped his hands from her body and created space, taking his warmth and her dignity with him.

"You're… you're right," he said, sliding his gaze back to his lap. He played with the cuts on his knuckles, the ones she'd only caressed moments before. "I should go before your aunt comes."

It was like being tossed out to sea. Maggie couldn't speak. She couldn't even turn her head to watch him go. It took many minutes before she could even move after he closed the door behind him.

Now Maggie was the stone. And she did what stones did best: she sank.

Chapter Four

THE FOLLOWING MORNING, Maggie blamed her headache on her lack of sleep. After Michael had left—no, vanished—she hadn't been able to close her eyes. Her mind repeatedly spun, working through the events of the day, wondering where everything had gone wrong, wondering what *she* had done wrong. Because, in the end, she could only blame herself.

A cad would always be a cad. How could one blame them for acting in a disreputable way? Maggie had known better. She had known exactly who and what Michael was… what he always had been. A wolf in sheep's clothing, a gentleman with rakish intentions, a boy who refused to grow up.

And still… being so completely aware of Michael's limitations, his devastating ineptitude, Maggie had fallen into his trap. Just as she'd fallen time and time again in her childhood. She never understood how he could do it, but one genuine smile from Michael could always wipe the slate clean. One kind word, one authentic sentence, could erase a weekend full of slights and being overlooked.

But even as Maggie used her fist to pound the down in her pillow, wishing the morning light away, she couldn't comprehend her reaction to Michael's latest ambush. The boy she'd thought she knew would have taken advantage of the situation. He would have kissed her and avoided her the following day. Though she had very little experience—or absolutely no experience—in these sorts of matters, she'd heard that rakes took advantage of silly girls, trading sweet words for kisses, and then avoided them when the fun had ended. However, last night there had been no fun, or at least the kind rakes usually enjoyed. Michael hadn't forced it. And even when Maggie was right in front of him, practically begging for him to claim her, he'd broken away.

He'd been… honorable? Was that the right word? *For Michael?*

But why did it not *feel* right? Why couldn't Maggie just accept it and let it go? Why did she always have to think the worst when it came to him? Because if he weren't being honorable, there could only be one other reason why he recoiled from touching her.

He simply didn't want to kiss her.

And for some sad, insane, bewildering reason, that torched her heart and ego more. In what world was Maggie the type of girl who wanted this loathsome creature to kiss her more than she wanted him to reject her? Was her confidence truly that lacking? Or did she really not consider Lord Michael to be that loathsome of a creature?

She couldn't answer those questions.

Or wouldn't.

Which was why she hid in her room that morning, nursing a headache that made her teeth vibrate and her vision double. Unfortunately, her stomach wouldn't be denied, and eventually, she had to face facts *and* all of her friends and leave her room. She just hoped that Michael had the grace to avoid her.

When Maggie entered the dining room for breakfast, she pleasantly noted that most of the party had already eaten. Only a few stragglers were left behind, nursing their coffees and teas, partaking in light conversations, or reading the various newspapers strewn about the long table. They nodded to Maggie as she perused the sideboard, loading her plate with a couple slices of bread and sausage, thinking that if her mouth were always busy chewing then she wouldn't have to engage in any inane chitchat.

Unfortunately, she was not that lucky.

"We missed you last night," Lady Every said over her teacup as Maggie took a seat across from her at the table. She should have known better. She should have steered clear of the widow, who never rested on politeness when she had something on her mind. It was one of the reasons Maggie liked Jo so much; they had it in common.

"Yes," Maggie said, buttering her bread. Her hands had to move so they wouldn't shake. "I decided to stay in after—"

Jo cut her off. "After Lord Michael *carried* you to your room."

Why did she have to say "carried" in that way? It sounded so… clandestine.

Maggie attempted to control her breathing, but something hot and overwhelming was gaining steam inside of her, and it wasn't embarrassment. It was anger. "He left right away," she explained quickly.

Jo nodded. With her neatly styled hair and demure ensemble, she was the height of sophistication. She had married young and married well; unfortunately, she'd also become a widow early. But her worldliness was always apparent, and Maggie had always appreciated her on-the-mark quips involving other members of the cricket club. However, that was all before she was on the receiving end.

"Of course," Jo said. Maggie thought she heard an entire conversation in those two words. Maybe she was being paranoid?

The scraping of fork tines ripped Maggie's attention from the widow. She turned to the head of the table, where the cricket club captain, Mrs. Myfanwy Everett, sat, finishing her eggs with a single-minded abandon. Maggie had never seen another person eat so much and so fast before. It made her feel slightly better about her own healthy eating habits.

Unaware of her audience, Myfanwy scraped every last morsel off the plate and into her mouth and reclined in her chair. She patted her lips with her napkin, resting one hand on her lovely, round belly.

Her large brown eyes widened when she noticed Maggie's rapt attention, and she smiled sheepishly. "I'm always so hungry," she said, a hint of apology in her voice. "I woke up and all I could think about were eggs. I can't explain it."

"You don't have to," Maggie replied easily. It was almost disconcerting witnessing Myfanwy behave so bashfully. The cricket captain was always so forthright and commanding, always so sure of herself on the pitch. Maggie had assumed that she would recognize Myfanwy as being more human now that she was a wife and almost mother, but that wasn't the case. Even on the sidelines, barking orders, and watching her teammates play, Myfanwy was still as daunting as ever.

"I think I'm a little sad too," Myfanwy went on. She picked up her fork again, but quickly put it down with a frown when she noticed nothing was left on her plate. "Our tour is open. We have nothing on the schedule until we play the Matrons at the end of the summer. What am I supposed to look forward to now?"

Maggie suppressed a smile and shared a look with Jo.

"Well… you do have a baby coming," Jo said gently. "I have a feeling that might take up some of your time."

Myfanwy chuckled, but Maggie could tell that she wasn't completely sold on the idea. "I suppose you're right," she began. "I just feel like I need you all more than ever. I've loved spending this last month with all of you. It felt like we were a real, professional team. And now we're all going back to normal… back to life."

Maggie nodded, understanding exactly what her captain was trying to say. The London Ladies Cricket Club had spent the last four weeks touring cities around the country, playing exhibition matches with town teams, trying to drum up excitement for women in the sport. Crowds were always plentiful in London, and they'd been wary about how some of the towns would take to them, but they'd been met with resounding support. Maggie had even felt like a quasi celebrity for some of it. Going back home—with Aunt Alice, no less—was similar to climbing to the top of a mountain and seeing the path to the ocean only to be told to go back the way you came.

Nevertheless, at the end of the day, the women of the cricket club had to stay realists. They understood the lives that were waiting for them. Most of Maggie's teammates would eventually marry, have children, and most likely give up cricket, looking back on these short years with pride and amusement. They would all move on.

Everyone but Maggie. She hadn't been lying to Michael. Marriage was not in her future, and it never would be.

On second thought, maybe she should have thanked Michael for his abrupt departure from her bedroom. He'd only reminded her that her convictions were right. People did not make dependable companions—not in the long run. That was what dogs were for.

"What is it?" Jo asked.

Maggie froze, realizing the table was staring at her. "What?"

Jo placed her teacup down with a demonstrable *click*. "Your face," she explained. "It's become frightfully pale. Don't you agree, Ella?"

Sitting next to the widow was Lady Ella, a young, plain-faced blonde woman who'd joined the team right before the tour. Maggie liked Ella because she didn't talk much, but always scored plenty of runs. In Maggie's estimation, one couldn't ask for a better teammate.

Lady Ella scrutinized her with frank appraisal. "She's not that pale, just rather gray. Is something the matter? Do you want us to fetch your aunt?"

"Or Lord Michael?" Jo quipped with a smile.

"What? No, I'm… I'm fine. I just didn't get enough sleep," Maggie blustered, shutting her eyes the second she realized her silly mistake.

"Oh, you didn't?" Jo replied with a distinct lilt to her tone. She gave Myfanwy a look, but the captain missed it because she was already up from her seat, moving to the sideboard for a second helping.

Maggie glared across the table. "Don't say it like that."

"Like what?" Jo replied innocently. "I didn't say anything."

"Yes, you did. And you don't know what you're talking about."

"Lord Michael's not here anyway," Myfanwy called over her shoulder, piling bacon onto her plate.

"What do you mean?" Maggie asked. Her gaze fell when she noticed Jo's interest in her question. Why was the blasted woman so insightful?

Myfanwy moved on to potatoes. "He left early this morning. At first light. The baby puts so much pressure on my back and I couldn't sleep—which means that I wouldn't let Samuel sleep." She faced them with a devilish grin. "I made him search the kitchen for some biscuits. He said he spoke to Michael on his way out."

Maggie played with her fork, trying to ignore the drop in her stomach. "Did Samuel say *why* he left so early?"

Myfanwy shrugged, stiffly walking her plate back to the table. "I don't know. I have a hard time hearing things when I'm eating. Lately, it takes all my focus."

Maggie didn't have the heart to laugh with all the others. Instead, she stabbed her fork into her sausage. And then stabbed it again. And then one more time.

Sadly, it didn't make the pain go away. The only thing that vanished was her appetite. And that only made Maggie more furious.

AN HOUR LATER, Maggie and Jane were putting the finishing touches on the packing when a knock sounded.

"It's Lady Everly and Lady Emma," Jane announced, coming back from the door. She bent over to snatch a chemise out of George's mouth before he hid it under the bed. "Do you want me to tell them you're busy?"

Maggie opened her mouth to say *yes*, but something stopped her. The ladies had never come to her room once during the entire tour. They must have a good reason for stopping by, especially since everyone had already said their goodbyes after breakfast. "No, that's all right," she said, folding a pair of gloves and stacking it on top of a pile. "Do you mind taking George out for a walk? I'm sure Aunt Alice will finally be ready to leave by the time you return."

Jane nodded and, after a little chasing, shoveled George into her arms and left the room.

Maggie waited for the dog's unruly barking to subside down the hallway—as well as for her nervousness to abate—before addressing her arriving guests. She did not like the way the ladies were looking at her.

Jo fired first. "What happened with Lord Michael?" she asked, almost knocking Maggie off her feet with the bluntness.

"Nothing, why… why… why do you ask?"

Jo cocked her head. "Because each time I brought him up this morning you looked like you were going to jump out of your skin."

"Then you shouldn't have brought him up!"

"I was just teasing," Jo replied tetchily. "But now I think something happened and I want to know. I'm not leaving this room until you tell me."

She nodded at Ella, who seemed to snap into action. The younger woman crossed her arms in solidarity. "Neither am I."

Maggie's gaze darted around the room. She was fairly certain she could escape. If push came to shove, she could snap Ella like a twig; however, getting past Jo would be no easy feat. That stark realization blew the obstinance out of her. She flopped down on the bed, the disappointment and abandonment from the night blanketing her like a shroud. "I already told you, nothing happened!"

Jo eyed her. "And I take it… that's bad?"

"No… Yes…" Maggie held her head in her hands. "I don't know."

The widow trod closer, pulling Maggie's hands down. "It was good that he left," she said firmly. "Trust me. You wouldn't have wanted it any different."

"No, I understand," Maggie said, "but…" The words clogged her throat. Tears pooled in her eyes as an avalanche of emotions began to build, threatening to tumble down and ruin everything. "*You* don't understand."

"I think I do."

"No," Maggie repeated. Why couldn't she get past that word? "I didn't want more…" she continued, searching for the right words to convey the onslaught of feelings battling for supremacy in her head. It was too damned difficult. There were too many. "I wanted him to want more and then… I thought he did… and then he didn't… and now I'm mad." She shot up from the bed, forcing Jo to step back. She balled her hands into fists. "I'm so incredibly mad. Because *I know* him. *I know* who he is and what he's like. *I know* his reputation and *I know* he would never want someone like me, and for one brief moment, I thought that he would… I thought he *did* want someone like me. And I was so stupid. I let myself believe it. I let myself actually think that he wanted me, and instead of being repulsed, instead of laughing at that ridiculous notion and throwing his interest back in his face, I fell. I fell for it. *All of it!* I fell for his smile and his curly hair that desperately needs a cut, and his stories that are always a little sadder than expected, and his body that doesn't fit his suit right but I wouldn't change for anything. I fell for him. Like I was ten years old once more, and he was teasing me, and I was too infatuated to want him to stop. Because even when he was teasing me, at least he was giving me attention. It's pathetic. *I'm* pathetic!"

Maggie's lungs seized. She swiped her hair off her face and her hand came away wet. She was crying. A lot. Over that fool! Why? Why couldn't she let this go?

Jo's calm voice came over her unexpectedly like a hug. "You're not pathetic."

Maggie shuddered and her shoulders immediately fell to their rightful place. "Don't lie."

"I'm not lying," Jo said. "It's only natural to feel how you're feeling. The man is a menace, like most men are, and he abused your good nature, as most men do."

Maggie accepted a handkerchief from Ella and wiped her nose. "I suppose. I just don't know why I'm so upset. And nothing I do or say to myself will release this anger. He made me feel like such a… a… *girl*."

"Powerless," Ella remarked.

"Yes, exactly." Maggie nodded. "Powerless. And I hate that. I hate the fact that he'll never know what that feels like. And he deserves to!"

Jo lowered her forehead and began to walk around the room. It was an easy pace, one made for contemplation. Maggie's heart swung inside her chest like the pendulum of a grandfather clock as she waited for the woman to speak.

Finally, Jo spun to her. "What if there's a way to make him feel that way?"

Something crawled up Maggie's spine. It felt dangerous and wicked and so very right. "What are you saying? Do you think I could make him fall in love with me?"

Jo's smile was thin, but full of promise. "Why not? You're pretty enough; you come from a good family. You run in the same circles."

Now Maggie's head was the pendulum as she shook it back and forth. "He would never—"

"But he almost did," Ella cut in. "Which means he would again. You just have to make it easier for him."

"Easier?"

Ella stepped forward stoically, squeezing her hands in front of her like she was about to divulge to them the whereabouts of the Holy Grail. Maggie supposed that giving an unmarried woman the secrets to gaining a man's undying affection was equally important to some.

"My mother has… *opinions*," the girl began.

Jo arched her brow. "Opinions?"

"I have four older sisters," Ella explained patiently. "They're married to two marquises, one earl, and one viscount." She bobbed her shoulders. "My mother considers herself something of an expert on the topic of marriage and attraction."

"I think I would too," Jo said, laughing.

"She says there are certain things a woman must do to grab a man's heart."

One part of Maggie wanted her to shove cotton in her ears and never broach the subject again; the other part of her wouldn't have abandoned her seat for all the money in the world. "Go on," she urged.

Ella swallowed a lump in her throat, or maybe it was her inhibitions. "She says women should appear soft and gentle. We should talk as little as possible, and when we do, it should be about the man and his interests."

Maggie was already bored. And yet she persisted. "Really? And that works?"

Jo *tsked*. "I hate to admit it, but this is crucial, sound information."

Buoyed by Jo's confidence, Ella went on. "Mother says women should dress as femininely as possible, with lots of bows and feathers. We should act helpless so that we play to the man's desire to be a knight in shining armor. And we should never, ever, ever, ever, *ever* argue."

Maggie's mouth almost dropped to the floor. "That's it?"

Ella shrugged. "Mother says that men are simple creatures."

"Your mother is a wise woman," Jo added.

"And you agree with this?" Maggie asked the widow. "You've

been married. Is this how you settled on your husband?"

Jo hesitated, and Maggie couldn't read her expression. "My situation was different. My husband was different," she said stiffly. "However, Ella's mother is sadly correct about the average man of the *ton*."

"But what if Michael isn't average?"

Jo rolled her eyes. "I've met him, darling. I'm afraid he is *very* average."

That notion rankled Maggie. Michael had always been many things to her, but average wasn't one of them. If he were, what did that say about her?

Ella snapped her fingers. "Oh, we mustn't forget competition. Mother always made sure another man was sniffing around my sisters when she wanted to pressure their suitors to propose. She'd pay them sometimes with gifts and trinkets. It worked marvelously well."

"That woman should really start a service. Mothers would flock to gain her knowledge." There was no hiding the admiration in Jo's voice.

Ella's face turned crimson. "Do you think? I've always considered it a little devious and calculating."

"Well, of course it is! But it's also remarkably effective." Jo pursed her lips for a few seconds before clapping her hands. "I know just the man. He'll be perfect. His attention will be enough to pique Michael's curiosity."

Maggie cringed. "Please don't pay anyone. It makes this whole situation seem tawdry."

"Oh, *now* you're worried about this whole enterprise being tawdry?" Jo didn't wait for an answer. "Besides, I wouldn't dream of handing this man a pound. But don't worry, he'll do it. He owes me a favor."

"So that's it?" Maggie bristled. "All I have to do is put more effort and frills in my wardrobe, speak softly, and be as malleable as possible?"

Jo returned a pitiful look and patted her hand. "I know, this will be difficult for you. Try not to get discouraged."

"I'm not discouraged," Maggie snapped, softening it with a little chuckle, "just… disappointed. It all seems too easy and so passionless."

"There's not much room for passion in the *ton*," Jo replied blithely. "A little romance, a bit of wooing, but not much passion. However, you don't need to worry about that. You just need simple, basic adoration."

Maggie frowned. There was nothing simple or basic about her feelings. Nevertheless, they weren't talking about her feelings; they were talking about Michael's. Could she truly make him feel this way? Could she make him besotted with her—if she pretended to be an entirely different person, of course? A woman worth being besotted over?

Maggie's gaze fell helplessly on the two women as she slowly but surely came to terms with the plan they were drawing out before her, becoming more comfortable with the act she was about to put on. "So, what then?" she asked. "I mean, how do I know when I have him?"

Jo lifted her nose, her expression turning dangerously serious. "You'll know you have him when he freely gives you his heart to hold. Even though it will hurt for him to breathe, he will willingly place it into your hands for safekeeping. You will feel the weight of it in your palm and hear the beats deep inside your soul. It is a monumental and all-encompassing thing but can happen in an instant. If you aren't careful, you can miss it."

Maggie was hanging on the woman's every word. "And then what do I do?"

Jo huffed, blinking out of her stupor. "Darling, then you do whatever you want," she replied quickly before hardening her voice. "But I suggest you crush it."

Chapter Five

MICHAEL HEARD THE long, forthright footsteps and turned to face the door. Seconds later, his father commanded the frame, stopping as if sitting for a picture, and marched into his study. "My dear boy," he exclaimed, stopping in front of Michael. For a moment, Michael thought his father would hug him as he used to. The older man raised his arms as if to embrace him, but they abruptly fell. "I'm sorry to keep you waiting. I wasn't sure if you were coming."

Michael noted a bitterness in the man's tone. He gave it right back. "I said I would in my letter."

Lord Arthur Conroy, the seventh Earl of Waverly, clucked his tongue and skirted past his only son, picking up a letter from a stack on his desk. Making high drama, he held it right up to his eyes. "It says here that I wasn't to expect you until tomorrow." He let the paper fall from his fingers back to the pile. "I have a distinct feeling that you weren't in a hurry to see me, so why the rush?"

Michael grimaced and ventured to the bar cart his father kept in the corner of his study. He took his time, pouring himself a brandy before continuing. "Can't I just want the pleasure of your company?"

Arthur laughed. It wasn't mean-spirited, but it lacked

warmth. "Of course you can. I only wish you wanted *the pleasure* more."

Michael twisted his amber drink around in his hand, taking another sip before answering. "You know how Mother is. She keeps me busy, always asking me to accompany her to this party and that. I can't leave everything to come to Leicester every weekend. You chose to live here, Father, not me. If you want to see me more, you should come to Town. I'm sure your wife wouldn't mind."

Arthur laughed again, and this time there was no mistaking the sourness. He followed his son to the cart and poured himself a matching glass. "Your mother and I have a beautiful arrangement," he replied dryly. "We see each other as little as possible, and we stay blissfully happy." He clinked glasses with Michael and swallowed his liquor in one gulp. "We are a match made in heaven. But I didn't ask you to meet me here to discuss *my* love life. It's yours I'm interested in."

Michael dropped his head and instantly moved away. He tried to make his movement casual, but he knew his father rarely missed a thing—especially a perceived slight. All discussions of his father's "love life," as he put it, were always off the table. Michael once believed that he would be open to the topic if his father wished to confide in him, but the chance never presented itself. Arthur liked his distance—both the literal and figurative kinds. The country gave him the space—and privacy—he valued. He wasn't hiding in Leicester, but his lifestyle still had a whiff of secrecy that always grabbed people's attention and spurred their wagging tongues.

Michael flopped on the leather couch, careful not to upset his brandy, and lay supine on the cushions. "I don't have a love life," he said, hooking one foot over the other.

Arthur regarded him shrewdly. "That's precisely the problem, my son, and it's why your mother asked me to speak to you."

Michael's ears perked up. "Mother? She wrote you?" That couldn't be true. Michael was almost thirty and only retained a few memories of his parents even being in the same room together. They conversed via middlemen. It was their "beautiful arrangement," and it worked for them.

"Don't be so surprised," Arthur said, following him to the couch. He peered down at his son, startling Michael with their similarities. It was almost like looking in a mirror. They each shared the same dark-brown hair and sharp blue eyes. Their cleft chins were identical, along with the high forehead and curls that covered the tips of their overly large ears. Though they never spoke of it, Michael assumed that his father wore his hair a little longer like him because of those ears.

Perhaps if Michael visited his father more, their resemblance wouldn't always hit him like an anvil to the chest.

"She's worried about you," Arthur explained, dragging Michael from his thoughts. "And I am too, for that matter. You should be married. My heir should have an heir by now. However, I hear stories about you with a different—I'll use the word *lady*, although we both know I don't want to—lady on your arm each night. And when you're not cavorting with… *ladies*, you're getting your face beaten in. Are you trying to punish me? Are you doing this to prove something?"

"Prove?" Michael came back to sitting and finished his drink, slamming it on the table next to him. "What the hell do I have to prove? I am a boxer. It's what I do."

"You are a viscount. And you will be an earl soon enough. That is what you do!"

Michael raked a hand through his hair. "I can be all of those things. Who says I can only be one?"

"This!" Arthur cried, throwing his hands out around him. "This place, this Society, this world we live in. It dictates. It says who you are and what you are, and you are my heir. I'm sorry that you got the notion in your head that you would be able to change all that or that you had some sort of power over it. I'm sure I didn't put it there."

"Oh yes," Michael growled. "How could you when I never

see you, when you're playing house here?"

Arthur blanched, and Michael almost wished he could take the nasty comment back. But it was too late.

When Arthur spoke again, his voice was softer, as if Michael's rudeness had sucked the energy out of it. "I'm sorry, my boy, truly I am," the earl started, blinking much too quickly, "but there's no use arguing. You are what you are and that's that. So stop this foolishness now and get married. Start a proper life like everyone else."

The resentment stirred inside Michael once more. Even though his father was like a wounded animal before him, Michael still had the desire to strike. "Like you?" he spat. "You want me to be married like you?"

Arthur jerked as if his son had punched him in the face. Michael had a hell of a fist, but even he wondered if it would have hurt half as much. "My marriage is wonderful. Your mother is the perfect wife. She is everything a man like me could have ever wanted."

Michael stretched his long fingers over his knee, admiring the scars and why they were there.

His mother was a wife in name only.

He told himself to stay quiet, told himself to let it go, but he was exhausted. He hadn't been able to sleep in Manchester, which was why he'd decided to leave so early. He couldn't stay in that house, not after his time with Maggie. What the hell had he been thinking?

He hadn't been thinking. That was the problem. He'd been *feeling*. And that was the same thing his father was now warning him about. Their world had no place for emotions, only duty. And hypocrisy. Because Michael apparently couldn't be a boxer and a viscount, but he could lead two lives in the *ton*—one in the light with his wife, and the other in the dark with a mistress. Just like every other man. Just like his father.

Michael ran a hand over his haggard face. He was tired of juggling two lives, tired of analyzing the repercussions. That was one of the things he loved most about the boxing ring. There was no time for all of that. It was all instinct and reaction. One could plan, one could train, but in the end, all that mattered was the will of the body.

The words lashed out of him, free and terrifying. "If mother is so perfect for you, why do you treat her with such disrespect?"

"You don't know what you're speaking of."

Michael wouldn't back down. Tommy Jones had trained that weakness out of him. "I do know. Do you think she was silent all those years? Who do you think she spoke to when you weren't around? Who do you think she cried to? *Me.* I heard it all. And I fixed everything. Even when I was a boy, I was the man by her side that you never were."

"Stop it!" Arthur yelled. His top lip curled back, his eyes as dark as night. Michael never could fathom why his peers teased him when he was younger, picked on him and raised their fists as they'd called his father so many things—an Aunt Nancy, a buggerer, an invert. They'd never known him. They'd never seen him like this, like he could dig up a mountain and throw it into the ocean without breaking a sweat.

His classmates had only heard the stories bandied about in their circles, whispered in dark corners, and laughed at over cigars and brandies in dining rooms. That the Earl of Waverly wasn't welcome in his own home in London. That the Countess of Waverly was finished being embarrassed by her husband's vulgar scandals and loose morals.

That the weak-wristed earl had given up everything—even his young son—to live with his male lover in the country.

Michael couldn't blame his peers entirely. The salacious stories were more entertaining. And the earl was never around to defend himself or his family—which was why Michael had to. And when his words continued to fall on deaf ears, he found his fists made for a more persuasive alternative.

Fighting was so very effective, and Michael liked doing it so very much, that he didn't stop even after the taunts died out. And now his father was asking him to leave it behind. How could he?

Boxing had been there for Michael when his father had not.

Just as quickly as the fury overtook the earl, it relented. Arthur released a ragged sigh and walked to the opposite wall, leaning the back of his head against the wood paneling. "I didn't ask you here to argue," he said gently, staring at the ceiling. "Believe it or not, I wanted to spend time with you, enjoy your company… and dare to hope that you would enjoy mine."

Michael inflated his lungs and allowed the anger to filter out of his body with his breath. He answered with a chuckle. "Enjoy my company and then order me to get married to the first girl who bats her eyelashes at me."

"Not the first girl," Arthur joked. "But maybe the first girl with a decent dowry."

Michael groaned. "Father—"

"You're just being stubborn. And there's no reason for it. Not much has to change. Marriage is a business. You will have your life, and your wife will have hers. Just make sure you both understand that. A man has his private life and his public one. It takes some balancing at first, but things eventually settle down."

Michael yearned to ask Father how *he* had fumbled it. If it were all so easy and expected, how had he managed to wreck his entire life? Or perhaps he hadn't. Michael wondered if his father was actually leading the one that he wanted, the one where his son played a minuscule part. At school, he'd smashed in every boy's face who'd dared to say the earl had deserted his son without a backward glance. But sometimes, only sometimes, Michael questioned if it had been true.

He opened his mouth and closed it. There was so much he wanted to say, so much he wanted to ask, but he didn't have a clue on where to start. Arthur straightened away from the wall, watching his son. His eyes were large and intense. Michael thought he saw a trace of yearning.

"I… I…" Michael focused on the carpet, afraid that he wouldn't be able to speak if he were looking at his father. "I don't want to live two lives," he said. *Not like you. Not like Mother.* Not like every other man he knew. "It doesn't seem right."

Michael wanted one life. *His.* He'd seen his father live in the shadows for so long; he'd seen the effect it had on him even in the snippets of life he'd been privy to. Shadows always felt safe at first, but they had a way of keeping out so much sun that one's very soul paled and shriveled into nothing.

Michael heard his father's footsteps and felt his large hand on his shoulder. He didn't see it coming, which was why he didn't flinch at the touch. It was tentative, ill-fitting and foreign, like wearing someone else's clothes. "Listen to me, my son. You have the girl in your grasp. She wants you; it's what everyone tells me. Why didn't you just do it and get it over with when you had the chance?"

Michael's gaze snapped up to his father. "When I had the chance? I couldn't even kiss her." The words tripped out of his mouth like drunken sailors. "She would never… Maggie would never…"

How had his father known about Maggie? Who could have told him? He recounted their conversation. Had he let something slip?

It wouldn't have been that difficult to believe. Michael's mind had been on the lovely, troublesome woman all day. His conscious tortured him with pictures of her sultry eyes when they'd sat next to each other on her bed, the way her laughter tickled his chest whenever he teased. He loved that sound, which was why he teased her so much.

But he could never consider marrying Maggie. Michael couldn't imagine putting her through that arrangement, nor did he think she would ever stand for it. Maggie needed a man who would give her the kind of love and passion that would make her toes curl in her slippers. The man that could kiss the frown from her face, who could taste the ardor on her lips despite her cutting words. She needed a man who lived as freely and fearlessly as she did. Surrounded by her damn yapping dogs.

Now, why did that odd, tumultuous picture make Michael want to laugh and cry? Why did it make his chest light and his head dizzy?

His father chuckled in his drink. "Maggie? Who's Maggie? Are you talking about the Marquis of Amesbury's daughter? The odd one? No, I meant… Lady Wendy. My friends tell me that she follows you around like a lovestruck kitten at all the events. Just ask her to be your bride and get on with it. You know what her answer will be."

Michael fumed from his blunder.

The earl went on. "The Marquis of Amesbury," he mused, "I haven't talked to him in ages. I wonder if he's still traveling all over Christendom with his wife. Such a lively couple—too lively. Maggie, that's right—the little girl. They used to drop her off with the old Lady Emma whenever they went abroad. Now *that* was a woman. Insane. Incredibly forthright. I once caught her smoking a pipe at Sullivan's, and she wouldn't leave the table until she'd cleaned out every man's pockets." He laughed at the memory. "Lord knows, the girl must be positively feral if she spent most of her childhood with that one."

"Sh-she's not." Michael cleared his throat. "And Lady Emma died last year."

His father frowned. "Ah, damn, how did I not know that? I should have sent a card. That's the problem with living in the country. You're always the last to know things."

Michael sniffed. "That's the only problem?"

"Never mind that," his father huffed. "Let's get back to Lady Wendy."

With one ear, Michael listened to his father drone on about responsibility and duty, but it was fruitless. He wasn't in the listening mood. Something felt off, uncentered, and he knew it had everything to do with that kiss—or *almost*-kiss.

Why hadn't Michael done it? He'd wanted to—his body had made that more than evident—and the scary thing was that Maggie had wanted it as well. Michael had recognized the passion in her gaze, had felt the electricity sparking between them. She had mesmerized him, and all he could think about was staying with her. When she'd told him to leave, he couldn't stop himself—he had to touch her, had to feel her silky skin beneath his fingertips one more time.

But then his conscience took over. Nothing about that night was normal. Maggie wasn't normal. And kissing her like she was seemed wrong. There was a spark inside Maggie that needed more, wanted more from life. She was outspoken and spontaneous, quick to anger and even quicker to smile. She deserved someone who lived just as freely, just as wantonly with their affection.

Michael could never be that man. His father had been that man—with the wrong person—and now his son was paying the price for it. If Michael wanted to toe the line in his fights, he'd have to toe the line in the *ton* and be the future earl that his parents wanted. He would be stern and passionless in the light of day with his wife by his side and let out all of his frustrations and inhibitions at night in the ring. His father declared he should have a mistress; Michael's mistress would be boxing.

And he and Maggie would cross paths from time to time and never have to wonder about what might have been. Maggie had boasted that she would never marry, but Michael didn't believe that for one second. She would never marry a lackluster, bloodless man of the *ton*. She would marry a man who gave her his soul along with the world. Because a woman like Maggie asked for nothing less.

If Michael had allowed himself to kiss Maggie, his life as he knew it would be in jeopardy. He had a sinking suspicion that loving Maggie had the power to transform a person, and he couldn't have that. He was already trying to juggle being two different people as it was. He couldn't handle being another.

No. He'd made a good decision. A sound decision.

But then why did he keep wishing he had done the exact opposite?

Arthur pounded his son on the shoulder. "Why the scowl? I don't know why you're making this difficult. It's not. All you have to do is make one choice and then everything will lay itself out for you neatly. You won't even have to think. Talk to the girl. Get it done."

Michael eventually nodded and got up to pour himself another drink. In the end, his father knew what to say.

Michael didn't want to think. As always, his body would be his guide.

But then why did it feel like he'd just gone twenty rounds and couldn't find his feet to save his life?

His father moved to stand in front of him now, commanding his attention. Michael watched him shuffle his feet. He recognized reluctance in the man's expression, the hesitation on his lips as he grew increasingly uncomfortable. "I..." Arthur closed his eyes and tried once more. "I'm not trying to be a tyrant with your life. But I know how cruel this world can be for... some people. Things are less complicated when you fall in line, behave like everyone else. I don't want you to have a difficult time. I need you to understand that. I love you. You're my only son. I just want what's best for you. I want your life to be easy."

Michael's limbs were impossibly weary. He couldn't have defended himself if he tried.

"But does an easier life mean a happier one, Father?"

The earl's smile was packed with sorrow. He shrugged his wide shoulders, the ones he shared with his son. "Who can say for sure?"

Chapter Six

THANKS TO JO, Ella, and Ella's indomitable mother, it only took one week for Maggie's new plan to make its debut.

Originally, Maggie hadn't considered making an appearance at Ella's mother's ball, but the ladies insisted it would be the perfect opportunity to lay her trap for Michael's feral feelings. When Maggie had informed Aunt Alice about her change of heart on attending (and asked her advice on what to wear for the night), the older woman had almost fainted from joy. However, excitement soon won over shock, and five hours later, Maggie walked up the stairs to the Viscount and Viscountess Weston's enormous and glittering ballroom wearing four pounds of feathers on top of her head and petticoats so stiff that she was sure they could walk themselves.

However, she had to give her aunt her due. As Maggie had reviewed her reflection before setting out for the night, she'd been pleasantly surprised by the handsome woman staring back at her. Usually, she had no patience for embellishments, preferring a more efficient and decisive style of dress, but she could appreciate this new version of herself, and even allowed it to bolster her confidence. The crimson satin skirts rustled when she walked, imbuing her with the notion that she was a great ship splitting through dangerous seas. She felt exotic and otherworldly. Didn't everyone wish to live in someone else's skin every once in a while?

Ella and Jo noticed Maggie the moment she entered the ballroom and could hardly wait for the butler to finish announcing her before swarming like bees around a fresh bouquet of lavender.

Jo, who usually played her emotions closer to the vest, couldn't hide her astonished appraisal as she surveyed Maggie from head to toe. Maggie was almost hurt by the amazed approval, though she decided to let it go and take it as a compliment.

"Is he here?" she asked her friends, surreptitiously darting her gaze about the room. She fidgeted with the top of her dress and longed to retrieve her shawl. Thanks to Alice's low-cut gown, she worried everyone would notice when her bumbling nerves turned all of her creamy skin pink.

"Yes, no, wait, who?" Ella replied breathlessly. The lovely girl's waist was snatched so tight, it was a wonder she could think or breathe. Maggie blamed the draconian corset on her befuddled answer.

"Michael!"

Jo stepped in, flicking her head toward the far side of the room, past the young couples lining up to begin the quadrille. "I spotted him earlier, pretending to be bored and miserable like all the other urbane gentlemen."

Maggie resisted seeking him out. She could already imagine the disinterested, haughty expression, the restless movement of his shoulders. It was enough to satisfy. "Are you sure he was pretending?"

Jo rolled her eyes, her irritation evident in the wave of her fan. "Of course he was. All of the men like balls even though they pretend not to. They want us females to believe they're dark and brooding, all Mr. Darcys, no Mr. Bingleys."

Ella scrunched her brow. "I liked Mr. Bingley."

"Not as much as Mr. Darcy, you didn't," Jo replied.

Ella's slim frame deflated. "Yes, I suppose that's true."

Maggie stepped between the two. The suspense of the night was killing her. "Can we focus, please? I can't just stand here. What should I do? Do I look at him? Do I smile at him? I practiced in the mirror this afternoon and I'm really starting to get how to coquettishly bat my eyelashes. What do you think?"

She leaned toward Jo, fluttering her eyes as seductively as she could until Jo grabbed her forearm. "Please, don't do that anymore. Ever."

Maggie retreated, quitting the action. It was probably a good thing, since she worried she'd pull a muscle from all the practicing. "All right, then," she began slowly. "Why don't you just tell me what to do?"

Jo faced the dancers, her back straight, her neck effortlessly graceful. Not for the first time, Maggie wondered why the widow hadn't remarried. Her mourning period had ended. Still young and still beautiful, Jo would be a catch for any man there, though there *was* the matter of her intense demeanor. "Good Lord," she exclaimed, "haven't you been to a ball before? You ignore the man. And then ignore him some more. If Michael comes toward you, walk the other way."

Maggie wanted to laugh, and then cry. The horses had officially bolted. "I don't understand. When do I speak to him?"

"You don't," Jo cried as if Maggie had just asked when she should strip off her clothes and bathe in the nearest fountain. "Not if you can help it. Tonight is not about speaking to Michael. It's about making him want to speak to *you*. How did you not know that?"

Maggie felt like a silly child again. It was like the time she'd asked her mother if she could wear her father's old trousers and her mother had laughed as if she'd told the funniest joke. Maggie had had to wait to visit her grandmother to try them on for the first time. Her grandmother had taken her seriously and shown no qualms. It had been glorious. "You didn't mention it," she replied sullenly.

"It was clearly implied."

"Not that clearly," Maggie grumbled. "I could have just ignored him from my home."

Jo's long neck fell back, and she scowled at the ceiling. "No, you couldn't have," she said, "because you need to be here to dance and appear to be having the time of your life without him. Only then will he realize that *he* wants to be the time of your life."

Jo appeared so sure of herself, so in command, but something inside Maggie pinched—and it wasn't only because of the dozens of pins holding up her hair and feathers. "I don't know…"

"Well, I do. Trust me. I know exactly what I'm doing."

"And my mother would completely approve," Ella chimed in. "Although… if that woman has limits, I haven't found them yet."

"Fine," Maggie said. "Oh, did you ever ask your friend for that favor?"

The muscle under Jo's right eye twitched. *Interesting.*

"Of course. I wrote to him last night." Her voice was as tight as Ella's corset. "He's agreed."

Either Ella couldn't discern the confusing note in Jo's tone, or she chose to ignore it. "Who is it?" she asked excitedly.

Jo's muscle twitched once more. "He's not here… yet. I don't think."

Maggie focused on the widow, sadistically enjoying her discomfort. "Are you not telling me his name for a reason? Do I not *want* to know?"

Jo's laughter was unnaturally high. Maggie had never seen her like this; it was like watching Aunt Alice giggle like a girl in front of Michael—out of place and off-putting. "I just want you to relax a bit more before I tell you," Jo explained quickly. "You're rather highly strung at the moment."

Maggie rolled her eyes. "What's the matter?" she teased. "Does he only have one eye?"

Ella perked up. "I find eye patches to be most dashing."

Jo's lips thinned. "No, though he *can* be a bit high and mighty at times."

"High and mighty?" Maggie smiled as Jo continued to squirm. "Is he some German prince?"

Ella clapped her hands. "Princes are so regal!"

"They're far too common." Jo clucked in disapproval. "My man—I mean the man I've chosen—has more of a... history."

Maggie sighed. *History?* "Please don't tell me he's old enough to be my father."

Ella stared off dreamily. "Older men are so distinguished."

Jo's gaze remained on the dancers, but the tendons in her neck flared. If Maggie didn't know any better, she'd think the woman was worried. "Just be careful," Jo ordered her, shielding her mouth with her fan. "He's sharp and silver-tongued. Don't believe a word he says. Always remember—the more truthful he sounds, the more he's lying."

"I don't think I want to meet this man!"

Jo lashed her with a side-eye, but her voice remained weightless, even helpless. "Oh, yes you do. That's the problem. Everyone always wants to meet him. And his faults only make people want him more."

Maggie couldn't contain her irritation any longer. "Why are you nervous? You're making *me* nervous. You said he was going to help me and now I'm on edge and on guard like I'm about to be dealing with Calico Jack." Her shoulders slumped when it came to her. "Please tell me he's not a pirate, Jo."

That brought out a laugh, relieving some of Jo's unnerving tension. "He's not a pirate... although I think his brother might be one. And he *is* going to help you; he promised me. The only issue is that I don't know if he's capable of helping someone without also helping himself."

"What does that mean?" Maggie asked.

Jo opened her mouth to answer, but a deep, amused voice from behind them beat her to it.

"Yes, what *does* that mean, Lady Everly?" the smooth voice purred. "I have to say I'm waiting with bated breath. And by the way, there *are* some of us who like Bingley more than Darcy. That stodgy fellow acted like a miserable prat half the time. Aren't you going to introduce your friends? Don't tell me I left my bed and came all the way out here for nothing."

The voice should have prepared Maggie for the man; however, she would forever believe that nothing could ever prepare someone for meeting Lord Oliver, Duke of Winchester, for the first time. Tall and commanding, dark and lean, he was the man writers conjured when they wrote about princes in their fairytales. With his ink-black hair and high cheekbones, Lord Oliver brought dreams to reality. He was the cad that made women rethink rules and propriety. He was indomitably impressive… to everyone except Jo.

"Your bed?" She snorted. "You're never asleep at the time."

"Sure I am," he quipped, the smile on his face never budging. "I just haven't started my day yet."

Jo tapped her front teeth and turned to Maggie. "Do you understand me now? Pure fox. Poor. Ruin."

Lord Oliver laughed, a great, booming laugh that brought half the room's attention their way. "But a quasi-honorable one, at least give me that. I'm a fox who repays debts."

The tendons strained in Jo's neck once more. Why was she so angry? The man was clearly a rake, but at least he was an entertaining one. "If you think this makes us even then you are terribly mistaken," she replied evenly.

Finally, there was a change in the man. A slight alteration in his carefree façade. Most wouldn't have even noticed it. He cocked his head. "Wouldn't be the first time, Lady Everly. You and I both know I haven't had a first time in a long time."

Maggie gasped. She wasn't entirely certain what the duke was referring to, although she could guess it wasn't fit for ladies' ears. She swiveled to Ella, but the poor girl had already vanished. Probably for the best. "Perhaps this was a bad decision—" she began.

Jo cut her off. "Lady Margaret, may I introduce Lord Oliver,

Duke of Winchester."

Maggie curtseyed. "It's a pleasure, Your Grace."

Something washed over him, and in seconds the rakish demeanor vanished, in its place the regal duke. He returned a low, somber bow, placing one hand on his heart. "The pleasure is all mine, Lady Margaret. Or Lady Maggie, I thought?"

Maggie couldn't help her smile—or her giggle. The man could melt ice. "Yes, my friends call me that."

"Then that is what I shall call you. Because we are friends now, the very best kind, the ones with benefits. Like dancing. Shall we?"

Had the quadrille finished? Maggie didn't have time to answer her own question before the duke swept her onto the dance floor, where couples parted as eagerly as the Red Sea to Moses. The music surged and Lord Oliver whisked her through the steps, commanding the waltz as he, no doubt, did most things, with utmost certainty and suavity. Maggie had never considered herself a good dancer—proficient, but nothing to write home about; however, in the duke's assertive and steady embrace, her feet barely skimmed the floor. His confidence rubbed off on her. She couldn't have been more grateful.

"I… I think I should start off by saying thank you," Maggie stammered, hoping the duke wasn't one of those men who preferred his dance partners to be silent. That was not her nature, and now that it was evident that he and Jo had some sort of a rocky history, Maggie couldn't rely on the widow to be their go-between. Rules and expectations needed to be stated and heard. "I don't know what Lady Everly did to convince you to help me. In fact, I didn't know you were acquaintances."

The duke gazed past her shoulder like he was recounting a sad memory. "Jo and I go back so far that we don't even remember who we used to be." His brow furrowed. "Or when she started to hate me. I suppose it's better that way."

Maggie doubted that. Women like Jo didn't seem to forget easily. Or forgive, for that matter. "Well, regardless, thank you."

The pleasant façade rolled back in like a storm over the ocean. "Not at all. The plays in London are boring at present. So I thought this would be a chance to star in my own. I always thought I would be great on the stage."

Maggie shook her head. "Oh, no, no, no, you won't have to do anything. Dancing is quite enough." Her voice rose hopefully. "Maybe one more dance tonight? And that would be all. I wouldn't want to put you out."

"How about two more?"

Three dances! "That might be too much."

He smirked. "For a duke? Nothing is too much."

Lord Oliver was like a fairy come straight out of the Green Forest just looking for trouble. Maggie tried again. "I don't think it will be necessary. Half the room is looking at us—at you—as it is. We've made our point."

"At *us*," he corrected her. "They're staring at *us*, and it's more than half. Much more. But we only care about one person, yes? Is he here? I'd hate for all these feathers to go to waste. By the way, did you murder a peacock before you came here tonight? It's fine if you did. They're such vain creatures."

Maggie blushed, ducking her head. "Yes." She blinked. "I mean, he's here. I didn't murder a peacock, although my aunt may have."

"Sturdy woman. I'd like to meet the audacious minx," he replied. "Now, where is *he*?"

"In the corner by the door, next to Lady Wendy. No, no, don't look!"

Naturally, Lord Oliver didn't heed her warning.

His face screwed up in confusion. "Oh, Christ! Lord Michael! You're in love with that old bruiser? Look at him scowling over there. Always so serious! And look how hard he's making poor Lady Wendy work for his attention. Bad form. Bad form all around."

Maggie's chest burned so hot she was shocked she wasn't immolated right there in the middle of the dance floor. "Shh, keep your voice down," she hissed. "And I'm not in love with him."

His cool eyes studied her warily. "But you want him to be in love with you so you can break his heart? That's awfully devilish, my lady. I respect revenge; it's a lovely way to spend an afternoon or two. However, did you think about just kneeing him in the bollocks once to get this whole thing over with quicker? You'd be surprised by how effective it is. I tell you from experience."

Maggie tilted up her nose as he glided her into another seamless turn. "Who said I want this done quickly? Besides, you and I both know the heart hurts more."

The duke's smile was slow to form, but when it did, it took up most of his face. "You are evil—another thing I respect, by the way." He leaned back, peering at her with newfound fascination. "By the by, did you ever consider that you should be worried about me?"

"And why is that?"

"Because I like women with a little bit of spirit. If you're not careful, I might propose by the end of the night."

Now it was Maggie's turn to laugh loudly enough to catch stares. "Will you please stop making me laugh? This entire party probably thinks we're insane."

Lord Oliver's eyes sparkled. "Everyone's insane when they're in love. So keep laughing, my dear. You hired me for the night and I'm ready to play my part. Let's give these people something to talk about."

Chapter Seven

LORD OLIVER WAS true to his word. An hour later, the duke still hadn't left Maggie's side, and she was certain the *ton* would be living off stories of his smitten performance for the rest of the summer.

"Would you like some punch?" he asked, guiding her off the dance floor after their *third* dance.

"Oh, you don't have to," Maggie insisted, waving her fan over her flushed face. She was actually sweating. And having fun. At a ball! Who would have thought?

Lord Oliver's eyes slid around the room as he spoke to her. She noticed he did that a lot, as if he couldn't help but make sure all attention was centered on him. The only time he hadn't done it was when he'd spoken to Jo. "I'm a duke," he replied, adding a playful little bow. "From time to time I allow myself to be charming and gallant. If I were you, I'd accept it while it lasts."

"Why? Do you turn back into a pumpkin at midnight?"

"No. Just an arse."

Maggie sighed through a chuckle. "Punch would be lovely, thank you."

The smile stayed on her face as she watched Lord Oliver press through the crowd. He didn't have to work too hard; the instant someone noticed him, they fell over themselves to give him room. What must that feel like, to have so much power? The duke wore it easily, as one did when they knew nothing else; nevertheless, behind his easy countenance and cutting quips, Maggie sensed something lonely inside of him, something almost mournful. And he wasn't the kind of man who would ever tell anyone why, at least not her.

"I didn't expect to see you here tonight."

Maggie's smile evaporated as she followed the voice to the man at her side. The man she'd been pretending not to watch all night. The man who—she was certain—had not been watching her.

Maggie told herself it was just Michael; however, being this close threatened to throw her off-kilter. His clothes were somber and still a smidge too tight around his arms and chest, and his hair had been styled back away off his forehead, leaving his face open and direct.

Maggie's fan picked up speed.

Michael reminded her so much of Lord Oliver. But men carried themselves with poise, a self-assuredness that made them charge when others hesitated, but where the duke hid his feelings behind a composed, teasing veneer, Michael was more forthright. His emotions floated too close to the surface, and his disappointment was evident in his tone.

Maggie couldn't let it bait her. *Be serene. Be gracious. Don't argue!* She replaced her smile quickly. "Lady Ella encouraged me. She thought I would enjoy myself."

Michael jutted his chin toward the refreshment room. "It certainly looks like you are."

"I am."

"Good."

"Yes. Quite."

Michael's tone had lost some of its verve. Was her agreeableness *really* working?

"I didn't know you were acquainted with the duke," he said, almost too nonchalantly, as if he didn't even care if she answered.

"For a man who's said he knows me so well, you don't seem to know much tonight."

Michael *humphed*, and Maggie cursed herself. So much for agreeableness. But it was difficult, more difficult than she'd thought it would be. Acting this way felt so unnatural, like asking a kitten to fly.

But the thunder in his expression abated. "I suppose I don't," he replied softly. "I don't mean to upset you. I just…" He glanced at his hands, and Maggie yearned to ask him to remove his gloves. Were his knuckles still bruised and broken? "I don't mean to bother *your fun*; I just came over to say I'm… You know, I'm sorry the way I left you the other night. I didn't wish to… confuse things."

Where had all the air gone in the room? Had someone sucked it all up? Maggie blinked. *Confuse things*? Did he honestly believe she was upset and pining for him? Did he think she was some newly out, fresh-faced, naïve chit who couldn't control her attraction for him?

Maggie grabbed the reins inside her. She wouldn't give him the satisfaction of fixating on those words. She'd fixate on others.

"Left me?" Her question dripped with condescension.

Michael's gaze latched on to hers, searching. "In Manchester, in your room."

Maggie huffed. "Were you in my room?" She tapped her fingers against her chin. "Oh right, after I was overcome with the episode at the wedding."

"You weren't overcome. Your aunt—"

"My aunt asked you to carry me to my room. Thank you again, so kind. I don't know what I would have done if you hadn't been there."

"You would have walked," Michael replied with bite. "You would have been fine."

Maggie bobbed her shoulders. "If you say so." The sentence landed with an audible thud. She scanned the room jovially, waiting for him to leave. Inside, well, she wasn't nearly so placid.

When he continued to stand in front of her, Maggie returned a questioning smile.

Michael cleared his throat. "How… how have you been?"

She covered her laughter with her fan. "In the week since I last saw you? I'm fine, of course." A swath of people scattered behind Michael and Maggie looked over his shoulder to see the fuss. Perfect timing. Lord Oliver returning with her punch. She made her voice cloyingly hopeful. "I'm better than fine, actually."

Michael scowled, and a piece of hair fell over his face. "What the hell are you mooning at? How can you even see through all those feathers on your head?"

"What?" Maggie's hand flew to her headpiece, and she stroked a feather as if to apologize for the ogre's offending words. "You don't like them? I thought they were rather nice. A little large, perhaps—"

"They're much too large. You won't need a carriage tonight. You'll be able to fly home."

Stay calm. Stay poised. Stay sweet. Maggie's stomach churned from the effort. "They're no longer than anyone else's," she replied, upset that she could hear the hurt in her voice. Why did he always have to be so honest with her? What was next? Another cruel name? "My aunt said I looked lovely. I suppose I'll let her know that you disagree."

"I didn't say that—" Michael clapped his mouth shut as if afraid of what might come out. "I just… I'm not used to seeing…"

"Me looking lovely?"

"Stop putting words in my mouth!"

Maggie threw up her hands. *So much for poised and sweet.* "I'm sorry. The *last* thing I want to do is make *you* upset."

"I'm not upset," he boomed, losing composure as swiftly as she had. "*You're* upset."

"I'm not upset."

Michael ignored her. "And you're not being honest with yourself. You love making me upset, teasing me. It's one of your greatest joys!"

Maggie searched for the duke over Michael's shoulder once more. The man was walking incredibly slowly and stopping to chat to anyone who would listen. He was doing it for her, Maggie realized. Lord Oliver didn't want to interrupt this moment. Little did he know it was swiftly morphing into a catastrophe. She had to contain herself. *Stay sweet. Stay poised. Be the girl that every man wants.*

It took effort, but Maggie managed another unbothered smile. "Maybe when I was a child, Lord Michael, but let me assure you that I'm not a child anymore. No more games."

Michael scoffed, folding his arms in stark defiance. Why didn't he believe she was gentle and tender, dammit!

"Even if I let you win?" he goaded her with a sly grin.

Maggie released a frustrated breath. "You've never let me win a day in your life. And you never will."

"But that's why you like me so much."

"I don't like you."

He showed all his teeth. "Oh, yes you do."

Where had her plan gone? What had Jo told her to do? Be nice and accommodating? Something like that? Maggie couldn't remember anymore. *Oh well.*

He held out a hand. "Dance with me."

Maggie's voice was impossibly faint. "I've already danced."

"With the wrong man."

"Oh," Maggie said, chuckling, "there's nothing wrong with that man."

"There aren't enough hours in the day for me to tell you what's wrong with that man."

Lord Oliver was a few feet behind Michael now. Michael had to feel him. How could he not? And yet he refused to turn from her.

His deep, fathomless eyes bored into her. "He's not a man who will stay. You know that, don't you? He'll leave you just like everyone else—" Shaking his head, he rubbed a hand over his mouth. "Forgive me. I shouldn't have—"

"Leave me like everyone else?" Maggie replied. "Is that what you shouldn't have said?"

Michael's jaw flexed.

Maggie stopped fanning herself, keeping her gaze sharp. "I'm not the lonely little girl I used to be, Michael. I think it's best if you remember that when you speak to me."

"I didn't mean…" Michael fought to contain himself. "I just meant you deserve better. You shouldn't let yourself get distracted by peacocking men."

Maggie sniffed. "And here I thought I was the one wearing all the feathers."

Michael let out a mirthless chuckle and reached up to touch a bright gold feather hanging over her ear. His smile was a little sad as he pinched it between his fingers. "You don't need these to get him to look at you. All they do is disguise who you really are."

Maggie could feel that invisible string again, the one that always appeared ready and willing to pull her toward him. Her words came out like a whisper. "And why do you think you know who I really am?"

Michael's hand was still outstretched before Maggie, waiting for her to accept it. He broke into a sheepish smile. "Because I've always known. We were children together—"

"But we're not children anymore, are we?" Maggie stared at his hand, willing herself not to take it. Something clicked inside her.

She turned her neck, moving the feathers out of his touch. He might have thought them ridiculous, but they served their purpose. They'd gotten his attention, and they'd reminded her of the part she was playing. Michael thought he knew her, but he was wrong. This Maggie, with the fiery dress and the fancy admirer, wasn't her. This Maggie was meant to entice, to tempt, to win Society's long game with the only cards that women were dealt.

Giving in now would ruin everything. Allowing Michael to

hold her would only grant him the power *she* craved.

This was only the beginning.

Maggie lifted her chin. "I appreciate your concern, my lord, but I'm a grown woman and I get to decide whom I want to be, *and* whom I want to spend my evenings with. It was a pleasure speaking to you tonight. I hope you have a lovely time."

The hand fell, but Michael remained. A reluctant smile forced its way past his scowl. "You never did like to back down from a challenge, did you?"

Maggie slid past him, reaching for the glass the duke offered. But before she left, she leaned into Michael's side and whispered, "Oh, my lord, you have *no* idea."

Chapter Eight

FOR DAYS AFTER the ball, Michael had the overwhelming urge to run. He yearned to run and run and run and run until his legs melted to pudding and his lungs threatened to explode. But he was in London enduring another afternoon. Running wasn't something one did in Town unless you were a thief pilfering pockets or a young buck late for your first appointment with your new mistress. He'd considered riding in the park, but he got no farther than a few lengths from the mews before he spun around and returned home.

There was no explaining it. Michael was decidedly out of form. And it was the worst possible time. Tommy had scheduled a fight for that evening, and it was a big one. Tim O'Shaughnessy was fresh off an impressive streak of wins in Ireland and considered the top contender to be the next bare-knuckle champion. The Irishman and his people considered Michael a mere steppingstone before getting a chance at real competition—the current champion, Jack Harrison.

Michael also had his eye on Harrison, but arranging a fight with the star had proven difficult. For a man who'd barely been told *no* his entire life, Michael had been hearing it a lot over the past few years. Fighting was a sport for the common man, and there was nothing common about Michael. Although, on paper, the idea of beating an aristocrat to a bloody pulp looked appealing, the practicality of it often turned men away. The repercussions could be too great. Many of the fighters who didn't know Michael considered him a liability, a fancy lad who was out searching for a lark. Fighting, though enormously popular in both the upper and middle classes, was still illegal. Men died all the time in the ring, or shortly outside of it from complications. No one wanted to *accidentally* kill a lord—a viscount, almost an earl—and have to deal with the questions.

But that hadn't stopped Tommy. Michael's unflagging trainer had worked just as hard to get Michael the matches he needed as he did to get his trainee ready for them. The Irishman was his latest miracle. Perhaps O'Shaughnessy assumed that if the match went belly up and Michael turned up worse for wear, he could hide out across the water until matters settled. Michael didn't care what his rationale was. He had no intention of hitting the ground, let alone settling in for the long sleep six feet under tonight. His toe would make it to the line as many times as needed.

But the day dragged on. Michael still had hours until he had to meet Tommy at the gym, and this tortuous restlessness continued to plague him. He placed most of the blame on the excitement for the match; however, Michael knew that didn't explain all of it.

And when he found himself navigating London's streets lost in meandering thought all the way to Maggie's aunt's townhouse, that only proved it.

He pushed his top hat lower over his brow. *What the hell am I doing here?* he wondered. This was the kind of insane thing lovesick puppies did, although they usually knocked on the door and presented flowers or chocolates. What was it about Maggie that kept dragging his mind and body back to her? Why did he see her face before he fell asleep each night? And why did he constantly ponder what she would say about things? Just that morning, he'd read a story in the newspaper about the charity that Harry Homes was starting for the poor immigrant families arriving in droves from Ireland, and he'd wondered what she thought of the idea. Why did he care about what Maggie thought?

Because *Maggie* cared what Maggie thought. That was why.

Her confidence had always scared him. As a boy, it had given him pause because his own mettle had been so weak. He could admit that now. He'd been intimidated in his youth, which was why he'd been the first to call her names and dismiss her accomplishments along with the other children in their parents' friend group—*all* her accomplishments over him.

Michael was grateful to realize he and the others hadn't broken her spirit with their stupidity and childish jealousy. She'd always been worth ten of them, and they'd all known it. Michael liked to think that he'd grown into himself, that the intimidation had waned as the years passed, but seeing her with that old duke, that irrepressibly charming and good-for-nothing scoundrel, at the ball had brought back all those old feelings of inadequacy.

The woman had changed her tune rather quickly on marriage. It only took one handsome duke's roving eye to fall on her before she backtracked. Of all people, why Lord Oliver? And what did he see in Maggie? Well, Michael knew what *he* saw: a beautiful woman who could make a man's belly hurt with laughter from a clever comment. A woman who was equal parts wild and soft, who knew her own mind and couldn't resist letting you know it too. A woman who once rode a sheep better than any boy and threw mud in his face when he dared ridicule her for it.

But how could Lord Oliver know all this? How could he appreciate it the way it should be?

Michael stopped pacing and stared at Lady Alice's door once more. His side ached as if his fight had already started, and O'Shaughnessy was aiming to break as many ribs as possible.

Michael wasn't the biggest fighter. Compared to most, he was tall and wiry but made up for the lack of bulk with speed and stamina. The pain in his stomach had nothing to do with nervousness from the upcoming brawl. He was scared. Again. And, again, it was Maggie's doing. Because in this one moment of his life, Michael was terrified that he was the one who had been too slow. He could admire and value all the little idiosyncratic things that made Maggie *Maggie*. But what if it was too late? What if Lord Oliver accepted and loved them first?

The door opened, startling Michael from his plaguing thoughts. With her ridiculous dog in tow, Maggie came out into the sunlight and started down the sidewalk. She was a far cry from the girl he'd bantered with at the ball. Gone were the feathers and yards of silk. She wore a simple light-blue day dress and matching, perfunctory parasol. Her bonnet was tied tight, protecting her wavy butterscotch hair from the reliable afternoon breeze. She walked steadily with a determined air. That was why Michael fell into step behind her. He wasn't following her, he told himself. He was merely curious. Her expression wasn't an ordinary *I'm going to the park* expression, though that was exactly where she was headed.

Michael gave her space, wanting to watch her for a time before addressing her. There was something exciting about studying Maggie when her guard was down. She smiled politely and nodded to the people she passed, always apologizing for her ill-mannered dog and all his insufferable yapping and attempted ankle bites.

However, the more Michael followed, the more he sensed something was awry. A couple of times, Maggie's footsteps slowed, and she twisted her neck to scan behind her. Michael made sure to hide from her view. When she was done searching for whatever she was searching for, she picked up her pace one more, still steady but less relaxed.

Just as Michael decided to catch up with her, Maggie ducked into a skinny alleyway, one that Michael was positive was a dead end. *What the hell is she doing now?*

He bided his time, waiting for her to come back. After a few minutes, his patience ran out. Michael had ideas of what happened to unsuspecting ladies in dark alleyways and none of them were good. He picked up his feet, hurrying into the alley.

Michael was just about to call out her name when—

"Oof!"

—the sharp brim of a bonnet slammed him right in the chin.

Michael grabbed hold of two arms to steady himself, holding tight despite the wiggling. Maggie's eyes came up from under the brim, violent and bright. "What are you doing here?" she said, yanking free. "Were… were you spying on me? And why are you always bumping into me?"

There was suspicion in her gaze, but also relief.

"Maybe because you never watch where you're going. And no, I wasn't spying on you!" he lied. "Why would you even think that?"

Maggie wrapped her arms around her chest. The day was far from chilly, but goosebumps erupted over her pale upper arms. "Because I saw… I thought I…" Her neck wilted, but not before Michael saw the flush in her cheeks. She was scared. And it was because of him.

"What?"

She chewed on her lower lip. "Someone was trailing me. I hid in the alley to see if they would follow me in." She paused. "But there was only you."

Guilt flooded him. "How do you know someone was following you?"

"I felt it. Don't look at me like that. I did. And it's not the first time. It's happened before—and recently. Don't tell me I'm imagining things."

"I'm not," Michael said, rubbing the back of his neck. "But there are many people walking about. It could have *felt* like someone was following you."

Her gaze narrowed. "Like yourself?"

"I wasn't following you," he lied—again. "I saw you— actually, I heard your barking, hairy sausage—and came to inquire about your day. And now I'm glad I did. It seems like I warded off a pickpocket or maybe even a kidnapper."

Michael hated lying, and he wasn't sure why he was doing it now. He felt lower than a snake. Lower than her precious sausage dog, who wouldn't stop growling at him. Little George eyed his ankle like it were a Christmas ham.

Maggie pushed past, breaking onto the sidewalk once more. "Don't tease about things like that. Dognappers are running rampant in the city. It's always in the papers."

"I'm not teasing," Michael replied, falling into step beside her. The pain in his stomach subsided. How could the blasted woman be the source *and* the cure of his discomfort? "I wouldn't dare. Well, you're safe now anyway. No one will get past me."

Maggie barked an acerbic laugh. "I don't need you; I have George."

The animal was staring at Michael's boots. If that damn thing tried to bite him… "I won't dignify that with an answer."

A silence fell. Michael would have liked to consider it a comfortable one, but it was not. Maggie was still on edge, and he was… whatever he was.

When he couldn't stand it any longer, he asked, "Are you off to the park? I am as well."

From the corner of his eye, Michael saw her frown. "I've never taken you for someone who enjoys a long walk," she replied stiffly.

"Well, I do," Michael lied again. Why was it so hard just to be himself around her? Maybe he'd navigated his life between two selves for so long lately that he couldn't remember which one was the real him. "It's good training, actually," he went on, struggling to stay nonchalant. "It strengthens the lungs."

"Oh."

Michael thought he heard a tiny sliver of interest, and it buoyed him forward. "So many people believe that it's all the hitting that takes a fighter out of a match early."

Maggie raised her eyebrows. "Isn't it?"

"No," he replied eagerly. "It's the lungs. All that punching and swinging and ducking. It's exhausting. If a man is not properly fit, he'll lose the match before he even takes a few swift jabs to the jaw."

Maggie's steps slowed as she appeared to mull over his words. Michael appreciated that she was taking him seriously. He rarely discussed fighting strategies with anyone outside of Tommy. His parents didn't wish to hear about it, and his friends were most interested in the outcome rather than the preparation. It was a rare person who wanted to know how the food was prepared; they just wanted to eat it.

"I had no idea," Maggie replied, gently yanking her leash before George could jump on a passing little boy who was enjoying a fresh hand pie.

"Now you do."

"So, you walk…"

Michael's smile widened. "Well, I'd prefer to run, but now isn't the time. Can you imagine me loping through the park with one hand on my hat and the other pumping beside me? I'd probably get thrown straight into an asylum."

"And they'd throw away the key," Maggie said, laughing, and the sound scratched at something inside Michael's chest. He rarely considered a woman's laugh—not like he did Maggie's. Deep and throaty, her laugh was a far cry from the sweet and demure giggles of other ladies in their set. Nevertheless, Michael noticed that it didn't happen often, most likely because Maggie didn't lie. If she found something amusing, she saw little point in hiding that fact. The same could be said for what she didn't find amusing—which was usually him.

"Or worse," she continued, thankfully oblivious to his thoughts, "they'd gossip about you in the papers."

"My mother would love that, I'm sure," Michael drawled. "Another crazy Earl of Waverly. Must be in the blood."

Maggie stopped and regarded him. Her face was exquisitely round, perfectly so. Michael had once heard that the sun was the only perfectly round object in nature. He had an inane desire to find the person who'd said that and debate them until they changed their mind.

"Your father isn't crazy."

Michael grimaced. The last thing he wanted to do was talk about his father. But by the resolute way Maggie looked at him… Even George had shut his trap, sensing the seriousness of his mistress. With a sigh, Michael relented. "No, but my mother likes to think of him that way. It's easier for her to understand."

Maggie nodded, beginning to move again. Her forehead puckered as she considered her next words. Again, this was rare for Michael. People asked him about his father even less than they asked about fighting. "I suppose a wife doesn't want to believe her husband is in love with someone else."

"Especially if that someone else is a man."

Michael froze. He couldn't believe he'd just said that. To a woman, of all people. What the hell was he thinking? He wasn't. That was the problem. Somewhere in the conversation, he'd stopped *trying* to be someone—not a fighter or a viscount. Michael was just *being*.

"I apologize—"

Maggie twisted her neck to him, one brow arched. "Are they? I mean to say… do they… love each other? Your father and his"— she swallowed a lump in her throat—"valet?"

Michael gave the question the gravity it deserved. "I've only been around them together a few times," he began slowly. "My father tends to keep Mr. Brown away when I visit."

"Is he ashamed?"

"I don't know," he replied. Honestly.

Maggie went on, completely oblivious to the fact that these were not the kinds of questions that one asked a man on a walk. But Michael wasn't just a man, was he? He was more. And he desperately wanted her to recognize it too. "Does he want to protect you?"

"A little late for that." Michael chuckled. "Half my childhood was spent defending myself from the boys who said that since I looked just like my father, and acted just like my father, that I must prefer men as well."

"Yes, I remember."

"You remember?"

She shrugged. "I was present at most of those weekend parties with the same children. They never made it a habit to speak to me, but I heard things."

Another lightning strike of guilt. Michael hadn't made speaking to Maggie a priority either, though she had the grace not to mention it now.

"And that's when you started fighting?" she asked, moving the conversation forward.

Michael shoved his hands in his pockets and stared straight ahead. "And I never looked back. We really shouldn't be speaking about this. It's hardly appropriate for a lady."

Maggie waved her free hand in front of her. "Don't worry. Grandmother was always telling me inappropriate things. She had views on everything and liked nothing better than to share them."

"Is that so?"

"It is." Maggie hesitated. "She… she said your father was a 'damn fool' but that what he did was one of the most romantic things she'd ever seen."

Michael's brow furrowed. He let out a short laugh. "Yes, I suppose someone might say that if they thought giving up everything for his lover was romantic."

"No." Maggie shook her head. "Not that. It was what he did for your mother."

Michael's voice was tight. He got the words out before his throat closed. "Wh-what are you talking about?"

Maggie went on before she lost her nerve. "Grandmother said that so many men are too open with their mistresses, regardless of their wives' feelings. After the incident… I mean to say… when your father left, most of the whispers stopped, most of the gossip. Grandmother said that staying away was the best thing your father could do for his wife. He may have got to keep his love, but your mother got London." Maggie flashed a wry smile. "And Grandmother always said that your mother came out on top. London was better."

Head down, Michael stayed quiet, mulling over her words. "I suppose I never contemplated it that way before."

Maggie shrugged. "There are as many ways to think about something as there are stars in the sky. It's how you solve problems."

That managed to bring out a smile. "Your grandmother was a smart woman," Michael said. "I wish I would have taken the time to know her better."

"She *was* smart." Maggie glanced up at him from under her dark lashes. "But I came up with that one."

Chapter Nine

MAGGIE BEGAN TO fidget. She'd assumed that Michael would leave her once they'd entered the park; however, she was nearing her destination and Michael still held close as if he hadn't a care in the world… as if he didn't *want* to leave.

After the mention of his father, they'd kept up a light conversation, mostly because the thought of walking in silence made Maggie even more jittery. Because then she might have to admit to herself that she was enjoying his company.

"You know, you never did tell me what you're up to today," Michael said, the side of his arm casually brushing hers as they climbed a short bridge over the park's single pond. It wasn't the first time they'd touched; every time Maggie tugged George's leash, she accidentally elbowed Michael in his ribcage. But this innocent act, this careless brushing of clothes and skin, felt deliberate in its spontaneity, enough to make Maggie's heart quicken.

Michael sent her a lazy grin. "Off to practice your cricket?"

"With George in tow? Impossible." Maggie snorted, and the dog glanced up at them, sensing he was the topic of conversation. "Once he snatches the cricket ball, he never gives it back."

"Haven't gotten that far in your lessons, then?"

"George is a work in progress."

Michael laughed. "Aren't we all?" He bent over to ruffle the top of the dog's head, and for once, George had the good manners not to bite his hand off in the process. Maggie was a proud mother.

She mirrored his action and also gave George a little love behind his long ears. "No, this isn't just an ordinary walk in the park. I'm meeting a man."

Michael tripped at the end of the bridge. "What?"

Maggie smiled. "A man. Mr. Burnham. We've written back and forth a few times. I've agreed to meet him. He suggested the old greenhouse just around the bend. There it is. Good. Now we can finally get to know one another and see if our situation is mutually beneficial."

Michael tripped once more. He grabbed Maggie's elbow, commanding her to stop. His mood had changed quickly. His face had been as calm and carefree as the pond they'd passed, and now he was growling as bad as George.

Michael maintained a low voice, but the warning was apparent. "What the hell are you talking about, meeting a man? You don't need anything 'mutually beneficial.'" Michael whipped off his hat and combed his hands through his wavy hair. "And why the hell did you bring George?"

Maggie couldn't understand his frustration and could feel her own rise to meet it halfway. The old Michael had returned. He had no right to an opinion on what she did or didn't do, and with whom! She threw back her shoulders, preparing to square off. "Well, it's George's decision. He has the last word on the matter."

"Oh, yes, that makes perfect sense," Michael replied sarcastically. "And what if George isn't happy?"

Maggie didn't appreciate that tone. "Then there will be no coupling."

Michael blinked so much that she almost asked if a fly had got stuck. He released her elbow and rubbed his eyes. "All right. I'm about to explode. Explain what's going on or I'm going to carry you back home over my shoulder. And try not to use the word *coupling* again. That would be helpful. Thank you."

Maybe the man should have gone running today, Maggie thought. Too much tension was not good for the body. Nevertheless, she took a deep breath and explained. "A few weeks ago, I received a letter from a Mr. Danbury. He'd become aware that I had a dachshund and wanted to know if I'd be interested in bringing mine and his together. It's simple, really."

"How did he become aware? That you had a dachshund?" Michael's tone had lost some of its bite.

Maggie cocked her head. "I'm not sure." She shrugged. "I suppose it's not much of a secret. I walk him most days and they are unusual dogs, quick to catch attention."

"And you just decided to meet him? What did your aunt say?"

Maggie tapped her teeth together, avoiding his gaze. She didn't like the way a blue vein bulged in the middle of his forehead. That couldn't be a good sign. "Nothing. I didn't tell her."

"Why the hell not?"

Maggie was lucky that she was strong. That question had the force to knock a lesser person to their knees. But she wouldn't be intimidated by him. Her decisions had nothing to do with him, and the sooner he came to terms with that, the better. "I didn't think she'd want to know," she replied, raising her voice. "She's not particularly interested in the breeding process. Not many people care to understand how the food is prepared; they just want to eat it."

Michael gave her a funny look before continuing his argument. "Very clever," he shot back. "But she would probably care to know why her only niece is gallivanting off by herself to meet an unknown man in a random location."

"I'm hardly gallivanting!"

"But you are meeting a man."

"About a *dog*!"

Maggie hadn't meant to scream, but the man was incorrigible. His exasperation was like a river feeding into her lake.

Michael turned toward the greenhouse in the distance and then rounded on Maggie, planting his fists on his hips. "You're not going."

"I *am* going. And you should just leave." After a pause, she added, "And stop trying to tell me what to do!"

"Well, someone has to!" he shouted back. "Your aunt is a terrible guardian, and you have her wrapped around your fingers, so she's no help. And your parents are, yet again, off on one of their trips to God knows where, doing God knows what. Your brothers are in boarding school and all you have is this dog, who, I'm fairly certain, is a cruel joke the Lord is playing on humanity. You are alone. Always alone. To your ridiculous devices and whims. Well, I'm not leaving you, Maggie. Not now. Not here. Someone needs to save you from yourself."

How did he… Who told him…?

It didn't matter.

Michael's blue eyes morphed into a stormy gray, and every word he threw at Maggie charged like a thick gust of wind. But she locked her knees and stood her ground. "And you think that person should be you?"

The question hit him, straight and clean, breaking the stress from his body. The blinking had returned. Michael straightened away, though his gaze still clung to hers. "Who else would it be?" he replied softly.

Maggie couldn't respond. So many answers shuffled inside of her, but none seemed to fit. Because she wasn't completely sure what they were talking about anymore. When he reached for her hand, Maggie flinched, but she didn't pull away.

Michael's expression was so incredibly open. She searched him for guile, for a mocking lift of his lips, for any trace that this might all be a misunderstanding, but found none.

"Who else would it, Maggie?" he asked again.

"I… I…" she stammered, hoping an answer would come to her the longer she stalled. There wasn't one. There never was.

Maggie *was* alone most of the time. But not now. Not with

him.

Which had been the plan, she told herself. This was what she'd wanted, wasn't it? The way he looked at her with such exquisite longing; the way he leaned closer to her as if he were ready to whisper a precious secret in her ear. But then why didn't this feel like she was winning? When had this stopped being a game?

George, bless his heart, saved her from answering that question. In an instant, the little muscle released an onslaught of erratic barks and lunged down the path, almost yanking Maggie's arm off in the process.

She jerked forward, smacking her nose against Michael's. "Ooh!" she cried, clutching her face. Through the slivers in between her fingers, she watched Michael do the same. "Are you all right?"

He grumbled through his palms, "Yes. My nose is used to it. You?"

"I'm *not* used to it, but I'm fine. This dog… I don't know what came over him. Still"—Maggie hid her disappointment as she started for the greenhouse—"I'm late. I… I should go."

Michael unleashed a mighty exhale and caught up with her in two impatient strides. "I thought I told you that I wasn't leaving you."

Maggie gasped as he tore the leash from her hand and guided the dog toward the meeting place, growling commands at the excited animal whenever it charged after a squirrel or bird. Maggie kept pace behind them so Michael couldn't see the smile on her face as the two males battled for supremacy. By the time they reached the greenhouse entrance, she surmised that George had been the victor.

The building wasn't currently in use and hadn't been for some time. The windowpanes were covered in so much dirt that the light inside was dim at best. Most of the plants and pots had been taken, though some were left on the tables in various states of decay.

"Are we sure we're not early?" Michael asked, touring the dismal space. When he stepped on a broken piece of glass, he scooped George into his arms without thinking, dodging the dog's incessant, loving tongue.

Maggie's stomach flipped and flopped as she watched Michael attempt to dodge the grateful kisses. "No, we're definitely late. Maybe he couldn't stay?"

"Maybe."

"That's a shame," Maggie said. "I'll have to write a letter to apologize and schedule another meeting."

"You will not."

Not this again. "I will too."

Michael cursed and switched the dog to his other side, directing the tongue away from him once more. "Don't you understand how dangerous it is? You can't just meet men alone. They can't be trusted."

Maggie crossed her arms. "And yet you think it's safe for me to be alone with you."

He glowered. "Don't be clever. Of course you're safe with me—"

"You know, I keep hearing that men can't be trusted. Lady Everly said the same thing about Lord Oliver, but he has only been a true gentleman."

"Damn it, Maggie," Michael groaned as he came toward her. "I don't want to hear his name on your lips."

Those very lips curved devilishly. "What? Oliver?"

Three more strides and he was glaring down at her. Maggie cocked her head, enjoying the emotions flailing across his face, the fleeting discomfort warring with desire. Was he jealous? *Oh, yes.* Jealous over her.

A boldness overcame Maggie. She petted George a few times before allowing her hand to wander to Michael's chest. Her fingers tripped up the buttons of his jacket. "So... I can't say his name. I can't say *coupling*. What do you want me to say?"

Michael snatched her finger. He held it in the air between

them just as surely as he held her gaze. Seconds passed with no sound other than their breathing as a million different scenarios played through Maggie's head. Anything could happen at this moment; anything was possible—and yet, in the end, it was inevitable that he placed her hand flat against his chest.

Maggie watched him direct her; she watched him smooth out her palm until it rested over his heart. Only when he had it exactly where he wanted it did he cover it with his own.

An audible breath escaped her as she felt his heartbeat radiate up through her arm into the corners of her body. The rhythm excited her; the base animalism heated her, urged her on.

"What do you want me to say?" she repeated in a whisper, leaning into him. "Tell me."

Michael shook his head, the attraction all-encompassing, continuing to draw her in like she was the polar opposite of his magnet.

He bided his time, lengthening the heightened moment, until his lips were just about to skim hers and he answered, "Nothing, dammit. Nothing at all."

Michael's lips were soft, surprising Maggie when they brushed hers, almost timid and searching, waiting. The kiss was like a knock on the door, asking her to open. Maggie did, shyly at first, pressing back on him, reflecting his motions as only a novice could. But when he surged inside her, sweeping into her mouth with his tongue, Maggie realized that she didn't want to follow. Following wasn't natural, and kissing Michael seemed like the most natural thing in the world. She gave herself up to him, canting her head to his, inviting him into her space, exploring the depths to which he opened to her.

He tasted of adventure. He tasted of unknown places and thoughts you couldn't divulge. He tasted of want and pleasure, wrapped limbs, and blueberries bursting in your mind at peak ripeness.

His thumb caressed the back of her neck, and Maggie clung to him. With one hand remaining on his heart, she cupped his face with the other. Her skin sizzled when she heard the rasp of his whiskers against her nails, the chuckle that came when he felt her shiver.

The kiss turned hot, primal. As Michael's lips came back to her again and again, Maggie claimed him before he could claim her. She rubbed her thighs against his, groaning when she felt the insistence of his pelvis, confused and so very curious about the myriad tingles it elicited in her own.

Staying alive was the only thing that tore her away. Maggie needed air, but even then, she didn't relinquish her territory. She rested her head against his chest while her lungs pumped, and she grinned when she heard the effort of his own against her ear.

Ready to get back to it, Maggie curled her fingers into his jacket and readied herself to capture Michael in another kiss but stopped short.

Someone had beaten her to it.

She found George taking advantage of the space she'd left, licking Michael's cheek with wild abandon.

Michael's expression was comically baleful. "This really is a terrible dog."

"He likes you!" Maggie took him into her arms and scratched his head, feeling the erotic moment thin until she surmised it was over. She spied Michael from under her lashes as he made no move to touch her again. "I should have remembered that men don't like it when women speak."

"What?

Maggie continued to give George affection, a vulnerability coursing through her making her suddenly shy. "Someone told me once that men don't like it when women talk too much. You proved that when you told me to be quiet."

Michael regarded her curiously. "I told you to be quiet so I could finally kiss you. I... I like it when you talk. Why wouldn't I?"

Oh.

Maggie was incapable of lifting her head. "Why *did* you 'finally' do that? You know… kiss me." *Especially when you stopped yourself before.*

Michael shrugged. "Because I wanted to."

Maggie pursed her lips. That bland answer should have infuriated her, made her storm out of the greenhouse in a huff. A week ago, it might have. But not today.

Michael ruffled George's ears and the animal's tail wagged. Maggie knew exactly how he felt.

"I want you to come to my fight tonight."

Maggie flinched at the non sequitur. "A fight? A real bare-knuckle fight? How? Why?"

Michael's grin was sheepish, boyish. "Why not?"

"For one, I'm certain it's not in a reputable place regarding women."

He huffed. "Since when do you care about reputable places?"

Maggie tried again. "And the last thing I want to do is see you get your head smashed in."

Michael cupped her chin in his hand, tilting her head to meet his gentle gaze. "That's funny—I thought that would be enticement enough." The lines fanning from the corner of his eyes softened. "Look, I know I shouldn't ask you. I know these fights aren't the sort of place for a lady." He dropped his hand and backed away. "Actually, you're right. Don't come. I'll never forgive myself if something—"

"Why do you want me to?" Maggie broke in. She could still feel his touch on her chin and desperately wanted it back. "Give me an answer. A real one."

Maggie watched as his smile turned wistful. "Because I want you to see me. The real me. Doing something I'm good at. Something I love."

"Does it matter if you love it?" she asked, already knowing that only certain death could keep her from that match.

His expression brightened and he dodged George's tongue to caress the side of her face. "Oh, my lady, you have no idea."

Chapter Ten

TIME WAS TICKING. Maggie spied the carriage waiting on the opposite side of the street, but she wouldn't leave until she heard Aunt Alice's telltale breathing. She plastered her ear to her aunt's door, listening for the signs that usually followed her aunt drinking three glasses of sherry. Ordinarily, Alice stopped at two; however, Maggie may have induced her to partake in a third after dinner when she asked her aunt about the gossip currently making the rounds of the *ton*. She didn't usually present herself as an enjoyable gossip companion, so Alice hadn't been able to resist the temptation.

When the whistle-like snores drifted through the bedroom door, Maggie finally had her answer. She shrouded herself in her black cloak and hurried down the stairs, making sure not to run into anyone as she escaped out the servants' entrance.

The carriage door flew open the moment Maggie came into view. An arm appeared from the darkness, and she wasted no time, grabbing hold and launching herself inside.

Lord Oliver appraised her from his seat. "You're strong," he remarked with a chuckle. "Not many women would have been able to do that."

"Cricket," was Maggie's only answer.

"Ha!" He squinted at her as if she were a curiosity in a museum as the carriage started to pick up speed. "Yes, Jo did mention that. It all makes sense now."

The duke's carriage was enormous. Five more people could have been inside, and Maggie still would have had ample legroom. She settled in her plush velvet seat, trying to act like this was an everyday occurrence and not the first time she'd asked a man she barely knew to drive her to an illegal boxing match outside the city.

Maybe Michael was right. Maybe Maggie did need someone to save her from herself.

When she couldn't straighten her dress or tug at her cloak anymore, Maggie faced her partner in crime, the man who had had no quibbles answering her letter this afternoon, informing her that he would be delighted to accompany her to the boxing match.

"So… you know where the fight is being held?" Maggie asked, cringing at how high her voice sounded.

"Of course," the duke replied, draped lazily in his seat. His inky hair was disheveled, and Maggie understood what the bloodshot redness clouding the whites of his eyes meant. Still, his black jacket was impeccable; his linen shirt was whiter than whipped cream and just as stiff.

Lord Oliver was the epitome of a gentleman, even if he didn't make a habit of speaking like one. "I told you to wear something bright," he spat, lifting his lip as he surveyed her clothing.

Dumbfounded, Maggie looked down at her dress. "It's yellow. It *is* loud."

He made an unintelligible noise. "That's light yellow, baby's-breath yellow, for Christ's sake. And why are you wearing a black cloak? You look like you stole it off a corpse."

Maggie was stunned by her perplexity. He'd told her to dress nicely; this was her nicest cloak! She squirmed in her seat. "I assumed that the point was not to be noticed, to blend in with the crowd. I don't want anyone to notice me and tell my aunt."

"But you're with *me*," Lord Oliver explained in a terribly

snobbish tone. "I never blend in."

Maggie threw her hands up. "I don't understand."

"Ugh, fine, let me explain, little one," he drawled. Lord Oliver uncrossed his long legs and leaned his elbows on his knees. "I am a fixture at these sorts of things, and it is customary for me to have a woman on my arm. Or two." He rolled his eyes. "Fine, sometimes three."

"I'm a woman."

The *cluck* Lord Oliver made with his tongue almost made Maggie slap him. "A *different* kind of woman. If someone—*you*— seems out of the ordinary, people might stare, ruining your little subterfuge."

The realization came hard and fast. "You mean a harlot. You wanted me to dress loud… like a harlot?"

"That's rather rude," he said, sniffing. "I prefer to call them paid companions."

Maggie balked, unable to tell if he was serious, which was a growing problem with the duke. "Well, I'm sorry, but this is all I have. We will have to make do."

Lord Oliver slumped back into his seat. "I suppose so."

"I suppose next you'll order me to hang on your arm or sit on your lap during the fight? Will that prove to everyone that I'm one of your *different* girls?"

Lord Oliver surprised her with a grin showing all his straight teeth. "That sounds like a lovely plan. Should we practice before we get there?"

He widened his legs and patted his lap while Maggie lobbed him a savage glare. "Are you ever serious about anything?"

The duke unearthed a flask from his jacket pocket and took a long drink. He made a dramatic "ahh" sound before returning his attention back to her. "What do you think?"

"I think I'm not sitting on your lap."

"That's too bad."

"Why?" Maggie asked despite all her misgivings. "Because you'll only ask this one time?"

The duke's face screwed up in confusion. "Are you mad? I'll probably ask five more times tonight." He shrugged. "I just thought it would make your Michael jealous, that's all." He rested his head back against his seat and lowered his hat over his eyes. "Just give it a think. You know where to find me if you change your mind. Until then, be a dear and don't talk anymore, all right? And wake me when we get there."

IN A LITTLE hamlet thirty minutes outside London, the Oyster Inn was not what Maggie had been expecting. The inn was quaint and lovely, a white beacon in an otherwise barren landscape; it was the kind of place that one only ventured to when one was trying to get to somewhere else.

After she woke Lord Oliver, slapping his cheeks lightly for the fun of it, he hurried her out of the carriage, fighting through the substantial crowds, insisting that they didn't have time to spare. Maggie had never seen so many people outside of London, and all of varying degrees of income. In the flat field behind the inn, day laborer mixed with landlord, duke mixed with tavern owner. All were equal in the eyes of the gambling gods.

"Will you stop dawdling?" the duke muttered, grabbing hold of the top of Maggie's arm. Impatiently, he hustled her toward the center of the storm, deep into the field where a ring was set up for the event. The ring was actually a square, set off on all four sides with two ropes. A crush was already settling in, squeezing as close to the ropes as possible for the unencumbered view. Even in the outdoors, Maggie wished to pinch her nose closed. The awful, masculine mixture of tobacco, sweat, and hair grease was entirely too suffocating.

Lord Oliver, on the other hand, didn't seem to have the same problem. Trudging through the throngs, flicking a disinterested nod to some of the men who called out his name in greeting, he situated Maggie a few rows back from the action. It was there that the stares began to come her way. Maggie fixed her cloak, making sure it still hid most of her face. "Why aren't we up front?" She balanced on her tiptoes, relieved that she could make out the ring behind the medium-sized man in front of her, whose top hat was the only tall thing about him. "Surely someone would have given up their spot for you."

The duke snorted at her blatant naïveté. "We have the best spot here," he explained. "You don't want the front row. Too much blood splatter. I learned that lesson the hard way. My father took me to watch Billy Gains when I was fifteen. Old Billy took a hard right to the eye and blood spilled all over my new necktie. My mother was furious with me. A perfectly good tie was ruined forever." He side-eyed her cloak and sniffed. "On second thought, maybe I should have placed you next to the ring. Christ, I hate waiting. When will the damn thing start?"

Lord Oliver wasn't the only one growing impatient. The longer the minutes dragged on, the rowdier the crowd became. Maggie was protected by her placement next to the duke, but she would still have a number of bruises by the end of the night based on all the elbows going around while people jockeyed for position. She was relieved to notice that she wasn't the only female in the crowd, though thanks to the duke's tutorial in the carriage, she surmised that most, if not all, of the colorfully clad ladies were being compensated for their time. Hopefully *well* compensated.

"Fuck," the duke griped, glancing at his pocket watch. "Have I told you that I hate waiting?"

"You mentioned it."

"Well, I do. I can't abide lateness. I don't know why it's so bloody hard for people to be on time for things. If I can do it, anyone can."

Maggie eyed her companion. He'd looked pale and withdrawn in the carriage, but in the brilliant light of the moon, the poor man appeared at death's door while he whined like a child.

She reached into her reticule. "Are you hungry? Is that why you're so surly? Here, I think I packed some cheese…" She rifled through her bag, taking out a few wedges wrapped in cloth that she'd packed for the carriage ride.

Lord Oliver sniffed at her generosity. "I'm not surly. I'm just annoyed." He snatched a wedge out of her hand. "Oh, fine, since you brought it. I *am* feeling rather peckish."

He finished the cheese in two bites and returned the cloth. Maggie wouldn't say that he was a transformed man, but the food brought a little color back into his pallid cheeks.

"Now," the duke began, brushing off his hands, "why don't you tell me why you're here? I thought the idea was for you to avoid the viscount. Make him follow you around like a helpless puppy."

Maggie had been waiting for the question. The duke was too insightful and ill-mannered to let it go. She'd prepared an answer while she was getting ready in her room earlier, one that seemed to fit the plan she'd concocted. Only now, in the center of this hive of activity, enjoying the buzz of anticipation, she didn't want to lie.

"Michael asked me to come," she said. "And I wanted to see him."

The duke stared at her for a long beat before snorting. "And what if your being here makes him want you less? What about absence makes the heart grow fonder and all that rot?"

The crowd stirred and a loud cry went out as a bustle of people started to move near the inn. It would have been impossible to see Michael's opponent if he hadn't been a whole head taller than most of the horde. The ground seemed to rumble with his every step. Maggie had never likened Michael to King David before, but it was the only way to describe him now, since his opponent was clearly Goliath.

In what world could Michael fight—and win—against someone like that? But instead of regretting that she'd come, Maggie felt her conviction only intensify.

"Are you going to answer me?" the duke prodded.

Maggie swallowed the nervousness in her throat. "I'm not here to make him fall in love with me."

"Then why the hell are you here?"

Maggie's eyes were glued to the ring. "I'm here to watch him win."

IF ONLY *WATCHING* weren't so painful.

Thirty rounds and forty minutes later, Maggie confirmed that watching someone you know fight must be infinitely worse than actually being in the fight. Because even though Michael was the one taking the punches, he at least had the aches and strains that went along with them. All Maggie had was her imagination, and it was running wild.

"How much longer can this go on?" she asked, cringing as the Irishman ducked one of Michael's punches and responded with a smack to his gut. Sweat flew from Michael's hair, and he stumbled back, catching himself on his heels before he could lose his balance.

"As long as it takes," Lord Oliver answered. He let out a *whoop!* when Michael rebounded with two quick jabs to O'Shaughnessy's face.

Maggie found that watching the fight was so much easier when she did it through her hands. There was only so much she could take. "Why does he keep doing that? His punches are only making O'Shaughnessy madder!"

Oliver threw her a disgusted look. "That's the point! Don't you see? Michael can't take the giant down with one punch. He knows that. Hell, O'Shaughnessy knows that. So he has to make him mad, throw him off his game. Tire him out. It's the only option."

The duke was right. At first, Maggie didn't see much rhyme

or reason in the fight. Each man threw punches, and the other one took them; however, the longer she studied, the more she recognized patterns and strategies. Michael didn't have the Irishman's height or bulk, but he did have speed and long arms. Whenever Michael saw a window of opportunity, he would get inside the giant's body, launch a series of attacks, and then withdraw before getting too damaged. It didn't happen often, but it was just enough to keep the giant guessing, *and* on his toes.

"Do you see that?" Oliver called out, pointing toward the ring. "Look at how hard he's breathing. O'Shaughnessy is almost down. Michael's plan is working. I can hardly believe it, but it is."

Maggie frowned, trying to see the same clues that Lord Oliver highlighted, but she would need more convincing. In her limited opinion, Michael was breathing just as heavily as the giant, and had more scrapes and bruises on his face than Maggie ever wanted to count.

Although his body *was* moving better. Where O'Shaughnessy was stiff and flat-footed, Michael was spry. He bobbed and weaved, changing up his stance like a dancer, forcing the giant to come to him. And that made O'Shaughnessy furious.

"Ah, it's over."

Maggie whipped to Lord Oliver. "What do you mean? They're still fighting. Michael's not down!"

"I'm not talking about your man," he replied sullenly. He tossed a hand toward the fight. "The giant. He'll go down in the next few minutes. Trust me. I've seen it before."

A rush of excitement gripped her. Maggie was positively giddy. "Then why are you so upset? Didn't you want Michael to win?"

Lord Oliver squirmed, avoiding her gaze. "Naturally, I wanted Michael to win," he said cagily. "However, I'm a realist, and a realist puts his money on a giant."

Maggie's mouth dropped open just as Michael landed another combination, causing the crowd to shake the earth with cheers. "You bet against him?"

The duke grunted.

Another cheer.

"How much?"

He shrugged. "Just a couple?"

Maggie's brow lifted. "A couple pounds?"

"A couple *thousand* pounds."

A bubble of laughter escaped her. It came out so freely and effortlessly, due in large part to the fact that Michael was getting out of the match with his life intact. "Serves you right," she chided the duke, smiling as the giant stumbled around the ring, grasping for a lifeline that was nowhere to be found. Now Michael was the hunter, tracking O'Shaughnessy, never letting up, not allowing one inch of refuge. "You shouldn't have bet against your friend."

Lord Oliver's top lip curled back. "Who said Michael was my friend? I can barely tolerate the sour bastard, although he is a damn good fighter. Besides, there's no such thing as friends when it comes to gambling, which is precisely why I like it so much."

Maggie scowled at the disreputable man but managed to bring her attention back to the ring in time to see the giant go down. The crowd erupted in chaos, and what seemed like a thousand arms appeared to pierce the night sky all at once. Breathless, speechless, Maggie watched a short, bald man climb inside the ring and hug Michael, allowing the fighter to hang on him while he accepted the praise.

Maggie balanced on her tiptoes, craning her neck as high as she could. Blood and sweat dripped from Michael in some places and dried and stuck to him in others; he looked like he'd just gone for a gory swim. His body glistened; the muscles of his arms continued to tense and flex as he attempted to relax. She waved her hands, hoping to catch his attention, but there was too much noise, too many others clamoring for his notice. Maggie's heart was fit to burst. Michael's face was a mixture of extreme fatigue and pride. He'd known he would win even when others hadn't, and he'd done it. He'd done the impossible.

Maggie understood what it was like to win, to feel that un-mistakable exhilaration. But she'd always experienced it with her teammates. Sharing it had always seemed right. Better.

Instantly, she made up her mind.

"Wait!" Lord Oliver cried, reaching for her arm. "Where are you going?"

Maggie fought free, setting her sights on the inn. "I need to see him."

The duke captured her again, paralyzing her with his somber expression. "Oh, no you don't. You shouldn't. Let's go now before this place turns into a powder keg."

"I'm not leaving until I see him. I just… I want…" Maggie couldn't explain it; sharing this experience with Michael seemed so incredibly important. She didn't want him to be alone after everything that had happened. She needed to be there for him. With him.

"You don't understand," the duke continued, shaking his head. "A man isn't himself after a fight. His blood is up. It takes a lot to bring him down. I know what you think of me, I know that I tease, but believe me now—inside that inn is not the place for you. For a lady."

Maggie considered him. This wasn't the playful man, nor was it the haughty duke. For once, Lord Oliver appeared genuine, serious, and she almost heeded him. But she was serious too.

"But I'm not a lady tonight. I'm a paid companion, remember?" She kissed him on the cheek. "I won't be long. I promise." Maggie flew out of his arms, elbowing her way through the crowd toward the inn.

"What's so important that can't wait?" she heard him call after her.

You have no idea.

Chapter Eleven

MICHAEL SAT ON a small wooden chair in the corner of the room. His hands trembled in his lap. Again and again, he shook them, but it didn't work. From experience, he knew that this could go on for minutes to hours depending on the fight. He couldn't just turn his body off with the snap of his fingers. Half the day had been spent in tense readiness, and even after what he'd just battled, his body still had more to give. Not fight, but something.

"Mike?" a voice called from the hallway. "Sorry to bother you, mate."

His trainer. Michael wiped a hand over his face. It came away wet. He'd been alone for ten minutes and still hadn't washed the blood away. It hadn't seemed important, not when he was still coming to terms with what he'd just accomplished. *The fancy lad,* the lord who posed as a bruiser, had gone toe to toe with one of the best, and he was still standing. And it was only the beginning.

"What is it, Tommy?"

A pause. Then the trainer's voice was uncharacteristically uncertain. "Ah, ya, mate, I've got someone here who wants to see ya... a woman."

Michael grimaced and immediately regretted it. His face felt like it had been run over by a cavalry. The Irishman may have been clumsy, but his ham-hock fists more than made up for it.

"I told you, Tommy. I don't want to see anyone tonight. I just want to wash up and get home."

"Ah, no, mate." The door cracked open, and Tommy peeked through. His face was ruddy with the fever of victory, and his bald head was dotted with sweat beads. If Michael didn't know any better, he would have thought the grizzled trainer was embarrassed. "It's not like that," Tommy said, opening the door all the way.

Maggie stood in the hallway, her head bowed, her hands clasped in front of her like she were waiting in line to confess her sins.

Michael launched from the chair, tearing a shirt from the bed and throwing it over his sweaty and battered skin. "What are you doing here?"

Maggie's chin jerked up. "You told me to come!"

Michael's feet glued into place. If he moved, he wasn't sure if he would kiss her or strangle her. "I told you it wasn't safe."

Maggie laughed nervously. "You said that, but you didn't mean it. You wanted me here. And I'm glad I came." She nodded to Tommy, who realized that he'd just been dismissed. Michael scowled at the man as he slinked out the door, taking more time than necessary.

"You shouldn't be here."

"Well, I am here, so you just have to accept it." Maggie shrugged, then took off her cloak and hung it on the hook behind the door.

"What are you wearing?" Michael asked.

She looked down at her dress. "Now what's wrong with it?" she asked with heat.

He pawed at the back of his neck. "Nothing," he said, surveying the bright yellow dress. "It's just a little loud, that's all. Not you."

"That's what I said!

"What? To whom?"

"No one," Maggie answered quickly. "Forget I said that."

She smiled shyly as a blanket of silence tucked over them. She walked into the room, touring the small space with a few strides. It wasn't Michael's room, but it still felt like she was inspecting him, his choice of life. Her gaze landed on the small, tidy bed. "Will you sleep here tonight?"

Michael cleared his throat. "No. The inn gave me the room so I could clean up in privacy… and I suppose, stay and celebrate if I wanted."

Maggie hugged her chest. Michael regretted not asking for a fire to be lit, but he hadn't expected company. "Are you… celebrating?" she asked.

Michael's body was again tense, strung tight. It was like being back in the ring, waiting for an opponent's move. He nodded.

"Alone?"

"It's better that way," he explained. Michael spread his hand out in front of him, regarding the mess he'd made of his knuckles. "I'm not the best company after a fight."

Maggie walked to the bureau, where a pitcher and basin sat filled with steaming water. She took off her gloves, picked up a clean linen, and dunked it in, wringing it out with both hands. "Maybe you haven't had the right company." She went to him and reached for his shoulder. Softly, she led him to the corner and pushed him down on his pathetic little chair.

Just as she was about to place the cloth on the corner of his mouth, he flinched.

"Let me," she whispered. "Please?"

Michael took a deep breath and nodded.

He stared straight ahead as she cleaned the nicks and scratches on his face. Every time he attempted to sneak a glance at her from the corner of his eye, his chest squeezed, hurting him more than any of the Irishman's blows. For the past few hours, Michael had been surrounded by blood and sweat, unclean men, hands slapping his bare shoulders, and rancid mouths speaking much too close. Maggie cleared his consciousness. She smelled fresh and clean, new and innocent. If the winner took the spoils, he only wanted her.

With Maggie's hands on him, Michael had no concept of time. Speaking felt like a sin. Her hands were sure and efficient as she worked quietly, mopping up the butchery done to his face. He sent up a prayer of thanks that he hadn't broken his nose; he didn't wish anyone to be confronted with that type of carnage.

But when she maneuvered to the other side of him, Michael's curiosity got the better of him. "So, are you going to tell me?" he rasped, mortified by the sensitivity in his voice. "What did you think of it?"

Maggie paused. His head was level with her chest, and he watched it rise and fall as she contemplated his question. The gown may have been loud, but it was demure and covered her from head to toe—yet Michael still believed it to be the most provocative thing she'd ever worn. Maybe only because she'd worn it to see him.

"I'm glad you won," she answered.

Michael huffed and grabbed at his side. His ribs hadn't been quite as lucky as his nose. "That's it?"

She bent in front of him, frowning while she patted the cut around his right eye. She bit at her lower lip while she focused, and Michael noticed that her right front tooth slightly overlapped her left. He decided that it fit her, along with the shallow dimples on her cheeks that were more pronounced when she scowled than when she smiled.

Her breath was sweet and warm and caressed his chin. Had it been mere hours before when they'd exchanged breaths in a kiss? Had she thought about it as much as he had?

"Have you ever watched a fight before?" she asked.

The question caught him off guard. "Of course."

Maggie straightened, holding the cloth in front of her. It was stained pink and probably would stay that way forever. Her brow pinched as she considered her words. "No, I... Yes, I understand that, but have you ever... watched someone you knew fight?"

Michael shrugged and palmed his shoulder. It was no better than his ribs. "Of course I knew them."

She was rattled. Maggie twisted the cloth in her hands. "I mean, not just someone you knew, but someone you… knew well… and, perhaps, favored."

Lord, he wished she wouldn't make him laugh. But Maggie looked so adorable and uncomfortable as she stood there trying to tell him that she liked him without actually saying the words. In all fairness, Michael didn't need any of her stammering. She'd come. That was telling enough. And all that mattered.

He rose from the chair, took the cloth out of Maggie's hand, and tossed it back in the bowl.

Her head bowed. "I was told not to come here," she whispered.

Michael smiled at her shyness. "*I* told you not to come here."

Maggie's laughter was weak, listless. "No. I was told not to come in here… with you."

"Who told you that?"

She ignored his question. and more words tripped out. "They said your blood would be up; they said it wouldn't be safe for me."

Michael swallowed the space between them, taking Maggie's hand. He pulled her toward him. "*I* told you that being alone with men wouldn't be safe."

"You said every man but you." Her voice was hushed.

Michael palmed her chin, tipping it up so she could see him, see the man he truly was. "I will always keep you safe, Maggie. I will never leave you."

Her eyes were clear, deep pools of faith and understanding. It humbled him.

"You shouldn't make promises you can't keep."

Michael brushed his thumb over her lips. Once. Twice. His senses had been pulled tight this day. He'd traded punches and felt the power of another man all the way to the marrow of his bones, but nothing had prepared him for this. For Maggie. For her trusting expression, her velvety skin. For the fact that she desperately wanted to believe him but wouldn't allow herself.

It brought out something savage in him. Michael had known that his body had more to give. There was so much left in him. And the dam was breaking. But he was not afraid for her.

If anyone could handle Michael in this state, it was Lady Margaret.

He held her tight, asking her to listen. "I'm going to kiss you, Maggie. And I won't be gentle, and I won't be sweet. But you are right. My blood is up, but it has nothing to do with the fight. It has everything to do with you."

Michael was rewarded when Maggie's eyes widened.

But she didn't retreat. She didn't run scared. To Maggie, curiosity was always going to be stronger than fear. She met him halfway.

Michael gathered her in his arms and seized his opportunity. He crushed his mouth to hers, unloading all the apprehension and awe, all the turbulence and relief that had coalesced that day. His ardor didn't cower her. Maggie opened for him and accepted his tongue, rolling it with her own in a carnal dance. Michael walked her back to the bed. His hands still shook, and now his legs were doing the same—from plain, limitless desire.

Michael didn't release her mouth as he covered her on the bed, drinking the sweet, insistent little sounds from the back of her throat while giving her his moans. His body screamed with pain—his ribs ached; his arms were on fire—but nothing could have dragged him from this moment. He'd dreamt of having Maggie underneath him, but it was nothing compared to reality. Their bodies undulated against one another, having their own conversation, but it wasn't enough. Michael ran his hand down her body, over the lively curves and enchanting dips, and gathered her skirts. He lifted them and searched for skin.

Maggie gasped in his mouth. For one brief moment, her body froze. But Michael was not deterred. The kissing stopped. His lips rested on hers as he flattened his palm against her calf, running up her leg until he reached the bare skin above her silk stockings. She was downy and delicate, luxurious and strong. Her muscles flexed and pulled; her inner thighs quivered the higher he wandered.

Maggie clung to his upper arms. Her hold was tight, almost suspicious, as she waited to see what he would do next. He used his fingers to tickle the plump fleshiness of her hips and was rewarded with a sweet giggle.

"Do you like that?" he whispered, trailing kisses to the side of her neck. Maggie sighed and lifted her chin to grant him more access.

"I… I don't know."

Michael laughed. "You don't *know*?"

Her nails dug deeper into his biceps as he settled his hand in the triangle of her thighs. Michael cupped her mound, playing with her soft, curly hair, toying with the idea of doing more. He shuddered from the possibilities.

Maggie rocked her pelvis into him, an untrained movement that fueled him even more. "My head says I shouldn't like it," she rasped, jerking when Michael slid a long finger along the seam of her pulsing entrance. "But my body… my body says it does."

Michael's own body felt so impossibly light. There was no doubt what it wanted and liked. *Her.*

He ran a tongue along her ear and smiled when she shivered. "Let your body win the fight," he told her, tugging the lobe between his teeth. "You can listen to your head tomorrow."

Michael captured her mouth once more at the same moment he urged a finger inside her passage, slowly at first, meeting her body's resistance with gentle pressure. She squeezed her legs against him, and he focused on winning over her anxiety. He worked her, listening to her body, testing her limits. When he felt her start to relax, he plunged further, stretching her and teasing her, inciting a flame that made both of them wild.

Maggie kissed him with abandon. Her hands were no longer keeping him at bay. Her restraint had reached an end, and her arms wrapped around his neck, pulling him impossibly closer.

Michael tried to keep a clear head. He needed her to find her release. He could anticipate its advent in her choppy puffs of breath and the restlessness in her limbs, but his own need was also pounding at the door.

Maggie was now the playful one, sucking on his lips, holding his head in her hands, moving him, canting him until she had him in the right spot. She became the aggressor, pumping her thighs, using him to reach fulfillment. They were sweaty and wet, impulsive and greedy. Michael could hear her growing impatience as she panted in his ear.

"Don't leave… don't leave me," she keened.

Michael groaned, rolling his thumb around the nub. She liked that. Maggie's head dug into the bed as her neck arched. "Never," Michael murmured, kissing the skin she gifted to him. Her mouth was open, and she screamed out. Michael couldn't stop himself. With his other bruised hand, he dipped a finger in between her pink lips. He almost lost himself as she sucked it with her moans and came in a splintering release.

Maggie went limp in his arms, falling back on the bed, all strain and tautness evaporating in a single, humid moment.

But Michael wouldn't leave her.

He continued to kiss her—on her sooty, full eyelashes that flickered whenever she was going to say something delightfully cutting; on the fantastically curved lips that smiled up at him whenever she thought she'd checkmated him with a witty remark. Those same lips that were now seductive and bashful over what they had just done.

Michael didn't smile back. A somberness overwhelmed him, a deep sensation that prohibited him from taking any of this lightly. He rested his forehead on Maggie's. "You need me," he said.

She didn't say anything, though her arms found life again. Michael's hair always turned curlier when it was wet, and she wrapped one of the tendrils around her finger. It was a simple gesture, casual, but it did something to Michael. Again, that lightness overtook him. Even after his victory tonight, it was only now that he felt impossibly whole. Not the viscount, not the boxer, just Michael.

But life would not be deterred for long.

"Maggie?" a voice called out from the hallway, followed by a few substantial pounds on the door. "Maggie, we have to go. I've worn out my welcome, I'm afraid."

Michael's head popped up and he shot her an incredulous look. "Are you serious? *Him?*"

Maggie squirmed, surprising him with her contrite expression. "I couldn't come on my own. And you didn't offer me a carriage."

Blood came rushing back, and with it all the pain he'd been suppressing. Michael winced as he rolled off Maggie and helped her to her feet. "I didn't offer you a carriage because I told you not to come."

She fluffed down her skirts and reclaimed her cloak from the door hook, then fanned it out dramatically before draping it around her shoulders. "You didn't mean it, remember? And it's too late anyway." Irritably, she fastened the clip around her neck and stared at the floor. "You..." She shook her head as she tried to find the words. "You're at least happy I came, aren't you?"

Michael ran a hand through his damp hair and settled his fists on his hips. When he tried to reach for Maggie, she stepped away.

"Aren't you?" she asked.

"Jesus Christ, just answer the lady!" Lord Oliver yelled through the heavy door.

Michael filled his lungs. "Fuck off, Your Grace," he shouted back.

"You fuck off," the duke returned. "You ruined my night and cost me a lot of money, now don't ruin the lady's!"

Maggie pressed her fingers against her forehead. "Your Grace, can you please give us some privacy?"

He answered with a sarcastic *humph*. "I've given you quite enough privacy, my dear. It's time to go."

Michael launched himself for the door. His hand was on the

handle when Maggie caught him by the arm. "Don't," she said, holding him until he contained himself. "He's not worth it."

Michael's gaze darted back and forth between her eyes. "But what is his worth to you, Maggie? Why do you keep company with the scoundrel?"

Another irritated noise interrupted them from the other side of the door. "I could ask her the same thing about you."

"You're not helping!" Maggie cried. She turned to Michael. "He's a friend. A somewhat helpful friend, since he brought me here tonight to see you." She ducked her head, her expression turning shy. "I won't forget a second of it."

Michael hugged her tightly, kissing her quickly. "Nor will I."

Oliver pounded on the door.

"I have to go," she said.

The thought of her leaving drove Michael into a violent panic. "Let me take you. Just give me a moment and I'll be ready—"

"No. I don't need help," she replied, softening her response with a reluctant smile. "You should stay. Celebrate with your adoring fans. If anyone deserves it tonight, it's you."

"No, I don't want to be with anyone other than—"

She cut him off with a much-too-quick peck on the lips and spun to open the door. The smug Lord Oliver was on the other side, leaning against the wall. His expression said that he'd heard everything.

He showed his teeth with a wide smile and locked eyes with Michael.

Maggie rushed past, but the duke lazed a few more seconds, his stare only intensifying. "You've had quite the night, haven't you?" he said in that low, teasing way of his.

Michael left his hand on the door, poised to slam it in the duke's pale, malnourished face. "I'm sorry yours didn't work out as well. There are always more fights to bet on. Better luck next time, *Your Grace.*"

Lord Oliver let out a lifeless chortle. "And there will always be more women, am I right, *my lord?*"

Michael studied the duke closely, trying to find his meaning. "There are no other woman for me," he said. "Only Maggie."

The duke returned a wistful smile and finally peeled himself off the wall. "Good answer, bruiser. Good answer."

Chapter Twelve

MAGGIE ALWAYS FORGOT which step squeaked the loudest. When she tackled the staircase later that night, she got her answer. The third.

"Maggie, dear, is that you?" Alice called out from the library. How was that possible? It was midnight. She was supposed to be merrily snoring until breakfast.

Maggie paused. She could pretend that she hadn't heard her aunt and—

"Niece? Please come here. I need to speak with you."

Maggie sighed and turned, yawning loudly the moment she entered the library. Aunt Alice sat comfortably on her settee, enjoying a tea and a plate of iced biscuits next to the fire. When she saw Maggie, she marked her place in the book she'd been reading and placed it at her side.

"I didn't think you had plans tonight," she remarked. Maggie couldn't tell if there was a warning in her voice. "Certainly not plans that involved your going out without a companion."

"I... I..." Maggie blew out a blustery breath, desperately searching for a plausible explanation.

"Don't bother," Alice replied blithely, massaging her eyes. "My headache is not in the mood for a lie."

Maggie hurried to her side. "I'm sorry. I should have told

you—"

"Yes, you should have, but no one has to know." Alice patted Maggie's hand. "I was once a girl too. I may be an old maid, but I know a clandestine meeting when I see one. I will let this go, but don't make me regret it."

"You won't!" Maggie replied, sitting next to her aunt on the settee. "I promise. And it wasn't what you think. It wasn't clandestine, not really… not *intentionally*—"

Alice held up a hand. "Please. I don't need to know. Unless I need to know." Her hawklike eyes felt like they were digging into Maggie's soul. She raised a brow. "Do I *need* to know?"

Maggie shook her head. "No."

"That's what I was hoping," Alice said, "but you did spend a lot of time with my mother growing up, so I wasn't sure. God only knows what you learned from her. Now, on to more important matters." She picked up a beige envelope from the side table. "I don't know if you're aware, but Lady Everly wrote to me, asking if we could join her at her brother's estate at the end of the week. It seems that a couple dropped out last minute and she wanted to see if we could fill in. I know it's late, but I thought you might enjoy it. I have to admit, I've always been anxious to see Lord Baxter's estate."

"Yes, of course," Maggie replied, hiding her surprise. Jo had failed to mention this to her. She wondered what the widow had up her sleeve. "Though are you sure you want to? As you said, it is last minute, and we've only returned from Manchester a couple of weeks ago. I'd hate to make you travel again."

A look came over the older woman's face that Maggie couldn't read. Alice placed the letter back on the table and picked up another. "I received another note today," she said gently.

Maggie's stomach tightened. Nothing about her aunt's tone boded well.

Alice continued, her expression incredibly kind and re-strained—incredibly un-Aunt Alice-like. "Your parents have written. It seems they won't make it back for Christmas like they told us. Instead, they've decided to travel more." Her voice lifted as if she were trying to make the news sound optimistic. "They have their sights set on India."

"India?"

The lines along Alice's mouth drooped. "Indeed. They are quite the adventurers."

Maggie attempted to rustle up some form of admiration. "Indeed. Adventurers."

The fire crackled. It threw light and shadows over the room, highlighting her aunt's roving emotions. Alice struggled to continue. "My sister said that they've already contacted the boys' school, informing them that they should stay on over the holidays. They write that it shouldn't be a problem."

Not a problem for them, no, Maggie thought bitterly. Nothing ever was *their* problem. But what about her young brothers, who hadn't been home in months? Or Maggie, who'd been palmed off on relatives so often in her youth that she didn't know where to call home?

But anger was fruitless. There was no one to cry and scream at. Her parents always made sure of that. There were always messengers.

Maggie forced a smile. Poor Alice's lips quivered. Was the woman sad for her, or sad that she had to deal with Maggie and her *clandestine nights* longer than she'd planned?

Alice tapped the letter against her hand, watching Maggie closely. "Don't worry about me, dear. I think a weekend in the country would be a lovely diversion—for both of us."

Maggie held her aunt's gaze, instantly understanding where Alice's sympathies lay—with her—and began to regard the woman differently—which shamed her. Hadn't she just told Michael about all the ways one could think about something? Why hadn't she shown her aunt the same grace?

True, the woman lacked the spirit and biting humor of Maggie's grandmother. In fact, Maggie could barely comprehend how her grandmother had birthed a child such as Alice. Maggie's mother had always made sense—she matched the old countess's joie de vivre and zest for running against the grain. However, Alice was a different sort of animal. She preferred the safety of the *ton*; she reveled in the dependable nature of Town life. The excitement that took place between the four walls of a ballroom was more than enough for her.

Maggie had considered Alice a know-it-all gossip, but that wasn't fair. At least she was *here*. At least she wanted to talk to Maggie. That counted for something. How could she forget that it was her aunt who'd served as her companion and allowed her to travel all over the country playing cricket last month? Without her, Maggie wouldn't have been able to go.

"Aunt, I don't think I ever properly thanked you for allowing me to stay here. I know it probably hasn't been easy."

Alice leaned back in her chair, slightly embarrassed by the attention. "You don't have to say anything, my dear. It is my pleasure. You're my niece."

"Still," Maggie continued, "I need you to know how much I appreciate your being here for me."

When Alice recognized that Maggie wouldn't stop with her silly show of emotions, she relented with a shy smile. She studied her niece for a long beat, her gaze narrowing as if she were coming to terms with something.

Her mouth opened, and she hesitated before speaking. "You know… you remind me of your mother so much sometimes. My sister and I are two very different people, always have been. My parents used to complain about how rambunctious she was, but I knew they were secretly enchanted with her. Everyone was. Despite our differences—and there were many—we were thick as thieves." She studied her hands, her voice taking on a far-off quality. "When she met your father, I couldn't believe she'd found someone to match her. I have to confess, I know I was young, but their love *frightened* me. They were always so intense with each other, so dramatic. I couldn't understand the appeal."

"You are not alone," Maggie replied.

Alice's brow lowered. "I don't mean to criticize them. It was just my observation. When she found your father, she never looked back. Sometimes I wonder if I would have been the same if I'd ever married. I doubt it. Whenever your sister and I would go swimming in the pond by our house as children, she would jump right in regardless of the temperature. I always started by sticking in a toe."

Maggie laughed. "You were sensible."

"I was cautious. But I think about it, and I wonder if she made me that way, or at least had something to do with it. You see, the world needs balance to work. So do people, and so do marriages. Your parents, for all their love, never had that. I used to think of them in terms of a scale. If you put one of them on each side, it would balance perfectly. But your parents could never bear to be apart, so they'd stay on the same end, inevitably toppling the whole thing."

Alice let out a quiet laugh and dropped the letter into her lap. The lines around her eyes appeared deeper, the sentiment in her voice more pronounced. And the guilt that Maggie harbored over her actions that night intensified. Was this a warning or just insight from the older woman? Either way, she welcomed it.

A loud crackle popped from the fire and Alice blinked. She picked up the letter, stacking it over Lady Everly's note in a perfunctory manner. "Listen to me, going on," she said, reclaiming her old self. "You're tired, my dear. Why don't you go off to bed, and we'll discuss our weekend plans tomorrow?"

Maggie nodded, accepting the fact that her aunt needed time to herself. She had thinking to do as well. But before she left the room, she turned back to Alice, who was surreptitiously wiping at the corner of one eye. "If you don't mind, Aunt," she began, "I'd like to write to my brothers and ask if they'd want to spend their holidays here. I know what my parents said, but I still think it's worth asking."

Alice's nod was firm and swift. "I'd like that very much. The more the merrier, as they say. It will give me an excuse to ask Cook to try out new recipes!"

THREE DAYS LATER, Lady Everly stared at Maggie with an expression akin to wonder. "You know, I hate to admit this, but when you first concocted your plan, I wasn't sure you had it in you to see it through. But the man is already kissing you. I'd say you're ahead of schedule. Well done."

Maggie looked down at her boots, unsure of how to respond. She didn't want to point out that Michael had kissed her more than once, and some of what they'd experienced together involved more than kissing. That information was only for her.

With Aunt Alice in tow, Maggie had arrived at Lord Baxter's estate early that afternoon. It was an easy ride, only two hours from London, so Maggie unfortunately couldn't claim exhaustion when Jo pounced on her the second she stepped from the carriage.

Even though more guests were scheduled to arrive, the widow hauled Maggie along her brother's spacious grounds in search of privacy and, more importantly, information.

"Ahead of schedule? Don't you believe it's time to end this game?" Maggie asked. Her tone was breezy, careless, not like she'd been worrying over the topic since the night of the boxing match. "I've been thinking, and I don't know if I want to do this anymore. It's lost its fun."

"Lost its fun?" Jo stopped in her tracks, her hand steady on Maggie's arm. "But the fun hasn't happened yet. The fun is when Lord Michael shouts his love to you and you rebuff him." She fixed her cool eyes on Maggie. "I thought that's what you wanted?"

Maggie continued to walk, needing to look at something other than Jo's damning disappointment. "It was. It *is*," she added quickly. "I just don't think I should be spending any more time with him. That's all."

Jo hesitated, and Maggie could sense the condemnation building. But her friend surprised her with one gentle word: "Why?"

Maggie kicked the loose pebbles on the path, her frustration winning out. Frustration for the insufferable woman and all her questions, and frustration in her own shortcomings. Jo and Ella were the only people she could discuss this ridiculous plan with. The only issue was that they didn't want to hear what she had to say. They'd assumed that it would all go so easily—maybe it was supposed to—but Maggie had been the problem. Because the more time she spent with Michael, the more she wanted to spend with him. She was a glutton for punishment. Rebuffing him was the furthest thing from her mind. Which was why she had to stay away.

She might not be her mother, but Alice was right: they had so many things in common. And Maggie's response to Michael the night of the fight had only pointed them out more. She didn't *want* to be her mother. She certainly didn't want a marriage like the one her parents shared—all selfish passion, no sense or regard for others. But she could feel Michael's pull. The invisible string that continued to tug her every waking (and nighttime) thought back to him. It was desperation. It was pure, utter madness. Resisting wouldn't be enough. Maggie would have to hide.

She feigned a smile for her friend's benefit. "It's nothing. Pretend I didn't say anything. I think I'm just tired from the drive."

Jo finally relented. "I'm sorry, Maggie. I shouldn't have dragged you on this walk right away. I should have allowed you to get situated in your room. I promise, the rest of the weekend won't be like this. The men will hunt, but the ladies don't have a schedule. In fact, you can stay in your room or hide away as much as you want. You won't even have to see Michael at all."

"What?" Maggie coughed on the word. "What do you mean, see him? He's not here."

Jo blinked. "I thought I told you. My brother invited him; they're good friends. That's why I invited you. I thought it would help, but that was before you told me all this." Maggie's face must have turned green, because Jo immediately became alarmed. "I'm so sorry! I really thought I'd told you. Or maybe Ella was supposed to tell you?"

Maggie waved a hand in the air. She closed her eyes, reaching for strength. Why was she behaving like such a weak ninny? Of course she could be near Michael! She would just take pains to not stay *that near* him. "I'll be fine," she reassured her friend. "I'll just keep my distance."

There was nothing subtle about the concern in Jo's voice. "Is there something you want to talk about—besides kissing? Oliver did say you were alone with Michael for more than a few minutes. A lot can happen in that time."

"What! Why would he say that? I didn't know the duke was recounting my actions like a gossipy grande dame! And I thought you hated him!"

Jo squinted at the sky. "I *do* hate him. Lord knows I do. But now that I've acknowledged his presence again, he's written me a few times. I never write him back. The scoundrel doesn't deserve it. But don't worry; he doesn't relay your every movement. He's just an old, clucking hen passing the time between amusements."

Maggie hated the fact that she was now considered one of the duke's *amusements*. But she couldn't blame him entirely. As Jo had declared, he *was* a scoundrel. And what was it that people said? *If you lie down with dogs, you get fleas.* Maggie had the urge to scratch her entire body.

"What did he do to you?" she asked, turning the tables on the widow.

Sadly, Jo was so much better at hiding her emotions than Maggie. Outbursts were not her thing. However, she did turn her nose up and stare off into the maze of shrubs, avoiding her friend's prying eyes. "He didn't break my heart, if that's what you're asking."

Maggie let the statement linger, waiting for Jo to say more. She was rewarded for her patience.

"I never let it get that far," Jo continued.

"Are you so certain it would have ended in that way?"

Jo let out a mirthless laugh. "Oh yes, my dear. Lord Oliver is a duke, and dukes break all their toys because they always know that someone will bring them new ones."

The defensiveness in Jo's tone tugged at Maggie's heart. There was so much she didn't know about the widow. She came across as so hard and unyielding, but the woman was flesh and blood, just like the rest of them.

"But you weren't a toy, Jo," Maggie replied gently.

Jo flicked a piece of hair out of her face. "Unfortunately, Oliver didn't see it that way… Men like that, when they look your way, it's like the entire sun is shining only for you—but when they give you their shadow, it's like you've never been so cold. And when they are done playing, and you can't make them laugh anymore, they move on. They leave." She gave her a tight smile. "So, bravo to you for taking matters into your own hands, for leaving Michael first. Whatever you do, don't give up. Remember why you started this in the first place. Remember what he did to you and what he will do again. You almost have him. He's almost eating out of your hand. So don't hide. Keep going until you win."

"I don't think there can be a winner in this game."

Jo patted Maggie on the shoulder, directing them back to the house. "Of course there will be. There's always a winner. Hasn't cricket taught you anything?"

Chapter Thirteen

MICHAEL DIDN'T KNOW what he'd done, but clearly it had been wrong.

He'd planned on canceling his weekend trip to Lord Baxter's; however, once he heard Maggie would be joining the party, the minutes couldn't have passed quickly enough until he was sharing the same room with her. But if he'd been expecting a warm welcome, he was disappointed.

Because the woman barely looked his way—barely acknowledged his presence. At first, Michael had tried to console himself, knowing that Maggie wouldn't act too familiar in front of the other guests; however, a little bit of familiarity wouldn't have been improper. She was acting like she could hardly remember his name when she'd been breathing it into his mouth only days before.

Had he been too aggressive after the fight? Too brazen with his need? He'd warned her; however, even Michael had to admit that no amount of warning could have prepared her for the fire that erupted when they'd come together. Even he had left the night amazed.

But not scared. If anything, he wanted to experience it again and again. Could he have frightened her? Maggie wasn't an ordinary woman; she didn't startle easily. He couldn't understand her coldness, nor could he abide it. With every blank stare, every span of space she kept between them, Michael found himself growing more and more confused.

There was a time and place for games at every country house party, but this wasn't it.

By the second day, when the guests were lounging on the great lawn past the gardens, enjoying a picnic and tea, Michael's patience had reached its end.

"It's such a lovely day. How about a game?" Lady Anne Baxter asked, brushing the biscuit crumbs from her hand. Lady Everly's sister-in-law was a round woman with a pleasing face whose entire mission in life appeared to be keeping everyone moving. She'd been married to Lord Baxter for five years, and Michael had heard rumblings of the couple's disappointment in their failure to produce children. He wasn't one to project onto others, though he could sense a nervous anticipation in the lady. She was always flitting about, never staying still. Michael recognized a kindred spirit when he saw one. He too had given up staying still years ago. Staying still gave the rolling, unmanageable thoughts a chance to present themselves and spread like a cancer in his consciousness. It was always best to keep busy.

Perhaps that was why he was the first of the group to stand along with their hostess and welcome an activity to pass the time when all the others avoided the comment, averting their eyes to their cups. It was kindness, but also an act of self-preservation.

"What do you suggest, lady?" Michael asked. "Croquet? Or maybe cricket?"

"Oh yes! What a wonderful idea!" Lady Baxter exclaimed, reaching down to tug her husband's arm until he stood with them. "I think we have a few accomplished cricket players in our midst. I confess, I am not much a sportsman; however, I am more than open to advice."

Her eyes landed on Lady Everly, who, after releasing a long, drawn-out sigh, proceeded to place her teacup on the blanket and find her feet. "I suppose we could put a game together," she said begrudgingly. The rest of her sentence faded into the breeze, though Michael thought he heard her gripe, "… although I *was* relaxing…"

The hostess focused her attention on the rest of the group. "Lady Maggie? You are also an accomplished player, is that right?"

Maggie smiled, and the effortless way it came to her face stabbed Michael in the center of his chest. Her smiles had been ready enough over the party, just not for his benefit. "I would not call myself accomplished," she said, "though I do play. I would be happy to join you."

"Wonderful. That's the spirit," Lady Baxter crowed, placing her hands on her hips. She studied the rest of the lazing crowd. "Now… who's next?

IT TOOK AN effort, but Lady Baxter managed to wrangle fourteen people onto the makeshift pitch—everyone except Aunt Alice, who had only laughed and gone back to enjoying her strawberries and cream when Lady Baxter invited her to join in.

She divided the group in no particular order, though Michael noticed that she was on the same side as all the females who were members of the London Ladies Cricket Club. Though it was only meant as an afternoon amusement, Lady Baxter clearly wanted to win, and she must have surmised that her best chance of doing that included Lady Everly, Lady Ella, and Maggie.

Maggie and her teammates opted to take the field first and did a respectable job holding Michael's side to thirty runs before getting their three wickets. It helped that four women on Michael's team had never held a cricket bat in their lives. Instead of going easy on the women, Lady Everly bowled out two of them in quick succession.

Michael tried to take the game in stride. He even attempted

to laugh off the lack of balance in the teams, but when it was his turn in the field, he asked to bowl. Competitiveness ran deep. He might lose the match, but he'd be damned if he didn't take a few wickets of his own, if only to wipe the haughty look off Lady Everly's face. That woman was a menace at the best of times.

Michael assumed it would be easy. Those ladies might play cricket regularly, but how good could they truly be against someone like him?

Unfortunately, he received his answer readily enough. Even with his stellar bowling *and* Lord Baxter and Lord Rutherford backing him up in the field, Lady Ella put in for fifteen runs. The lady's soft-spoken mien belied her tenacious manner, and when she swung the bat, she swung it like her life depended on it.

Naturally, Jo was no different. However, the biggest surprise was Lady Baxter, who had obviously been playing a joke on all of them. *Not much of a sportsman?* Ha! Her first turn at the crease resulted in a six when the ball sailed over everyone's heads past the line of hedges that marked the edge of the field.

At Michael's frown of incredulity, she merely shrugged her shoulders with a twinkle in her eye and said, "Did I fail to mention I used to play in the Singles vs. Matrons game? But I don't think I was ever this good back then!"

Lady Everly snorted. "You were *better*! That ball barely made it over the hedges. Don't tell me you're getting old, Anne!"

Lady Baxter stuck her tongue out at her sister-in-law, positioning herself for another go. Sure enough, when Michael bowled the next ball, she sent it even farther. She didn't even bother to watch it land, but rather raised an eyebrow at Jo. "Is that good enough for you?"

Jo finally smiled in appreciation. "Yes, darling, that's rather good. But perhaps that's enough. We don't want to embarrass the other side *too* badly."

The hostess in Anne appeared to win out over the blatant competitor. "Yes, that's very sensible of you."

She popped up the next ball, and even though Michael's side

cheered for the small victory, he was convinced that she'd dismissed herself on purpose. That stung his pride even more.

But that flurry of indignance was short-lived when Anne handed the bat to Maggie. Michael noticed she was back to her old self. She hadn't worn any ridiculously feminine outfits during the weekend. Her long brown hair was fashioned in an efficient bun at the back of her head, with no feathers or other gargantuan embellishments lining her plain bonnet. Though he could admit he'd grown to appreciate the loud yellow dress she had debuted at his fight, her muted, carefree appearance at the party relaxed Michael. It was like seeing an old friend.

Only, the feeling wasn't mutual. Maggie took her place in front of the stumps, raising the bat high, her grip sure and strong. Michael admired the leanness of her figure, remembering the way she'd held him in those long arms with the same self-possession and composure, the same self-confident intensity.

But the difference was in the eyes. A good cricket player never took his eyes off the ball, so Michael didn't begrudge her gaze as it stayed far from his; however, Maggie's darted all over the place as she waited for him to bowl. First it landed on Lady Ella, and then Lady Everly, and then back again. A secret conversation seemed to be taking place between the trio, and the longer it went on, the longer Maggie's face became.

"Just get on with it, Michael!" Lord Baxter barked from the field, a harsh note of resignation in his tone. "If they're going to beat us, let's get it over with so I can go inside. It's bloody hot and I need a drink."

Michael nodded and went into his run-up. As he released the ball, he readied himself for the inevitable strike from the bat, but Maggie's swing was so wild and clumsy, she missed the ball entirely and almost landed on her behind in the grass. Michael's ball just missed the stumps, almost gaining the last wicket.

"That's all right, dear," Lady Everly called to her friend. "That was actually so much better than the swings in our last match."

Better? That swing? A blind man would have had a better

chance of making contact. That swing was ridiculous! Remembering Lady Baxter's farcical popout, Michael's ego received another strong slap.

"Don't play with me," he growled, taking a few frustrated strides toward her. "I know that's not how you swing the bat."

"I'm not playing!" Maggie hollered back. "And you've never seen me play, so don't pretend that you know anything about my swing!"

Michael couldn't understand the vitriol in her voice. Why was she so upset at him? What had he done to deserve this?

He was taken aback by the vulnerability in his own response. "Just play straight. Play honest. We can handle it—"

Lord Rutherford appeared in the corner of his vision as the sanctimonious man ran toward the pitch. "Go easy on her, Burlington. There's no reason to be so rude. She's a woman. Why should you expect her to be any better than this?" He turned away from Michael, addressing Maggie with a patronizing smile. "I find you charming, my lady. In fact, I would love to offer you some pointers after the game, if you're up for it."

"You're too kind," Jo called out, giving Maggie yet another inexplicable look.

Michael stepped toward Rutherford. The men played nice amongst others, but there was no love lost between them. Michael couldn't stand the smarmy fellow who traded gossip like currency and took every married woman he could find to his bed. "Get back in the field, Rutherford," he seethed. "This doesn't concern you. I'm talking to my—"

He stopped short. Rutherford's brow pinched together. "Talking to your what?"

Michael shook his head. What the hell had he meant to say? His Maggie? His woman? His lover? Because none of those descriptions were technically true, and yet they still gnawed at him, wanting to come out.

"Maggie," he replied evenly. "I was talking to Maggie. Not you."

Rutherford laughed in his face. "So touchy, Burlington. We aren't children anymore. No need to pick a fight at the first chance. Girls are shite at cricket, you know that. Well"—he sniffed, lifting his eyebrows to the opposite team—"*normal* ones are, at least. I was just trying to help the pathetic woman."

Michael saw red, but before he could do anything about it, Rutherford was already jogging to his spot near Lord Baxter.

"But that's *not her*. I don't know who that is but it's *not her*," Michael muttered to himself, squaring toward Maggie once more. He held up the ball, showing her that he was about to bowl.

A haunted look clouded her face. Again, Maggie looked at Lady Everly—almost beseechingly—but the lady only returned a steady nod.

"I'm ready," Maggie announced weakly.

Michael began his run-up. He put more spin on the ball, anxious to see what she could do with it. But the woman acted like she'd never encountered a spinner before and hacked at it like she was scything wheat. She did manage to make contact, though. The ball skidded, petering out in the grass by Lord Baxter, who knocked the bails off the stumps before Maggie could reach it. The woman looked relieved as she handed the bat off to the next batter, taking a seat beside the others on the ground.

Completely bewildered, Michael watched as Lady Ella walked over to her, patting her shoulder in a way that reminded him of someone being congratulated rather than consoled.

He couldn't process any of it, but there was one thing he was sure of—something was definitely going on between Maggie and her friends.

And Michael vowed that before the end of the party, he would find out what it was.

UNFORTUNATELY, MICHAEL'S QUESTIONS had to wait. The minute

the cricket game finished, the party hurried inside to dress for dinner. Soon after, Michael joined the other man for a quick drink as they waited for the women to join them downstairs. The men were nursing their intolerable loss, while Michael was nursing his increasing confusion.

And it only got worse as the night went on.

By the time dinner was over—and Maggie had successfully avoided looking at him for all six courses—he'd had too much to drink, and his self-control was nearing its limit.

The party retired to the drawing room, where, thankfully, music was ignored in favor of more games. Lady Baxter's competitive nature had still not reached its capacity, and she encouraged pairs of four to break off for whist. Michael's prayers were answered when he noticed Maggie refrain from joining Aunt Alice at a table. It was his opportunity to pounce.

As he came upon her, Michael noticed she wasn't surprised by his audacity, but she wasn't overjoyed by it either. With self-restraint in abeyance, he launched right in.

"Why did you do that?"

Maggie swiveled her head to all the guests closest to them.

"Don't worry," Michael went on. "No one can hear us."

She returned a disbelieving frown. "Do you know how loud you're speaking right now?

Was he speaking loudly? Michael couldn't tell because of all the thoughts screaming in his head. Taking her hint, he tempered his voice. "Why?" he asked again.

"Why what?"

"Why"—he gritted his teeth—"did you play like that? So poorly?"

She had the nerve to act hurt! "That's not very kind to say to a lady."

Maggie placed her hand against her chest in feigned shock and started to walk away, but Michael would not be dismissed that easily. He leaned into her ear. "You're better than that. You've been better than that since you were ten."

Maggie made an unladylike sound, rolling her eyes. "Hardly. And I'm surprised you don't like it. Don't all men want a woman who constantly needs help so they can instruct her? Rutherford seemed to enjoy it. What did he call me... pathetic?"

Michael studied her. She couldn't hide the bitterness in her voice, and she chewed on her lower lip as if ashamed the words had come out of her mouth.

"Rutherford's an arse."

She bobbed her pretty shoulders. "Still. He proved a point."

A cheer came up from one of the tables as a game ended. Seizing the advantage, Michael guided Maggie to the corner of the room and lowered his head until she was forced to look at him. "Is that what the afternoon was about?" he asked. "Am I nothing but a game to you? If that's the case, you're playing me all wrong, my dear. Since when do you think I want a helpless woman?"

Maggie continued to gnaw her lip, and Michael worried she might break the precious skin.

"I thought, by now, you knew me better than that, Maggie. I thought you knew *me*."

"I don't know what I know anymore."

"You know I want you. Do I have to be more direct?" he said. "I want you. And not some silly creature you and your friends have concocted."

Her eyes found his, and Michael's suspicions were confirmed.

"Oh, yes," he went on. "I know that Ella and Jo are up to something. I just don't know how you're involved."

"Just leave it be. It has nothing to do with you."

"I think it does. And I want you to tell me."

Maggie matched his intensity, and when she sighed, the anxiety seemed to be released from her body. Michael was ready for a confession, but it didn't come. "I don't think we should spend any more time together, my lord."

"*My lord?* What—"

"You have your boxing, and I have my life and my friends and my dog to get back to. This whole situation has been distracting."

"You're damn right it's been distracting," Michael growled. "But that doesn't mean it's been wrong. It's been more right than anything I've ever experienced before."

Maggie grew increasingly agitated. She continued to glance over his shoulder. "You don't mean that."

"I do."

"Please don't do this. You don't understand—"

"Then make me understand!"

Maggie expression was racked with despair. "I can't. It's out of control. I don't know how—"

"Wo-ho, what's all this?" Rutherford announced gleefully, causing the entire room to fall silent.

Knowing who the bastard was directing his question to, Michael had no choice but to back away from Maggie. He could feel a crowd closing in. A hand smacked him on the shoulder, and even though his bruises were still fresh and tender, Michael did not flinch.

"Don't be such a sore loser, Burlington. It was only a game," Rutherford said, coming up beside him. "You're caging the poor woman. Besides, she's hardly the one to take your frustrations out on. She didn't account for any runs, isn't that right, Piggy Peggy?"

Spit flew from his mouth as he punched out the words, and Maggie flinched.

Michael turned around slowly. "Don't call her that," he stated icily, but Rutherford merely grinned. He was the type of man who was accepted and invited to everything, though no one could ever explain why. Loud-mouthed and unctuous, he never brought wit or anything new to a conversation. But his title and good looks afforded him a place in the circle. Most of Michael's friends, like Lord Baxter, considered him harmless because they had the distinct advantage of being equals and able to fight back against his bigoted tyranny. Women of any kind were never that lucky.

Rutherford's handsome face folded into a sneer. "Oh, relax, Burlington. Little Piggy Peggy knows I'm only teasing. We're old friends."

Michael lifted his chin and stared hard at the man from his elevated perch. Rutherford wasn't short, but he only came to Michael's nose. "You're not her friend."

Titters of polite laughter sprang up sporadically around them. It was nervous laughter, meant to deflate an awkward situation, and ordinarily, Michael would have heeded them and moved on. However, at this point, he was more than slightly drunk and not in the mood for diplomacy. He closed his hand into a fist at his side, and it felt so *good*. Like putting on a perfectly tailored jacket.

"Not her friend?" Rutherford chortled along with the others. "I've known Maggie since we were babies. Isn't that right?" he asked, searching for Maggie over Michael's shoulder. "In fact, I was there the day that you came up with the nickname. As I remember, Maggie had decided she would try her hand at riding a pig. She wanted to impress us with her skills. Didn't work out for her, of course, but it was a mighty try."

Michael's scowl deepened. Had Rutherford been there that day? He couldn't recall. But there was something he did remember. "Maggie didn't try to impress you. You"—he clenched his jaw—"*we* dared her to do it."

Rutherford blinked in confusion. From the corner of his eye, Michael watched Lady Everly draw Maggie out from the corner. Together they left the crowd, seemingly bored by the turn of conversation.

If only Michael could let it go so easily. His resistance was partly due to the role he'd played in that juvenile nickname, but also over Rutherford's insistent familiarity with Maggie. How dare he think he could speak to her, let alone use that abominable name? How dare he even look at Maggie when she was his?

Michael's chest swelled at the realization. Yes, Maggie was his. And her name would never come out of Rutherford's fucking mouth again.

"I'm afraid your recollection is faulty, my dear man," Rutherford continued, encouraged by the crowd's rapt attention. "We didn't goad her into anything. One minute we were all talking about the latest scandal and the next she was flailing about on the back of an old sow. It was… well, it was a sight." He cocked his head at Michael, his eyes gleaming. "Perhaps you have a bit of selective memory because of the scandal we were discussing. Or maybe it's all that boxing. Can't be good for the head. You know, you cost me a substantial chunk of money with that lucky fight of yours against O'Shaughnessy. Shame, really. And for what? A little fleeting glory? It's a poor substitute for a working brain."

This was why Michael never drank too much. It slowed his reflexes, and every fighter knew that he was complete shit without them. He should have seen the trap Rutherford was setting, but he let himself get drawn in. "What the hell are you going on about? That was years ago. How could anyone possibly remember what we were discussing? What scandal?"

Michael recognized his error the moment the words left his mouth. Rutherford was like a fighter, weaving and moving, taking punch after punch, just waiting for the right opening. He'd found it.

His smile widened, showcasing two absurdly crooked front teeth. He closed his mouth when he noticed Michael staring at them. "Your father, of course. That's what everyone always talked about back then. Do you truly not remember? What were we, twelve? Danbury was filling us all in on what the papers had printed that day. Something about a club—the Dark Angel, I think it was named—that had been raided by a bunch of Bow Street Runners…"

Panic threatened to strangle Michael as that day came rushing back. It was odd how he'd forgotten that shameful conversation. Maggie's outrageous behavior had eclipsed everything else.

Rutherford became buoyed by Michael's silence and looked around at his congregants while he continued. "You see, we were all so enamored by the gossip at the time because this was the first instance of hearing about these miscreants. It wasn't a club, it was a molly house where men cavorted and dressed up as women, even wearing face paint like French prostitutes." He laughed, holding his stomach as if the act hurt him. "I won't even tell you what else they did there, for the women's sake, naturally."

Lord Baxter stepped in, unease evident in his expression. "That's enough, Rutherford. This isn't decent conversation."

"Oh, I know that!" Rutherford chuckled. "It wasn't decent for us children either, but I'm glad Danbury told us. It's important to know what filth is out here, especially so close by." He lifted an eyebrow at Michael. "Isn't that right, Burlington? Some of it's rather *too* close by, don't you agree? Or maybe you don't. Maybe it's true that the apple doesn't fall from the tree?"

Michael squeezed his fists so tight he was certain the bone would break through the thin, scarred skin. A war raged inside. He wanted nothing more than to break every crooked tooth inside Rutherford's mouth, but he also didn't want to lose control. Because that was where men like Rutherford drew their power. These men had no skills, no intellect, no curiosity in the world beyond their immediate sphere, and their goals were to strip it from everyone around them. Michael hadn't understood that when he was young, which was why he'd swung his hands so readily. But he was different now. A man. And he could bear it; he could take everything these bastards threw at him and never fall. He would toe the line again and again until they tired themselves out with their hate and fear. Then he would watch them drop, and Michael would be the last one standing.

He returned a bored smirk. "As you say."

Baxter continued to play the peacemaker. He gave Michael an apologetic grimace before smacking Rutherford on the shoulder again. "You're ruining the party, my good man," he said. "No one wants to hear all this old news. Come back to the table. Let's see if we take the next game of whist from the ladies. We wouldn't want them to think that their men are completely hopeless today."

That seemed to do the trick. Rutherford relented, disappointed in Michael's bland response. He allowed the earl to string him back to the cards. Nevertheless, just as he was about to take a seat, he spun around to Michael once more. "But doesn't everyone want to know who was at the club that day?" he asked. "So many were, but not everyone was taken into custody. A select few had the money and influence to keep themselves out of handcuffs and the gossip columns. But I am privy to the information, so let me tell you—"

"Oh, good Lord!"

Glass smashed to the floor, tearing Rutherford's audience from his grasp. All eyes shot to the opposite side of the drawing room, where Maggie posed in shock with red punch splashed all over her dress.

Lady Everly sprang to action, grabbing a clean linen from the sideboard and rushing it to her friend with Lady Alice not far behind. "My dear Maggie, what happened? Are you all right?"

Maggie tossed her arms up at her sides as liquid dripped from her body. "I'm so… so… clumsy!" she cried, walking to the center of the space, granting everyone a full view of her mess. Michael couldn't comprehend how she'd managed to get the punch in her hair, but there it was, sprinkling from the copper curls buttressing her rueful face.

"I'm so sorry. Look at your floor!" she wailed. For all her histrionics, Maggie's eyes stayed clear, without a tear in sight. "I hope I didn't ruin the night with my blundering!"

Jo hugged her shoulders, being careful not to get any of the punch on her pale-mint gown. "Not at all, dear. How could you think that? Let's just go get you cleaned up, shall we?" Maggie resisted at first, fixing a forlorn countenance on the spill, but eventually followed Lady Everly out of the room.

Michael started to trail behind her. He wanted to ask her what all that was about. Maggie was the least clumsy woman he knew. But Lady Alice put an insistent hand on his shoulder as he passed her.

"Give her time, dear boy," she said with unexpected familiarity. "She likes her space."

Michael nodded and held his ground. Maggie *had* appeared visibly distraught. The day had been long, and he had approached her in an ungentlemanly manner. And he didn't even want to mention the uncouth argument Rutherford had pulled him into…

Reluctantly, Michael returned to the guests. He readied himself for more of Rutherford's attacks until he noticed that everyone had gone back to playing cards and milling about the room. His altercation with Rutherford had been completely forgotten—or, at least, dismissed.

These people were fickle, Michael thought angrily. Even if their capriciousness worked to his advantage, he still didn't want to spend another second in that room. There was no reason anyway, with Maggie no longer there.

He was about to leave when he heard a snicker.

"Piggy Peggy strikes again," Rutherford remarked to a low buzz of cackles. "Why am I never surprised with that woman? She's always been a catastrophe."

Michael froze—and then the floor fell out from under his feet.

All at once, he was like a lonely spectator in a theater observing a series of vignettes flashing before his eyes. A picture of Maggie as a child covered in mud looking at him with sympathy, as if she couldn't care less about what she'd done. A new picture of Maggie, stained in pale red liquid, mirroring that same expression—always in his direction. As everyone had stared at her, her only focus had been him. Then and now.

Michael shook the pictures from his head. It couldn't be. *Could it?* Maggie couldn't have done it… for him?

Heat climbed up his body, spurring him on. Coming to his senses, Michael headed for the exit, leaving the gossip and the titters behind. Beyond a doubt, he knew that Maggie didn't care about it anyway. Vengeance was unnecessary because, he now realized, she'd always wanted the laughs and nasty comments.

They'd been her gift to him.

But something nagged at him before he could completely leave the drawing room. Just as Maggie didn't ask for revenge, Michael hadn't asked for her to humiliate herself for him. He would give her this gift anyway because he enjoyed revenge. He never cared how it got there—hot or cold—as long as it was served in the end.

He set Rutherford in his sights. Michael's feet did not falter as he came for the man, who made the stupid decision to step forward in what Michael could only surmise was encouragement.

Michael's fist flew through the air so fast that he heard a whistling sound. And then he heard the delicious crack of bones as he connected with Rutherford's jaw.

The man hit the ground with a disappointing thud. Michael would have appreciated more flailing, more drama. He was certain there were gasps and shrieks, tumbled wine glasses and scattered playing cards; however, Michael was deaf and blind to them all.

He bent over Rutherford's body, picking him up by the collar. "I warned you not to say her name again," he rasped menacingly. Rutherford's eyes rolled back in their sockets. Michael doubted he could hear him, but that didn't matter. He needed to say the words. He needed the room to be his witness. "I hope you learned your lesson, because this was the easy one. Speak of her again and you'll wish you'd never been born."

Chapter Fourteen

MICHAEL STORMED INTO Maggie's room without a knock, without a warning. His body was hunched and in fighting mode, his expression fierce, his voice low and menacing.

"Did you do it on purpose? Tell me now. I need to know the truth."

Maggie paused in the middle of untying her corset. The moment she entered her room, she'd wasted little time and energy ridding herself of the sticky garments, piling them in the corner to worry about in the morning.

Michael's unrelenting gaze flicked to her shoulders, where her chemise hung lifelessly over her bare skin.

"What are you... I-I don't understand what you're asking," she stammered as he slammed the door shut behind him, making a great show of latching the lock. "You shouldn't be in here."

His grin had heat. "Both of us seem to make a habit of being in rooms we shouldn't be in."

At the start of the night, his hair had been swept off his forehead and tucked behind his ears, but now it was unruly, bracketing his face with its chestnut waves. He reminded Maggie of a wolf, one that had just zeroed in on its prey.

"I want you to tell me why you did it," he said, the calmness in his tone belying the severity he held just below the surface.

Maggie could see it in the way he stretched and fisted his hands at his sides, the way his shoulders were wide and fixed. He had the devil in him. His blood was most definitely up. But whom was he fighting? The only other person in the proverbial ring was Maggie.

Why on earth was he angry at *her*? What had she done other than save him from that dreadful situation? Oh, but he didn't know that, nor did she want him to. Grandmother always told her that a man's ego was a fragile thing, and she'd never known her grandmother to be wrong about anything—especially men.

She counted the minutes until she'd be able to leave. Tomorrow everything would go back to normal, and she'd be safe at home with her aunt and dog. George never asked too many questions. Maggie's love for George was uncomplicated and wholesome, light and easy—the only way she wanted to experience it.

It was safer that way—for everyone involved. Maggie trusted herself in that relationship. She never feared who she was or could become. The feelings that she held for Michael were anything but civilized.

"I... I..." She licked her lips, and her stomach fluttered when she saw his gaze dart to her mouth. Maggie wasn't feigning confusion; it was difficult keeping anything straight when Michael regarded her that way. So hungry. "You heard me. I was clumsy. It's that simple."

Michael was shaking his head before she finished. "Nothing is ever that simple with you. I'll ask you all night until I get my answer. The real one."

"I don't know what you want!" Maggie said. She watched her wolf's focus travel lower, and she wrapped her arms around her chest, hiding her inviting flesh. Her robe hung on a chair on the opposite side of the room. She had little hope that he'd allow her to put it on. "All I did was drop my punch—accidently."

"Not that," he snapped, and Maggie jumped. Michael never spoke to her that way. He was barely holding himself in check, furious in a way she'd never seen before. Nevertheless, as the silence stretched out between them, something gave. The lines around his eyes wavered, and he appeared incredibly exposed, defenseless. Vulnerable. "At my parents' estate. That day." Every syllable was spoken with great intention. "Why did you ride that animal?"

Maggie shrugged, growing more uncomfortable with what he was resolved to uncover. "You know why. I rode it because I was dared to. And I knew I could."

"No." Michael shook his head. "Don't lie to me. I remember now. No one goaded you. One minute we were all listening to that insufferable Danbury by the stables, and the next you were flying off."

"That's not how I remember it."

Michael's blue eyes were impossibly sad. The side of his mouth twitched up in a mournful smile. "Do you remember what we'd been talking about?"

"*We*? No one ever talked to me. I was the little girl whose parents always left her behind. A pitiful creature you all ignored."

His expression softened even more. "Fine. The others, then. Do you remember what they were talking about... *whom* they were talking about?"

Maggie pressed her lips together in a tight line. Of course she knew. It wasn't every day that a boy's father was ridiculed to his face—especially when that boy was Lord Michael, Viscount Burlington.

With tentative steps, Michael traversed the perimeter of the bed. The closer he came to her, the more Maggie panicked. Because she wanted to be sure of her actions when he reached her. She wanted to be sure she would push him away and force him to leave her room.

But she wasn't sure, not even close.

"Tell me what you heard," he ordered her.

Her throat closed off, and when she pushed the words out, they sounded harsh and unnatural. "Why do you want to recall such terrible things? Why do you wish to recount what horrible boys like Danbury and Rutherford said about your father?"

Michael's expression lost some of its somberness. The smile he gave her was genuine and so very kind. He lifted his hand, caressing her skin with the back of his fingers from her temples down to her chin. Maggie wanted to take it in her own and kiss all the scars that covered his knuckles because those were the only scars she could see. She knew he had so many more inside, and they were the kind she was helpless against.

Michael wrapped his other hand around her waist, pulling Maggie against his chest. "I don't care about those boys. I only care about you. I let myself forget because it was easy. But that's why I need to remember now. I need to remember how low and terrible they made me feel. Because only then will I realize that it was you all along who understood it. It was you, Maggie, who was my champion. You did it, didn't you? You embarrassed yourself to drag their attention away from me. And I rewarded you by poking fun. I joined them in laughing at you so they wouldn't laugh at me. No wonder you hated me for all those years."

Maggie rested her hand on his chest. Michael was so warm and large, so strong. But he was a man. And they broke and splintered as easily as women, maybe even more so because they lacked the practice that women had. Women were always made to be the lesser, and if they didn't continually guard themselves against the idea, they could start to believe it.

"I didn't hate you."

The statement floated between them, a living and breathing thing.

"No?"

"No."

"Why, Maggie?" Michael reached around her and took his time unraveling her hair from its tidy bun. He didn't speak again until her long locks draped down her back. "You had every right to."

Maggie sighed. It was too effortless, too straightforward. He was a temptation she could no longer resist. *He* was the boxer; he had the stamina, and Maggie was afraid that she had no more fight in her. "I could never hate you," she said, "because I was too busy loving you… just like everyone else."

Michael didn't speak right away, causing Maggie to immediately regret her honesty. She pulled out of his embrace and felt fresh tears scald her eyes.

But when Maggie attempted to spin from him, Michael held firm, his hands on her hips, his arms locked straight. "Say that again."

Maggie blushed. "Stop it."

"Please." That one word was like an incantation, and she opened up once more. Through all the hurt, the risk of rejection, Maggie would give him what he asked. What she wanted to give him.

She watched his Adam's apple bob over his collar as he waited. "I couldn't hate you, Michael, because I loved you too much. I always did. You pretended to be like the others, but I could tell you were sad. Sad like me. Alone. You were just better at hiding it, better at fitting in with the rest."

"You mean a coward—"

"No. Just a boy. Just a sad boy." Maggie inflated her lungs, filling herself with his musky scent, with his masculine courage. "So, now you know. I couldn't just stand by as those imbeciles berated your father and you. They wanted you to hate him, to be ashamed of him—your own father, who was always with you, always so loving toward you. I know I was young, but it still makes no sense to this day. So I did the only thing I could do. I made them look at me instead."

"But what about you?"

"What about me?"

"Who was ever there to help you? To pick you up. To carry you?"

"I didn't need anyone."

Maggie felt free, as if she'd kicked off countless chains fastened to her feet. But she didn't feel better; she didn't feel released. Those weights may have kept her in the same place for a long time, but they also had kept her safe.

She clenched her teeth to keep her voice from trembling. "So now what? I've told you everything. I've given my oldest enemy everything he needs to end me. What will you do, Michael? Will you be merciful, or will you use it against—"

Michael chose something else entirely. He chose to conquer.

He rushed in on Maggie, capturing her mouth and her words like a man who'd said enough, heard enough. A man capable of great action.

Maggie fell into him, luxuriating in the way he wrapped his arms around her waist, holding her tight and safe. This kiss was demanding and searching. It was a question. And Maggie didn't leave anything behind. She gave him his answer. There was no going back now. It was impossible. It was inevitable.

Without breaking their embrace, Michael walked her back until the back of Maggie's legs hit the bed. There was no hesitation. There was also no doubt. She knew very well where they were headed, and she was surprised by the lack of hesitation inside her. She wanted this. She wanted him, even though he hadn't said he loved her back—it didn't matter. Her decision wasn't about him, she realized. This night was about Maggie and about taking what she wanted.

Michael's fingers shook, but they worked quickly. "God, I need you. I need to touch all over you or I'll go mad." He yanked the laces of her corset, setting her free from the constricting cage. He stood above her and wrenched it from her body, casting it on the floor without a second look.

His seriousness scared Maggie, the way he regarded her as if she were this great, priceless thing that must be handled carefully. He focused on her thin chemise, and soon that too was on the floor.

It was only when she lay before him completely naked that

Michael stopped to appreciate his work. Maggie wasn't sure what to do. She smiled, but even that didn't break him from his trance.

"Michael?" she rasped, placing her hands on her belly. "Michael. Come here."

He shook his head. His expression was raw and open, unbearably honest. "I-I can't," he replied. "I never want to stop seeing this picture of you."

Desire built inside her. Maggie had never considered herself beautiful. Attractive, maybe. Tolerable, definitely. But the way Michael looked at her made her feel like a goddess. And goddesses had the power and confidence to do whatever they wanted.

Slowly, she sat up. Keeping her gaze fixed on his, she reached for his jacket. Michael's breath hitched as she began to unfasten his buttons, working first on his vest… and then on his trousers.

"I don't know what to do with you," he rasped, giving himself up to her.

Maggie returned a half-smile, arching a brow. "Don't fighters practice?" she teased. "Don't you have combinations and plans for every situation?"

He held the back of her neck as she spread his vest wide and pulled his linen shirt out from his trousers. "I'm not fighting you, Maggie. I'd be too afraid to. I'm going to make love to you. It isn't the same."

A whirlwind of excitement sparked in her belly.

Maggie squeezed her inner thighs against his legs and pulled on his shirt until his head was level with hers. "Why would you be too afraid to face me? Am I that fearsome?"

Michael braced his arms on either side of her, sinking his fists into the mattress. Maggie could smell the brandy on his lips, the cherry undertones as he resisted kissing her so he could answer her question. "You're terrifying. You're the fighter who will never back down. Again and again, you will find a way to get your toe on that line. You would break me with your tenacity, exhaust me with your sheer will."

Maggie had never felt so powerful. She skimmed her nose

back and forth against his. "Does that really sound so bad?" She moved her hands to his back and pressed him into her. Michael accepted the invitation. He knelt before her, tucking his hands under her thighs, gripping her flesh with a ferocious possessiveness.

"It would be a good match, yes?" Maggie whispered. Her skin was impossibly sensitive; everywhere he touched her felt like it was being singed.

Michael nodded. "A very good match."

"One you would never forget?"

"Never?"

"One where both people win at the end regardless of who's still standing?"

Michael's hands moved up her thighs, and he groaned as he laid his head on her belly. "Maggie, love," he said, licking her delicate, downy skin, "I guarantee you that neither one of us is going to be standing at the end of this night. Maybe not tomorrow either."

That was exactly what she wanted to hear. "Then meet me halfway, Michael. That's all I ask. Just meet me on the line."

Michael nodded, and something switched in him. His expression became warrior-like, his body ready for battle. He came to his feet and tore off his clothes, all while keeping his blue eyes on her, daring her to stay focused on him.

She couldn't have evaded him if she tried. It didn't matter where Michael was—she would always find him. His actions were quick, and he paid no heed to the mess he made of his garments, but Maggie recognized the difficulty. Michael's fingers were swollen, which made unbuttoning his shirt challenging. He winced as he slid it over his head. And the answer to it was right in front of her.

Michael had worn his shirt when she tended to his cuts after the fight, but now she could see the full force of what he'd endured. Nasty, violent splotches of purple and blue riddled his ribs. Small knicks and scratches were peppered everywhere else.

No patch of skin was free from the torment.

Maggie couldn't stifle her cry. "Oh, Michael," she said, reaching out, but stopping before she made contact.

"It's all right. Touch me, Maggie. I want you to touch me."

Maggie nodded and allowed her fingers to bind the hurt. She prayed with those fingers, begging that her loving touch could heal him right before her eyes. Her mouth followed her hands, kissing the vibrant colors, murmuring words of praise and worship.

Michael hissed from her fleeting touches, and the masterfully crafted muscles of his stomach flexed and rolled as she kissed him. He was like a sculpture, an ancient study of the gods, and Maggie felt blessed as he brushed the hair off her face and allowed her to provide succor and compassion with the one thing she had… love.

Michael fell to his knees once more and urged her back on the bed. Maggie licked her lips in anticipation as she watched him gently place his hands on her knees and nudge them apart.

"My God, Maggie," he said, in awe. "I never thought this could happen."

She laughed, trying to keep her nervousness at bay. "What? Have me in bed?"

Michael's expression was heartbreaking. "No. Be happy. So happy."

He came to her then, breaking off any response Maggie might have had. She was no longer capable of speech or thought as he licked between her legs, swiftly, tenderly, lingering at her sex. It was like a lightning bolt had been captured inside Maggie's body, and it struck over and over again, trying to find a way out. She was mindless, tortured, as he licked and tongued the delicate area. He was awakening something deep inside her, something that he alone knew how to rouse.

Maggie wanted more, wanted faster, and when she drove her fingers into Michael's hair, he answered. His mouth was a revelation, and when the sensations became too much, when her body became too demanding, when her life felt like it depended on those next few seconds, her earth shattered. She was unbearably heavy and depleted. And happy. So very happy.

Michael's eyes continued to feast on her. He kissed both sides of her inner thighs and climbed up her body, settling in the crux of her trembling thighs, fixing his limbs to hers like a puzzle piece finding its mate. They locked together in a breathless embrace that promised so much more.

"This next part might not be as…" Michael grimaced.

Maggie held his head, stopping him from looking away. "Will it make me yours?"

His eyes sank into hers; his expression was shattered but grateful. "Until our dying days."

"Then what is a little pain for a lifetime of happiness?"

Michael kissed her. It was sweet and light, leisurely. Maggie gave herself up to it and didn't notice him shift on top of her, fitting himself to her opening. She sucked in a breath when he pressed inside, stretching her, pleading with her to open for him.

She clasped the arms he caged her with, discovering the rolling hills of his sinewy muscles, leaning on his unwavering strength as he continued to invade her.

"Almost there," he gritted through his teeth. His chest pumped from the effort, and Maggie wondered if going so slow caused him as much pain as it was causing her. She felt herself breaking for him—breaking and becoming new.

"Michael?" she asked, waiting for him to look at her. "Do you remember what you said to me during the match today? You said you could take it. Whatever I gave you, you could take it."

He laughed, though it came out more like a grunt, and he pushed inside her even more. The act was different, unexpectedly hard and lovely at the same time.

"I can take it, Michael. Don't worry about me."

"I don't want to hurt you."

"You won't." Maggie moved her legs up higher, hugging his hips, smiling as Michael's eyes closed in what could only be considered bliss. "Take me, now. I want to be yours. It's all I've ever wanted—"

Michael surged inside her with one heavy thrust. Maggie screamed out, panting wickedly against the side of her neck. She stroked his face, caressed his back, ran her fingers up and down his spine—she couldn't stop touching him, couldn't stop reveling in the fact that she could never go back. She'd made her decision, as had he.

Michael balanced on his elbows and gazed down on her. His expression still signaled pain, but there was a clearness in his eyes, a lightness to his being. "Thank you," he said, pulling out of her only to slam inside again.

Maggie arched her back further, taking all he gave. It was an odd, unnerving feeling, to be filled by someone, but it also felt incredibly right. At times in her life, she had felt so out of place, yet she knew that here, now, with Michael, was exactly where she was supposed to be. With someone who unequivocally wanted nothing other than to be here with her.

The act took on a life of its own. Michael rolled and pumped inside her, faster and faster, encouraging Maggie to give and take, to yield and conquer. The pain was soon gone—or conveniently forgotten—and she rejoiced in the slickness of his body, the smoothness of his strokes, and also the power in herself. Because she had been right: Maggie could take him. As much as he gave her, she would accept, and she would do it well.

Michael's strokes became shorter, his rhythms choppier. He ordered her to hold on to him. To never let him go. And for once, Maggie did what he said. Without question.

Head to head, chest to chest, they allowed their primitive natures to take over, and when Maggie felt that butterfly wing of excitement climb up her inner thighs again, she urged him on, crashing against his pelvis, keening when it grabbed hold, throwing her over the edge.

Michael followed. He captured her mouth as they exploded together, cutting off their screams before they alerted the entire house. Later she would be thankful for his quick thinking. Maggie's awareness of others had fled the moment he touched her.

Still entwined, they fell into the mattress, weary and boneless. Even as Maggie's eyes began to droop, she kept her arms around his neck. The idea of his leaving her was untenable. How would she ever handle it? Michael moving to the other side of the bed seemed a journey too far.

His large hand stayed splayed on her belly. Every once in a while, he circled a finger around her navel. It tickled Maggie, but she wouldn't have moved it for all the world.

"What did you think?" His tone was nonchalant, but Maggie could hear the need and exposure. Her boy was sensitive. Always had been. And she was one of the only people in the world who knew it.

She played with his hair, considering the perfect words to encapsulate everything he was to her and the cataclysmic experience they'd just shared. She didn't want him to have any doubt.

She laughed when it came to her.

He lifted his head, giving her a little scowl. "That wasn't exactly the response I was expecting."

Maggie's smile widened. She shifted in the bed, forcing Michael on his back, then straddled him, placing his hands on her hips. "And what were you expecting, Michael?"

His expression darkened. "More."

"More?" Maggie rocked back and forth.

Michael nodded.

She squinted at the ceiling, tapping her finger against her chin. "What do I think?" Her grin took up her whole face. "It was quite something."

Michael chuckled, sliding his hands up her thighs to the edge of her breasts. The rough tips of his fingers played with her nipples until they were tight and straining. "Something, huh?" Michael raised himself up, and without preamble, captured a nipple in his mouth, sucking the swollen nub until Maggie gasped. He arched a brow up at her from the valley of her breasts and smiled. "Praise indeed."

Chapter Fifteen

"W HY WERE YOU acting so cold to me earlier?" Michael asked.

A glimmer of sunlight was dripping through the window, and he realized that he hadn't slept a wink that night. But he wasn't tired. He didn't think he'd be tired ever again.

Maggie shifted. She lay on her side, draped over his front with one arm flung passively over his torso. Michael loved it. He'd never liked the idea of belonging to anyone before, but that was before Maggie. Before he'd known who he really was, the true Michael—*hers*.

"I was scared," she said, rearranging herself so that she could look up at him. Her hands were on his chest, and she rested her chin on them while she answered him. Her hair was wavy and scattered over her shoulders onto his body, covering him like an overgrown perennial. She gave him warmth; she gave him substance; she gave him life.

Michael traced her lips from end to end, his fingers lingering on her impossibly soft skin. "You're never scared."

"I was."

"Why?"

Maggie lowered her face onto him, hiding. She stretched her hands over his arms, kneading his muscles, almost like the motions were helping her think. Michael approved wholehearted-ly.

"Why were scared of me?" he asked again.

She shook her head. "Not of you. Of us… of me."

Michael waited for her to collect her thoughts. She groaned against him, and he squirmed from the sensation. She popped her head up with a smile.

"Stop trying to distract me," he said, laughing. "Tell me why you were afraid."

Maggie's brow pinched. Her fingers walked up his arm, over his shoulders, down his clavicle. She stopped to explore the dip at the base of his neck. Apparently, lack of sleep wouldn't deter his ardor for Maggie. Yet again, he was hard and throbbing. He recorded that information. It was good to know.

"My parents…" she started slowly. "I never wanted to be like them. I love them, I do… but sometimes I think they should have never had children."

The hurt in her voice stabbed at him. Michael regretted ask-ing the question; he didn't want to mar their night together with sadness, but he also didn't want to leave anything in this bed. No misunderstandings or words left unspoken. When he left Lord Baxter's estate today, he would leave knowing that Maggie and he had only one place to go together—forward.

"Was it that terrible, having them as parents?"

"No, not really. When they were around they were lovely, more than lovely. They made me—us—so joyful because all they wanted to do was play and have fun, but then they would leave and we would flounder. Luckily, we had Grandmother, and the boys eventually had their schools, but…" Her voice shook. "They could never see beyond themselves. They had this great passion and only had room for each other. They made everyone else feel like secondary characters in their great love story. If I learned anything from them it was that I needed to be independent. I couldn't rely on anyone to take care of me or make me happy." She shot him a disgruntled look. "I suppose you think I'm too independent?"

Michael rubbed his thumb against her smirking lips. "No. I think you're perfect."

"You're too kind, but you're also delusional."

Michael *humphed* and rolled Maggie until they were facing one another. He rubbed his hand over her body, along the luscious slopes of her breasts and the crevices of her sharp ribcage. "Although…" he said, squeezing her delicate nipple until it hardened and reached for him. Michael couldn't resist and took it in his mouth, twirling it with his tongue while she waved and crested beneath him. He released her and blew on the rosy nipple, swollen and turgid from his attention.

"Again?" Maggie asked, though Michael knew she wasn't as put-upon as she sounded. She'd instigated activities throughout the night as well.

"In a moment," he said, moving to the other nipple. "I do love your independent nature; however, there are times when it's rather nice relying on someone else. Even better."

"Oh, yes?"

From the corner of his eye, Michael saw Maggie's heel dig into the bed while he doted on her. He licked his lips, meeting her heavy gaze. "Yes."

Without warning, Michael landed on his back, taking Maggie with him. She'd obviously assumed that he wanted her to straddle him again, but when he continued to position her higher on his body, she resisted.

"What are… what are you doing?"

Michael cocked his head. "Educating you."

He continued to arrange her until she was on her knees and her legs were splayed above his head. Her entire face had gone pink.

"Good girl," he said, petting the pretty opening above him, causing her legs to shiver. "Do you know that you can give yourself release? Men do it. Women do it. Have you ever tried, my love?"

Maggie bit her lip. Speech was not an option, and she shook her head.

Michael's smile was pure rake. "It's wonderfully satisfactory. More than that, really, but it fails in comparison to someone doing it for you like I'm about to do for you now."

Without warning, he grabbed hold of her thighs and lowered her to his waiting mouth. He coaxed his way inside her, flattening his tongue to entice her sex.

Maggie's arm shot out for the headboard, keeping herself from falling. "Good Lord!" she exclaimed.

Michael grinned against her silky folds. "Exactly. Stay still, darling. The best is yet to come."

Maggie's head dropped back as Michael went to work, energized by his tutorial. His expert tongue had her rocking and swaying against him in no time. This wasn't a languid, leisurely experience. Michael feasted on the woman like a starving man, at times holding her up when Maggie's body couldn't take any more.

But he was also devilishly attentive. The moment he felt Maggie's control slip, the moment her breathing came faster, the moment he felt her ecstasy rise, he lifted her off his mouth.

"What?" Maggie opened her eyes and glared down at him. "What are you doing? I was almost… I was *almost*."

"There?"

Her cheeks blazed. "Quite."

"Do you want me to bring you *there* again?"

Her lips widened into a tight smile. "If you could be so kind."

Michael ignored her sarcasm. "With pleasure."

He was always a man of his word. He lowered her succulent behind and continued, working her harder, faster, flicking the tip of his tongue over her sensitive nub until she writhed in abandon. Michael almost forgot the point of the whole exercise when she took her hands away from the headboard and clutched her breasts, massaging them in the rhythm of his tongue. According to his calculations, he was minutes away from spending; it would be worth it.

But once more, when the telltale signs occurred, and he recognized her reaching for that picture-perfect ending, he picked Maggie off his mouth. He'd been ready for her glare; the curse was a little unexpected.

"Why do you keep doing that?" she cried, her sultry mouth in an adorable pout. She didn't wait for him to respond—Maggie tried to climb off. "I'll just do it myself."

Michael held firm to her hips. "Oh, no you don't," he said, chuckling.

"This isn't funny. You're not being nice."

He matched her glare. "Oh, I'm being *very* nice. I'm teaching you an important lesson. Do you know what it is yet?"

Maggie crossed her arms, hiding her breasts. "That I should rely on you?"

Michael ripped her arms down. "Yes, you silly, stubborn woman, because relying on me is worth it. Because I will never let you down."

Her smile was sweet and deadly. "You're letting me down now."

"Not for long."

This time when Michael lowered her, he gave no mercy. He unleashed a torrent of passion, and Maggie had no choice but to allow him to be the master. When she was close to fulfillment, Michael used a finger to lead her to the edge. He surged inside her, massaging her with his tongue. Maggie cried and mewed with the sinful sensations, needing… aching for more.

"Tell me you need me," he panted, licking her juice from his lips.

"I need you."

"Tell me you want me."

"Oh, God. Oh, God, I want you, Michael. I want you."

"Now tell me coming is better when I make you do it."

Maggie shook her head, biting on her lower lip. "So much better. *So* much."

And seconds later, when she came on top of him, Michael was certain that the student had learned the lesson. Maggie collapsed on the bed, curling into his side. She sighed like a contented kitten. "I suppose I can rely on you sometimes," she murmured as sleep took over.

Michael stroked the top of her shoulder. "You do that, lady. You do that."

LEAVING LORD BAXTER'S estate was bittersweet for Maggie. However, she should have known that Michael wouldn't stay away for long.

Only one day after returning from the country party, she and Aunt Alice were enjoying a cup of tea when the butler informed her that she had a visitor. Michael strolled into the room with a devil-may-care smile and a bag in his hand, smelling rather like smoked meat.

George, who had been sleeping away the afternoon on his satin pillows on a patch of sunlight near the window, made a beeline for the man. He stood on his hind legs, pawing at Michael like the fiend that he was before Maggie could even rise from her chair.

Alice laughed at the drama. "If you don't have something to give that dog, then that's plain mean."

In answer, Michael reached into the sack, retrieved a small sausage, and tossed it to the overstimulated dog. Poor George wasn't the best at catching, and it knocked him on his nose before bouncing to the floor. "And I've got plenty more," Michael announced as George finished the snack in one gulp and scratched his pant leg for more.

"I hope not much more. He'll get fat," Maggie said, following her pet.

She could feel her entire body go red as Michael boldly

looked her over from her slippers to the top of her head. She didn't have to guess what he was thinking. Besides, she was thinking it too. She hadn't the faintest idea what was appropriate, given the situation. They weren't engaged, and Maggie hadn't told Alice about her intentions for Michael yet—she barely knew them herself—but curtseying and bowing in public seemed unnatural and distant. What she wanted to do was grab his head and bring him in for a toe-curling kiss, but she couldn't do that in front of her aunt—or George. The poor dog was much too young and immature for such things!

"He's already fat," Michael announced, laughing at Maggie's scowl. "But not for long."

"What does that mean?"

"Oh, never mind the dog!" Alice said, placing her teacup on the table. The look she gave Michael was playful, but stern. "I assume you're courting my niece, so what did you bring her? Don't tell me you came all the way here just to give her dog sausages."

Michael squirmed under her aunt's reproachment. Maggie covered her smile with her hand. Alice was just being ornery. She knew that Michael bringing gifts to George was the sweetest thing Maggie could have asked for.

"I... ah... Yes, um, I apologize, Lady Alice," Michael stammered, seemingly shrinking in front of the older woman.

"You apologize?" she returned haughtily. "Do you mean to say you are *not* courting my niece?"

"No, I am. I most definitely am."

"Good."

Maggie's heart almost beat out of her chest. Why had she needed him to say it to Alice? There had been no going back after their night together; however, announcing it to her aunt was like printing it on the front page of the paper.

Alice went on, her tone gaining verve. "So know that the next time you come to my house without a gift for my niece"—she sniffed—"or me, we will have problems, you understand? I am a great fan of French wines, by the way."

Michael cleared his throat. "Thank you for making me aware."

Alice's harsh veneer popped like soap bubble. "Good!" She smiled warmly. "Now, won't you take a seat? We were just having tea."

Michael frowned at the upholstered chair that Alice directed him to. "Oh, um… yes, that would be nice." He wiped sweat off his brow. "Ah… sorry… actually… I had no idea being a suitor was this stressful."

"It doesn't have to be," Alice said with a distinct lilt in her voice, "if you would bring presents."

"Right." Michael nodded. He regarded the empty chair once more and threw a beseeching glance at Maggie, who was trying not to laugh. "Actually, I thought Maggie and I would take George to the park. I had the idea that I might try my hand at training the little demon."

Maggie was already searching for her shawl.

Alice stood up, her expression frighteningly serious. "You mean you're going to *train* that horrible beast? Teach it not to scratch my lovely furniture or bark like a banshee every time someone walks past the front window?"

Michael's complexion had gone from tan to green. Those were quite the promises. And yet the silly man had made them. "Absolutely."

Alice hurried out of the drawing room and snatched George's leash off a table in the foyer. She punched it into Michael's chest. "Have a lovely time, dears. Take as long as you like."

The couple were happy to take Alice up on her offer.

Maggie would never admit this to Michael, but she had her doubts regarding his dog-training abilities. She couldn't remember if he'd had a dog when he was young. Certainly he hadn't immediately warmed to George on first take—however, even she could admit that the dachshund was an acquired taste.

But Michael surprised her in the first ten minutes at the park.

He had George sitting and staying in no time—which wasn't particularly difficult, since Maggie had already taught the dog those tricks. But when he stopped George from tugging on his leash during their walk, she considered that Michael might actually know what he was doing.

"Your little George thinks he's your master," he said as he guided the animal down the walking path in a perfectly civilized manner. "You can't let him think he's walking *you*."

Maggie nodded, but she didn't hold her breath. Each time she saw another dog (or a squirrel, kite, leaf, flower, stick, or fly) she tensed, waiting for George to forget his new teachings and try to run off. But it didn't happen. For a solid ten minutes, Michael had the dog behaving like a well-trained, good, normal dog. It was a miracle.

"I suppose I have been rather lax with George," she allowed. She bent down and rubbed the good boy's ears. "He's always been there for me, and I want him to be as happy as he makes me. I guess that has made me rather indulgent."

"You don't have to do anything special, Maggie. He already knows you love him."

"How did you learn to do all that… train dogs?"

Michael's smile transformed his face. Even with the bruises that lingered, he appeared so young and carefree when he allowed happiness to break through. "My father always kept dogs for hunting. He adored those damn animals. He had a man who trained them, but he liked to be a part of the process, said it would help the dogs respect him more. And he taught me to do the same."

Maggie liked the picture he painted: a young Michael sur-rounded by yipping dogs begging to be taken out into the field to run. No doubt, he ran with them half the time.

"I wish I could take George hunting," she said. "I know you don't believe me, but he's been bred to be a master hunter."

Michael rolled his eyes at the hairy, tube-shaped animal. "That is a lap dog."

"Look at his nose! George has a champion hunting nose. Oh! I didn't tell you. I received another letter from Mr. Burnham. He apologized for missing me before and has asked that we try again. He wants to meet tomorrow, see how the dogs get on."

"No."

"No?"

"Not without me."

Maggie looked around to make sure they didn't have an audience. She could sense a fight coming and there was no way she was going to back down. "I don't need your permission. I will go."

"No."

"Who do you think you are—"

Michael took a step, coming nose to nose with her. His voice was soft but steely. Matter-of-fact. "Don't ask who I am. You already know it. I'm your lover. I am your past and I am your future. I will not stop you from visiting this man because I know how important that silly dog is to you, but you will have to do it with me. You might be independent, Maggie, and you might not want to give me your soul, but you already have mine. And it cannot bear to think of you being in harm's way. And that is it. Do we understand each other?"

A feather could have knocked her down. Maggie's mouth latched shut. She'd told Michael that she loved him—had always loved him—but he hadn't done the same. Was this it? Was this his declaration? It felt like it. It was as close as it could be without his actually using the words.

But something still held her back. Half of her wanted to throw her arms around him and kiss him in front of the entire park, and the other half wanted to run. Because no one had ever looked at Maggie the way Michael was looking at her, and that old, childish fear crept up. The fear of losing herself.

She matched his conversational tone. "Fine. And you really shouldn't talk about George that way. He's not silly. He's misunderstood." It was a small tic, an imperceptible moment, but

Michael's face morphed from intense to confused as she sailed past all that he'd said. Maggie went on nervously. "Just because he looks a certain way doesn't mean he can't be something different. You're being prejudiced. What about you?"

"What about me?" he said so quietly that Maggie almost didn't hear him over the breeze.

She pulled her shoulders back. "People look at you and see a handsome, elegant, well-bred viscount."

"Repeat that part about my being handsome."

"Stop teasing," she said, relieved. Michael was back; the little blip of hurt was gone from his face. "I'm trying to make a point."

"That I'm handsome? I already knew that."

Maggie swatted him playfully. "That you look like one thing and are another. You are a viscount and a boxer. And you do both things well. Why does George have to be different?"

"Because George has the body of a sausage, and I have the body of a Greek god."

Maggie opened her mouth to inform him that (although he was right) she'd never heard anything so narcissistic and wrong and childish—

But he beat her to it.

Michael tipped off his hat and shielded them as he swept in for a quick kiss. Incredibly satisfying, but over too fast—Maggie's eyes were still closed when he backed away.

When she opened them, she expected to find Michael wearing a smug grin, but his expression was once again serious. He wound his pinkie finger around her own, ducking his head until their foreheads grazed. "Can I come to you tonight?"

Everything inside Maggie wanted to scream yes, but sneaking Michael into her aunt's house seemed an impossible feat, however godlike he thought he was. Battling a cyclops was one thing; battling her boisterous dog was another. "I don't think you can," she said. "George barks every time he hears a noise. It would be too difficult. He would alert the entire house."

Michael contemplated the dog, who was busy chewing on a

stick that was longer—but not thicker—than him. It was a minute before Michael came back to her. "What time is it?"

She shrugged. "Four? Maybe a little after."

Michael nodded. "Plenty of time." He tugged on George's leash, rousing the dog from his fun break. "All right, Georgie. Time for more lessons—when to bark and when not to bark—and we're not leaving here until you get it right."

Chapter Sixteen

THE FOLLOWING MORNING, Michael wasn't at his best.

"You were late today, scrapper." Tommy Jones circled him, keeping an eagle eye on his fighter's movements. The two had been training for the better part of an hour, and this was the first time Tommy had said anything other than "quicker!" or "harder!"

Michael lowered his head and continued to shadow-box, holding a weight in each hand as he threw a combination of punches. His arms were on fire, but he wouldn't quit. Tommy was right; he had been late.

"I know. It won't happen again," Michael panted. "Sorr—" He stopped himself from apologizing because he wasn't really sorry. He'd woken up to a delightfully willing Maggie, who insisted she make love to him one more time before he left. A man should never apologize for keeping his woman satisfied.

Tommy's face screwed up in thought. He tore his cap off and scratched his shiny head. "I know you were with that girl."

Michael smirked and then punched his imaginary opponent harder. "She's not *a* girl, Tommy. She's *my* girl."

Tommy muttered a curse. "Whatever you call her, you know how I feel about that. I told you, no distractions. We're so close to having everything we want. Everything we've worked for is finally paying off. Women weaken legs, you know that. And I don't need you losing sleep and getting all moony eyed over some chit."

Michael dropped his hands. "She's not a—"

"Don't tell me she's not a chit. I'm trying to explain something to you. Are you listening?" Tommy waited for Michael to nod. "I was worried that O'Shaughnessy might have knocked the sense out of you, but now I think it might be this woman."

"I was late today—that's it. I told you it won't happen again, and it won't."

Michael picked up his fists once more as Tommy continued to study him. His gaze was sharp. The man had trained boxers for most of his life and never missed a thing. If Michael was slipping in any way, Tommy would know it. But Michael knew he wasn't slipping. If anything, he felt stronger, faster, and smarter than he had before. Whatever anyone threw at him, he was confident he could take it.

And that was because of Maggie. Only Maggie. The woman made him feel invincible. The only issue still driving him crazy was her hesitance in needing him. Maggie wanted him; Michael knew that well enough. But he wanted more. He wanted her to need him. There was no weakness in that, and he wished she would acknowledge it.

"Will you take that silly grin off your face?" Tommy barked. "You're supposed to be imagining your opponent right now. Are you going to smile in the ring?"

Michael hadn't known he'd been smiling. He wondered how much he smiled throughout the day without being aware of it. No doubt he looked insane walking down the street. Insane but happy.

"Just stop now, that's enough!" Tommy cried, throwing a towel over Michael's bare shoulder. Michael grunted at the trainer and dropped his dumbbells, wiping himself down. The men walked to the outer edges of the gym, receiving congratulations and respectful head bobs as they passed. Michael was secretly chuffed. He'd rarely got such pleasantries from the other boxers. Usually, they remained politely aloof when it came to him. But ever since he'd put O'Shaughnessy down, he'd commanded a new level of admiration. Michael didn't encourage the attention, but he didn't dissuade it either—he'd earned it.

One of the young boys who helped out in the gym ran up to him with a glass of water. Again, that was new. Michael usually had to get his own. He drank it down in one gulp and wiped his mouth with the back of his arm. Tommy watched the other gym members go through their workouts, but something was different. The trainer seemed stiffer than usual, wound too tight—like a powder keg just waiting to go off.

Michael's curiosity was piqued. "What did you mean," he asked the trainer, kicking him in the boot, "when you said we were so close? What have you heard?"

Tommy still hadn't put his cap back on his head. The scalp was red and raw from his picking at it, something Michael noticed he only did when he was nervous. "It's nothing," the trainer replied dismissively. "You don't need to know yet."

Alarm sounded in Michael's ears. He kicked his trainer again. "Know what? What aren't you telling me?"

Tommy's heavy eyes had a shine, an excitement that Michael had rarely seen. But they also held a little trepidation. "Jack Harrison's man came to see me a couple of days ago."

The alarm only got louder. There was only one reason why Harrison's man would come sniffing around here. He was looking for a fight for his champion.

"Does he want me?" Michael asked. "Does he want a match?"

Tommy attempted to stay solid and professional. "Well, you know... he was planning on scheduling O'Shaughnessy, and you beat O'Shaughnessy. But he thinks it was a fluke. He thinks Harrison will put you down fast and easy. So... it's a match they think will benefit them."

Michael lashed out, grabbed the trainer, and kissed him on his shiny forehead. "Who cares why they want the match!" he exclaimed. "They're giving me a chance. I can't believe it. How did this happen?"

"I'll tell you how it happened," Tommy said, wiping off his forehead, battling a smile that wouldn't quit. "We worked hard. We kept going. We fought whoever they put in front of us, and we won. The only people that believed in us were us. And now we've forced everyone's hand. Now, they can't ignore us anymore."

Michael grabbed him for a bear hug. He picked Tommy up, bouncing him high in the air. "Did you hear that, boys?" he called out to the gym. "Jack Harrison wants to fight me. He says I'm going to be easy! But I'm going to make sure he eats his words along with the teeth I knock loose!"

The boxers stopped training to clap and cheer for Michael, for the first time making him feel like he was actually a part of something and not just a person with his face pressed up against the glass.

"We'll be rooting for ya, Mike," a voice called out.

"You deserve it, scrapper!" It wasn't lost on Michael that no one called him *my lord*. Not once.

He beamed, dropping Tommy back to his feet. "Thanks, boys. I'll make you proud of me!"

"All right now, let's not get ahead of ourselves," Tommy grumbled, shaking out his jacket. "I still have to settle everything with Harrison's man"—he narrowed his gaze on Michael, almost like he was testing the waters—"but he was thinking the fight could happen in a couple weeks' time. If you're ready."

"Oh, I'll be ready."

"So no more being late," Tommy said. "No more late nights. No more drinking. This fight is all I want you thinking about, morning, noon, and night. You understand?"

Michael nodded, his mind going straight to Maggie. He was supposed to meet her at Lady Alice's later in the afternoon so they could go together to meet Mr. Burnham about the dogs. He couldn't wait to see the look on her face when he told her everything.

Michael bent down to pick up the dumbbells again and headed back to his training area.

"Where are you going?" Tommy said.

Michael turned to find the trainer where he'd left him. "We have to train," he answered. "Where do you think I'm going?"

Tommy shook his head. "We have time for all of that tomorrow. Drop those weights, scrapper. We're going to the pub."

Still, Michael didn't move. "The pub? You just told me there was no drinking."

Tommy started for the door, waving a hand for Michael to follow him. "I meant tomorrow. Tonight, we're going to celebrate."

※※※※※

AUNT ALICE GAVE Maggie an apologetic look. "You shouldn't be angry with him. He's a viscount, you know. He probably had pressing business." She sniffed. "Perhaps he's searching for the perfect wine for me."

Maggie continued to pace around the foyer. George sat at the bottom of the steps watching her every irritated stomp. "I'm not angry, just… frustrated. He knew how important this was to me."

"Why don't you write Mr. Burnham?" Alice said. "Ask him to reschedule. I'm sure he'll understand."

Maggie shook her head. "No, I don't want to do that again. I'm afraid if I don't meet him this time, he'll just give up on me." She frowned at her boots, mulling over the prickly situation. "No, I have to go. I *will* go. If Michael ever deigns to come, tell him I waited as long as I could."

Alice's expression grew panicked. She followed Maggie as her niece gathered her parasol, reticule, and George's leash. "He told you not to go alone, and I agree with him. You shouldn't meet with a man we don't know."

Maggie attached the leash to George's collar. "He's not some man. He's Mr. Burnham. We've written numerous times. There's nothing to be worried about. Besides, we're meeting in the park where there are plenty of people. What could happen?"

"Still…" Alice trailed off, and Maggie knew that she'd won the argument. "Why don't you take Jane with you?"

Maggie stifled a grimace. She liked the maid well enough, but didn't want to spend the afternoon being followed around, forced to make polite conversation. "Jane's busy, and I don't want to pull her from her work. Honestly, Alice, it will be fine, and I'll be back before you know it."

With an encouraging smile, she stole out the door before Alice could say anything further.

The journey was so much quicker without having to pull George this way and that. Under Michael's tutelage, the dachshund was well on his way to becoming a model dog. Maggie couldn't wait to show him off to Mr. Burnham. She was certain the man would be impressed and demand they breed the animals. In fact, he should worry about her being the picky one. Not just any dog would be good enough for her George. She was a proud mother, and her son deserved only the best.

Maggie let her mind wander to the beautiful little puppies that would come from this partnership. It was safer for her because if she let herself think about Michael's forgetfulness, she would only get angry. Could he have forgotten? She'd reminded him before he left her bed that morning, though it had been early, and he had been singularly focused on something else. But that didn't sit right with Maggie. Alice was most likely right—he was busy. And Maggie couldn't expect him to always put her first.

Michael would be disappointed with her, there was no doubt about that; however, she would have to make him see reason. He couldn't expect her to wait around for him and not do what she'd planned just because he wasn't there. How was that fair to her?

The greenhouse came into view. It was just as vacant and dilapidated as before, and the lack of sunlight on the cloudy day made it seem even more sinister and lacking. Maggie's steps faltered at the grim picture, but when saw movement through the dirty glass, her dedication to the matter at hand strengthened.

"All right, George," she said, picking up speed. "It's time to meet your destiny."

But George wasn't looking at the greenhouse anymore. He stopped in his tracks, releasing a deadly growl.

Maggie tugged on his leash. "Not now, George. I'll let you chase squirrels when we're done, but you must behave for a little while longer."

George's bark heightened into something high-pitched and angry. And he wouldn't stop running in frantic circles as if he wasn't sure where he wanted to direct his alarm. "Stop, George!" Maggie cried, but George didn't pay her any heed. She was so intent on trying to wrangle him that she didn't hear the footsteps behind her until it was too late. When she finally turned, she ran straight into a body.

And then everything happened too fast to register. Someone tore the leash out of her hands and snatched George, squeezing the animal's mouth shut. Maggie screamed and raced after the thief, but he was too quick. He put distance between them in seconds and was at the edge of the park, climbing into a waiting carriage, before Maggie understood what was truly happening. She broke for the carriage, but there was nothing to be done. It was gone. George was gone. She was alone.

And she hadn't the faintest idea what to do next.

Chapter Seventeen

THE KNOCK ON the door came a short, distraught thirty minutes after Maggie returned home. She'd only just finished telling Alice everything that had occurred and finally been able to talk without crying.

The butler led a tall, gangly man into the drawing room. His clothes were shoddy but respectable, and when he took off his hat, the light from sconces reflected off his greasy, dark hair.

"Mr. Taylor for you, my lady," the butler said, barely hiding the contempt when he sneered the tall man's name. "He said it's urgent."

Maggie stood alongside her aunt, lost and exhausted. When they approached him as one unit, he didn't seem to find their frenzied demeanor disturbing or unusual. He held his ground with aplomb, as if this were all a part of the play that he'd helped write.

"I hear you're missing a dog," he said, not bothering with formalities. As distraught as she was, Maggie appreciated his forward nature.

"How do you know that?" Alice asked. "My niece has only just told me."

Taylor smiled, showcasing a gold front tooth. "I make it my business to know these things."

"What do you want?" Maggie asked. She'd intended more force behind her words, but she felt uncommonly weak, like an entire piece of her body was missing.

Taylor directed a smile at her. "I want to help you make a deal. Come now, ladies such as yourself know how this works."

They couldn't argue with him. Dognapping was big business in the city. You couldn't throw a stone without hitting someone who'd had it happen to them or knew someone who had. That Maggie was still a novice to this occurrence made her unusually lucky.

Alice placed her hand on Maggie's shoulder, nudging her to step back. "How much do they want?"

"Six pounds."

Alice gasped. "Six pounds? For a dog?"

"Well, it's not just any dog, is it?" He nodded to Maggie. "It's *her* dog, which makes it invaluable."

The tears threatened to fall again. Maggie didn't have six pounds, and she couldn't ask Alice to pay the ransom for her. She placed her hands over her cheeks, trying to keep her head from spinning. "I don't have it. But I can get it. I can get a banknote in the morning."

Taylor shook his head. "No banknotes. Only pounds."

Alice pushed forward. "I have jewelry. Will the thieves take that?"

"You're not giving up your jewelry!" Maggie cried.

"Well, we have to do something!" her aunt insisted. She turned back to Taylor. "How much time do we have?"

He reached inside his jacket and took out a card, handing it to Alice. "You have until tomorrow morning. I'll come back at eight. If you find the money and want to get in touch with me earlier, I can be found in Whitechapel." He tapped the card. "You can't bargain with these people, so don't think about trying. Rest assured, they will kill your dog like that"—he snapped his fingers—"if you go to the police or try any funny business. It's best to just pay them and get it over with."

"Just for them to steal him again?" Maggie blurted. "Fanny Albright's dog was stolen three times last year by the same people, and they asked for a higher ransom each time." She regarded her aunt helplessly. "And I knew something was wrong. Remember? I told you it felt like people were following me. I kept getting that weird sensation when I would take George out for walks. Wait a minute. Mr. Burnham! Was he a part of this?"

Taylor shrugged. "You've got yourself a different kind of dog there, miss. I hear the queen has one just like it. People would go out of their way to snatch a dog like that."

Maggie felt dirty and disgusting thinking about the letters she'd written. It had all been a lie, just a ruse to get her and George in the right place at the right time for them to steal him. How could she have been so dumb? So myopic? Why had she agreed to meet him away from her house? What had she been *thinking*?

Taylor sensed Maggie's anger in herself. He gave her a patronizing pat on the shoulder. Maggie was too dulled by the situation to flinch. "This is how the world works, miss. There are swindlers everywhere just waiting to take advantage of lonely women. Don't be too upset at yourself. Besides, what can a girl like you do about it anyway? Just pay them."

"I'm not lonely," she whispered.

"Oh, sorry about that." He chuckled. "I didn't mean lonely, I meant alone—a woman who was alone. The swindlers keep a close watch on them. Easy pickings, they are, if you don't mind my saying."

"So, what do we do now?" Alice asked.

Taylor considered his words, giving each woman another lengthy stare. "I already told you. If you want to see your dog again, your only hope is to pay the six pounds."

Maggie pulled herself from her depression. "Do you promise he'll be alive?"

For the first time, the man seemed unsure of himself. "Oh, I can't do that, miss," he replied.

Maggie's ire could not be held at bay any longer. "Then why should I trust you? Why should I rely on you to help us?"

Taylor rubbed a hand over his mouth. "Well, I guess it's because you have no one else. I'm all you got. And beggars can't be choosers, can they?"

HOURS LATER, WHEN Maggie still hadn't received word from Michael and she'd cried out all the tears in her body, she determined that Taylor was wrong. The bastard wasn't all she had. She had others who could help. She also had herself.

And Maggie had never let herself down before. She weighed all her options. She could do as Taylor said and find the money to pay off the thieves, or she could simply take her dog back. It was an audacious plan, but it was something the thieves were not expecting. How many ladies ventured to Whitechapel to steal back their dogs? It was too brazen—maybe even foolhardy—which meant that Maggie would need another fool to help her. And there was only one fool she had in mind.

She didn't bother leaving a note. If everything went to plan, she'd be back before Alice woke in the morning. And George would be with her.

Fifteen minutes later, Maggie asked the hansom cab to wait and stepped out wearing the black cloak she knew the duke admired so much. It was well past dark, but the garment added a second defense to prying eyes.

She heard peals of laughter on the other side of the door. She pounded as hard as she could.

The door whipped open, and Lord Oliver appeared brandishing a wine goblet. He was shirtless, with unbuttoned trousers that were in very great danger of falling to his feet at any moment. "Finally!" he slurred. "We've been waiting much too long for the pleashure of your—" He stopped. His trousers managed to cling to his narrow hips, but Maggie thought his mouth might have hit the ground instead. Hers too, for that matter.

His perennially bloodshot eyes widened to saucers as he tripped out onto the step and swiveled his neck back and forth. "What the hell are you doing here?"

The day had been too terrible to care about good manners. "What the hell are you doing answering your own door... and like that?" Maggie snapped.

Oliver frowned at his lack of attire before answering with a naughty smirk. "This is my home. I can answer the door and dress any way I please."

Maggie angled her head. Waiting.

Oliver relented. "Fine, I'm entertaining someone. Fine, I'm entertaining a few someones inside." He sniffed, raising his nose in the air. "And we were waiting for another someone. I thought you were her, but she'd never wear a drab little cloak like that."

Maggie pulled said garment tighter around herself. "I'm trying to go unnoticed."

"Brava, well done."

She sighed. "I came for your help. I need you to take me to Whitechapel."

Oliver slumped against the doorframe and took a sip of his drink with his wine-stained lips. "Darling, you know what Whitechapel is, yes? You know it's not the best place for pretty dukes like me and beastly ladies like yourself?"

"Of course I know that, but I still have to go. For George."

Oliver pondered her for a long moment. "Darling," he drawled, "I am currently hosting a group of... *energetic* people tonight. Why don't we take our little trip to Whitechapel tomorrow? I hear it's much less bloodthirsty in the daylight. We can help your friend then."

Maggie balled her fists. Why had she thought this would be a good idea? She'd never wanted to hit someone so much in her life. "Tomorrow will be too late."

Oliver yawned. "Yes, well, tomorrow is always too late.

That's why I prefer to avoid it as much as possible."

He was a lost cause, Maggie thought dismally. "Never mind, Your Grace. I'm sorry to take you from your fun." She spun around and marched back to the cab.

"Well, you don't have to be all rude about it," Oliver called after her. "Where's your precious Michael? Why isn't he helping you?"

"I don't need his help," Maggie yelled over her shoulder. "And I don't need yours either. I will do this on my own."

MICHAEL LAUGHED AT another of Tommy's jokes. The entire tavern laughed. Michael was positive that he'd already heard the funny story, but he didn't want to be rude—not when Tommy had been buying his drinks all night. He had lost track of the time hours ago, along with the number of drinks he'd consumed. But it must have been too many, because two Lord Olivers stumbled into the tavern, and neither looked happy to see him.

"You!" the duke said, pointing directly at Michael. "I have to talk to you."

Tommy rose out of his chair only to tumble back down. "You should congratulate him, Your Grace. We're celebrating. Mike, here, is set to fight Jack Harrison in two weeks. Get your bets ready."

Oliver smiled grimly. "I have a feeling Lord Michael might not be alive next week, or even tomorrow, for that matter."

"What's he going on about?" Tommy asked, and Michael could only shake his head.

Oliver disregarded the trainer, keeping his tipsy intensity on Michael. "I had a little visitor tonight."

Tommy shrugged. "Did you really come here to tell us about your whores?"

Oliver struck him with a death glare. "They're *paid compan-*

ions. Why do men have to be such insufferably cruel arses?"

Michael dragged himself up to his feet, hands on the table to keep his balance. He wasn't too drunk yet, but he was close. "What about your paid companions, Your Grace?"

"This isn't about my paid companions! This is about your…" Oliver slammed the table with his palm. "I don't know what the hell she is to you."

Michael's brain cleared. "Maggie? What about her? I was supposed to meet her this afternoon. How the hell did I forget that?"

"Because you're a son of a bitch," Oliver replied, "like we all are from time to time. But I thought you might want to know that she mentioned something about wanting to go to White-chapel tonight. I sent her home, but who knows what a girl like that might do. She's a tenacious one."

The blood drained from Michael's face. Whitechapel? He'd only been away from her for less than a day. What the hell trouble could she have possibly gotten herself into? "Thank you for not taking her," he said. "I'm actually surprised you didn't."

"Well, I was a little busy," Oliver replied, checking his nails, "and I'm *still* a little busy, but out of the goodness of my heart, I wanted to find you and make you aware."

Michael surveyed the man who looked even more worse for wear than usual. He hadn't shaved in days and his linen shirt was on backward. Michael was shocked he was wearing trousers. "The goodness of your heart, huh?"

Oliver rolled his eyes. "And… my last paid companion never showed up, so I thought I would come here and see if there were any other ladies in the mood to have some fun tonight. They don't say 'the more the merrier' for nothing."

"You really are a disreputable piece of shit, aren't you, Your Grace?"

Oliver flashed that smile that said he'd heard it all before and nothing Michael could say would ever harm him. "I most definitely am," he said with typical good humor. "But at least the ladies that talk about me do it with a smile. You can't say the same, can you?" His expression hardened. "So, find Maggie. I don't know if this is just another ruse in her little game with you, but I know many actresses, and I never took her for one."

"What game? What the hell are you talking about?"

Lord Oliver unearthed his flask from his coat pocket and threw back an interminably long drink. He blinked as if to remember what they were discussing. "Ah, the game... the game... You know the game? The one where she uses me to make you jealous and fall in love with her so that she can squash your heart—that game. Surely you've figured it out?" He leaned his hip on the table. "Between the two of us, I don't think she was ever going to do it. She's a different sort of girl, I give her that, but she's not one to go for the jugular. I told her to go for the balls instead, but for some reason, people don't like to accept my advice. I'll never know why."

Michael could have taken a blow to the head and still not be as astonished. "Oliver, focus. Look at me, Your Grace." He snapped his fingers until the duke stopped swaying. "What are you telling me? Why would she want to break my heart?"

The duke closed his eyes as he chuckled. "Oh, you dear, stupid boy, because you broke hers first. Why else?"

Chapter Eighteen

"ARE YOU SURE about this, my lady?" The hansom cab driver stuck his head through the window with a baleful expression. He'd stopped the cab a block away from the address Taylor had left on his card, saying he would venture no further. "I don't think you should be here. In fact, I *know* you shouldn't be here."

Maggie swallowed the lump in her throat along with the biting retort. She hadn't gone this far to back down now. The world truly wished women to be helpless. No one wanted to help her steal her dog back, nor did they want her to do it by herself. How was a woman supposed set things right when every opportunity was continually blocked?

"It's fine," she said evenly. "Will you wait?"

The driver's eyes were jumpy; he valued money but valued his life more. "How long?"

Maggie had no clue! But uncertainty would only make the fearful man even more jittery. "Ten minutes."

The driver made a meal out of contemplating but ultimately agreed. "If you're not back by then, I'm leaving you."

"I would expect nothing less, sir," Maggie replied curtly.

She opened the door onto the dingy street, taking pains not to step into a running river of trash and foul-smelling debris. Despite the late hour, the East End borough was loud and active, with groups of men stumbling down the thin, winding paths and gangs of tattered children harassing each other over their "takes" for the night. The pubs were crowded and noisy with people releasing steam at the end of the long workday. Maggie hoped that would work to her advantage. She wondered if Taylor was in one of the numerous pubs lining the streets, biding his time until he had to harass another family like hers.

Even with her cloak, Maggie was conspicuous. By the *ton*'s standards, her uninspired clothes were hardly worthy of mention, but in Whitechapel they were terribly out of place. Right away the children flocked to her with palms outstretched, begging Maggie for spare change or food. They covered her like bees on honey, prohibiting her from taking any more steps. She tried to tell them she had nothing to give—hadn't thought to bring anything—but they were all talking at the same time, shouting to be heard over the others.

A large, brutal hand came out of nowhere, smacking the children's heads, so hard and so fierce that Maggie cried out for them.

"Get back! Get back, you dirty beggars!" the man said, charging toward Maggie, taking her elbow in his large hand. "Leave the lady alone!"

"Please, don't hurt them," she said as he towed her away from the urchins. "They didn't do anything wrong."

The man was short and thick and had a full head of hair stuffed under his cap. His grip on her intensified the more she pleaded. "You have nothing to worry about, miss," he said. "I've got you now. Those little bastards will bleed you dry."

Maggie tugged, but he wouldn't release her arm. "You can unhand me now." Her voice shook. The man was walking her toward Taylor's address, but she didn't get the sense that he would be overly helpful to her cause. "Please," she tried again. "I appreciate what you did, but you need to let me be now."

"Ah, come on," he said over his shoulder. "Let's just go to the pub and have a good time. I have friends there that might take a shine to you. Everyone wants to make friends, don't they?"

"That's not what I came here for."

He *humphed*. "A fine lady like you in a place like this? Sure you did."

In a panic, Maggie reached into her reticule, where she'd stashed a small knife. She clutched it in her shaking hand and lunged, catching the man's wrist.

"Bitch!" he shouted, releasing his hold just enough for Maggie to turn on her heels and run. She didn't get three steps away before he caught her again, snagging the back of her cloak. Red-faced and furious, the brute spun her back toward him and raised his arm. Blood dripped down in thin red rivulets as he reared back to strike her. All Maggie could do was cringe and tense for the smack—

But it never happened.

She opened her eyes to find Michael behind the man, holding his wrist in the air, burrowing his fingers into the cut. Then Michael landed a blow. One hard shot in the kidney sent the man straight to his knees. Another shot to the man's face had him on the ground, unmoving, other than a few twitches from his legs.

"You're here," Maggie said, feeling equal parts awe and un-imaginable relief. "*How* are you here?" She hurried to him, thinking to throw herself in his arms, but Michael stepped back, keeping her at a distance.

"Wait. Just wait," he said irritably. His breathing was labored; his eyes were like slits. Maggie couldn't understand it. This was nothing like Michael after his boxing match. This was a whole other animal.

"Michael?" she tried again, but once more he dodged out of reach.

"Damn it, Maggie. Give me time. I can't touch you right now. I don't..." Anguish tore at his throat. "I don't trust myself."

"I'm sorry. I'm so sorry. I didn't mean for this to happen."

The man on the ground groaned, and Michael kicked him

again. "I'm not angry at you," he said. "I'm angry at this piece of shite. And I don't want to touch you until I'm sure all the anger is out."

He kicked again.

Maggie flinched. "He wasn't even groaning that time."

"I don't give a damn." Michael planted his hands on his hips. He looked around as if he'd just now realized where they were. "What the hell are you doing here?"

"What are *you* doing here?

"I'm looking for you, you daft woman."

"How did you know where to find me?"

"Oliver." He nodded at Maggie's disbelief. "He's a wastrel, but I think he spares a measly few minutes a day thinking about someone besides himself, and you were that person today. I hate to say it, but I'll forever be in that man's debt."

Michael released a long breath and finally opened his arms to her. He enveloped her in an embrace that made her bones pop. "What were you thinking, Maggie? What are you doing?" he whispered into her hair.

"They have George," she said against his neck. His hand settled on the back of her head, holding her, keeping her steady. Maggie closed her eyes and breathed in his scent, immediately going to a place in her mind that was safe.

"I know," he said. "I stopped to speak to Alice. She told me everything."

Maggie flinched out of his embrace. "She's awake? She knows I'm here?"

Michael's expression tightened. "I woke her up. She's furious, naturally. And scared. She told me that if I didn't come back with you, I shouldn't bother coming back at all." His hand traveled down her arm until it landed on the knife. He raised it between them. "What did you think you were going to do with this?"

Maggie squared her shoulders. "It worked…"

"Until it didn't. It wasn't smart, Maggie. None of this was."

"Well, what did you want me to do?" she asked. "I won't let

them hurt George."

"You should have waited for me!"

"Like earlier? When you didn't show up? You weren't there! I can't just wait for people to find time to help me. I needed to act. I couldn't just sit at home thinking about everything that George could be going through! You can't ask that of me!"

Michael's expression crumpled. "Shit. I know that! I know I wasn't there for you. And I'm sorry. Things happened, and I let it all get out of control. I'm sorry, Maggie, but that doesn't mean you should put your life in jeopardy." He wrapped his arm around her waist and led her back to the street.

Maggie swiveled her head. "Where are we going? I'm not leaving without George. You can go if you must. I will do this on my own!"

Michael shot her a thunderous scowl. "Oh, yes, you're doing a wonderful job so far."

"Did you come here to berate me or help me?"

"Both!"

Oh. "Well, how about this? Help me first and then berate me later. Please?" She threw out her hand for him to shake.

Michael's jaw clenched at the sight. Then he palmed the back of her head and snaked her to him, crushing her mouth with a devastating kiss.

"Damn you," he said, yanking back. "Let's go—you're wasting time."

Maggie stumbled slightly as she followed Michael down the street, ignoring his incredibly descriptive and foul words. Taylor's address directed them to a short, derelict building, badly maintained, like the others surrounding it. At first, Maggie had thought it a warehouse, but on closer inspection, it was clear that it was another poorly kept lodging house.

Keeping Maggie behind him, Michael opened the door and led her up a flight of stairs to a rudimentary kitchen. A hallway branched out with several doors. A few were open, showcasing crowded rooms with an impossible number of beds and tattered clothes hanging between the walls like ceremonial bunting. Raised voices and crying babies left little to the imagination on what was behind the closed ones.

"Why would he keep the dogs here?" Maggie asked.

Michael squeezed her hand. "The people here are poor, and half don't even speak English. Who's going to complain or ask questions?"

"But then, how will we get them to tell us where the dogs are?"

"I'm going to have to be persuasive."

Maggie frowned at the growl in his voice. Michael's brand of persuasiveness might be too loud for the current situation. If Taylor wasn't here, the last thing they needed was his getting wind of what they were up to.

Maggie spied a little girl sitting alone at the far end of the hallway. She sang quietly to herself as she brushed her doll's hair with her pudgy fingers. Maggie walked to the girl. She noticed the doll was missing an arm and the flower-patterned dress it wore was caked in dirt. But the girl held the doll as if it were a priceless antique. Maggie wondered if any doll had ever been loved as much as that one at that moment.

"Hello," she said, treading softly on the wooden boards. The young child didn't startle, but she stared at Maggie warily, as if waiting for signs of trouble. "I like your doll."

The girl paused then went back to the doll's hair. "Her name is Mary. My daddy found her for me."

"You have a good daddy. And that's a beautiful name. It looks like you love Mary very much."

The girl's demeanor softened. "She likes it when I brush her hair. She likes to be pretty."

"You are doing a very good job of that."

The girl nodded. "She's my best friend."

"I have a best friend," Maggie explained gently. "His name is George. I think he's pretty, though some people tell me he isn't."

The girl giggled. "Boys can't be pretty!"

"Well, George is. He's a dog with the body of a sausage, but he is the prettiest sausage in the world. Someone took him from me. And I'm very sad. Probably as sad as you would feel if someone took your Mary."

The girl's hand slowed and eventually dropped from the doll's head. She contemplated the floor. When she spoke next, her voice was hushed and furtive. "There are dogs down below," she said. "We're not supposed to talk about them. I can hear them at night when everyone is sleeping. They bark a lot." Her eyes lifted to Maggie. "Do you think one of them could be your George?"

Maggie nodded, stifling the tears building in her throat. "George loves to bark. It's what he does best."

The little girl stood up and took Maggie's hand. "Then let's go find him. He doesn't seem very happy, and I can't sleep with George here."

Chapter Nineteen

"H OLY HELL." THE smell hit him first. Michael opened the cellar door and nearly toppled over. Dogs. So many dogs stared back at him. And then the barking started. A cacophony of anxiety and agitation.

He heard Maggie gasp behind him. "There are so many. There are…"

Michael gulped, scanning the room. "Twenty-two. But I don't see—"

"George!" Maggie swept past him into the foul room. Along with five other dogs, George was tied to a post that had been pounded into the floor. Fresh fury scalded Michael as he watched the beloved pet cower and whimper while Maggie worked to set him free. He appeared a little mussed and dirty, but relatively unharmed. Some of the other dogs in the room weren't so lucky.

Maggie carried the dog back to Michael, crying and laughing as he licked her face. "I'm so sorry, George. I'm so sorry I let them take you from me."

Michael guided the duo out the door. "Hurry now. You can kiss each other as much as you want in the carriage. We have to go before anyone gets back."

Maggie glanced over her shoulder and scowled. "It doesn't look like anyone spends any time here." She was probably right.

Cleanliness was not important to the thieves. The dogs were surrounded by their own filth, and since Michael could spot no candles or lamps, he surmised that they spent most of the time chained up in darkness. Someone had to deliver food and water, though Michael couldn't see signs of either.

"Still," he said, pushing her toward the stairs, "we can't delay."

"No, wait!" Maggie wouldn't budge, and he already knew what she was going to say.

Michael blocked her with his hand. "I know. I know, dammit! You weren't going to leave without George, and now you're not going to leave without all of them. Well, neither am I!"

He ordered her to put George in the hansom cab and tell the driver to wait for the others.

Maggie was halfway up the stairs before she twirled around. "But what if he says no?"

The blasted woman always had so many questions! "Tell him I will pay him handsomely to say yes. And if he still says no, tell him that I will hunt him down and kill him."

Michael didn't expect her smile, but it was brilliant. "Wonderful!" Maggie exclaimed, taking the steps two at a time.

Michael returned to the room where twenty-one pairs of haunted eyes watched him expectantly. *Wonderful.*

None of this was wonderful. But it wasn't too late to make it *something.*

MAGGIE POSITIONED THE last pillow on the floor, not rising from her crouch until it was just right. When she stood, a white, curly-haired terrier sniffed at the pillow's corners, eventually deciding that the velvet accessory Michael's mother purchased twenty years ago on advice from the king was acceptable for his grubby body.

"There," Maggie announced, dusting off her hands. "I think that's it for the night. Do you think they'll be comfortable enough?"

Michael sighed, surveying his once-luxurious drawing room, which Maggie had spent the last hour transforming into a premium boardinghouse for dogs. All of the pillows and blankets his servants had been able to find were now scattered over the floor for the pampered little majesties.

"They'll be fine," he remarked dryly when he noticed two shepherds stretching their bellies in front of the fire, trading gaping yawns.

Maggie twisted her lips. She still needed some convincing but let it go. "I should get back," she said, casting another doubtful glance at the animals. "Alice is probably out of her mind with worry."

Michael spotted a Dalmatian chewing on one of his slippers. How the hell had it gotten that? He wrestled with the animal for a few seconds but ultimately gave up. "I had the driver take a note to her when we arrived. I told her that I would bring you back in the morning."

"Oh." Maggie swung her arms back and forth, unsure of what to do with herself now that the difficult night was at an end.

She had no idea.

"I've never been to your townhouse before," she said casually, wading through the dogs. She looked everywhere but at him. "It's large. A little too large for a bare-knuckle boxer."

"Well, I am also a viscount, if you hadn't heard. Besides, the dogs make the room seem smaller."

"The dogs make the room smaller *and cozier*." Maggie perked up. "Maybe you should keep them. I daresay they would be very happy here."

Michael placed his hands on Maggie's shoulders and directed her out of the room. "I think you're exhausted, my dear. That can be the only reason for your ridiculous statement." They tackled the staircase side by side. "You have nothing to worry about. I'll contact the police in the morning, and we'll put a note in the newspaper informing the public that we have missing dogs. The little ones should all be picked up and back in their own homes in no time."

"Oh, yes, that's a good idea," Maggie yawned, slumping against him.

Michael noticed the dark marks under her eyes and her sluggish feet on the stairs. If he were a real gentleman, he would drop her off in one of the numerous guest bedrooms and let her get some much-needed sleep. But Michael had needs too. And once they were fulfilled, she could close her eyes.

They'd made a deal, after all.

As exhausted as she was, Maggie still managed to read his mind. "Michael," she said as he led her down the hallway to his bedroom, "I know I promised that you could berate me tonight, but do you think it can wait? I am awfully tired."

Michael opened the door to his room and was beyond pleased with how readily she took to it. Yes, she *was* tired, and Michael's bed *was* fit for a dozen kings, but there was more to the story. She was comfortable with him… with their situation. It made everything he was about to say feel incredibly right.

He studied her as she strode around the room, lightly caressing the few items he kept on his bureau, skimming her palms over the gold-and-red damask covers on the bed. She gave him a wan smile. "Again… it's very big."

He chuckled. "Again, I'm a viscount."

She nodded, once more using her hand to cover a yawn. "Will you help me take off my dress? I assume I'm not getting my own room."

"You assume correctly." Michael adopted a harder voice. "But we have to talk about tonight first."

Her expression fell. "I thought we were going to wait."

"You thought wrong," he began. "But I'm not going to berate you for what you did. I'm angry about it—no, furious—but I have something else on my mind."

"What?"

Michael couldn't temper the hurt in his voice as he said, "I want to know when you plan on breaking my heart." Slowly, he came to stand before her. "You're supposed to, yes? You were supposed to make me fall in love with you and then stomp on my feelings."

They shared a long stare. The air thickened and Michael had to work to breathe, but he needed to see her reaction.

"Who told you?" Maggie rasped.

"Who do you think? Our very mouthy duke."

"Of course."

"Don't be angry with him. I'm glad someone told me about the little game. Why didn't you?"

Maggie willed strength back into her fatigued frame. "It was a silly idea. I was just so upset with you. I wanted to hurt you the way that you'd hurt me."

This was what he had been searching for, because Lord Oliver had failed to explain what Michael had done to batter Maggie's feelings so badly. This couldn't possibly be about what happened when they were children. Surely, after everything, they were past that. "What did I do, Maggie?"

Her laughter was anemic, void of life or color. "You didn't kiss me. That night after the wedding. I thought you were going to, and I wanted you to so much, and then you just… stopped. I thought you'd been playing with me and my feelings. I felt like a child all over again. But what made it worse was that I had thought those old feelings for you had died, but they'd only been lying dormant all these years. You'd dragged them out only to crush them again."

Michael recalled that night. He'd replayed it endlessly in his mind but thought all the torture had been on his end. He ran a hand over his face. "I wanted to kiss you. Good Lord, Maggie, you have no idea how much."

She shrugged, evading his gaze. "Then why didn't you?"

"That's the question, isn't it? I've asked it of myself probably a million times. I suppose I was afraid. My father always wanted me to fit in with the others, be like the lads who teased me mercilessly about him. Be the perfect viscount and earl that he couldn't be, which meant always going with the tide, marrying a respectable woman, living quietly, never making waves, or speaking about anything remotely interesting. I always thought I could give him that if I could have my boxing too."

He reached out and caressed tiny, fawn-colored hairs off her forehead. "But I knew if I kissed you, all of those good intentions would have flown away. Because you are not simple or quiet or easy, Maggie. And you are too interesting. You are everything I've ever wanted or ever wanted to be."

She smiled shyly and placed her hand over his. "I had it all wrong, didn't I? When I was trying to make you fall in love with me, I tried to act more feminine. I tried to be everything that your father wanted me to be for you."

"What do you mean?"

Maggie was confused. "I let Aunt Alice dress me."

"Oh, God, don't remind me of those damn feathers."

"I acted nicely and pleasantly to you."

"You argue with me constantly."

Her eyes narrowed. "I played horrible cricket because Ella and Jo told me that men love it when girls are terrible at things."

"That's why you swung the bat like a deranged blind person! I couldn't understand what you were doing."

"I was just trying to make you love me."

Michael held her face. "You never had to try, my love, and certainly not with those silly clothes or poor cricketing skills—not by making yourself lesser. By simply being you, you ensured that I never had a chance. You challenge me, and yell at me, and force me to look at the world in a million different ways, and I am better for it. So, I have to ask you again. When are you going to break my heart? Because you have it in your hand. And you will hold it forever. It is no longer mine, so do with it what you will. But do it quickly, because I don't think I can wait any longer not knowing if I will be kissing you in my bed tonight or merely dreaming about it."

Maggie's eyes darkened to emeralds, the tears giving them a luster that almost blinded him. She rested her forehead against his. "If you say I have your heart, then know that I will never let anything happen to it. I will keep it safe for the remainder of my life and for all eternity." Laughter bubbled from her throat. "And I will never give it back, so don't ever ask."

Michael wrapped his arms around her. "Like George with his cricket ball, eh? Like mother, like son. That's fine, my love. It is yours forever and always."

She squeaked as he swooped under her to pick her up. He rearranged her legs so that they wound around his hips.

"What are you doing now?" she said, giggling.

"I was going to carry you to the bed."

"Your bruises! I can walk—"

Michael groaned. "I know you can walk, I know you are perfectly capable of doing it yourself, but I *want* to carry you, my love. I want to feel the weight of you in my arms, knowing that you are all mine. And I know you want to argue with me, but you will have to wait until tomorrow. Tonight, you're going to let me do what I want."

"And what's that?"

"I'm going to love you. And you're going to have to learn that you have a man who wants to be relied upon, who wants to solve all your problems. It doesn't mean you have to let me— Lord knows you won't—but let me pretend sometimes. It's good for a man's ego."

"Grandmother told me that."

Michael snorted. "Such a smart woman. What else did she tell you?"

Maggie bit her lip and shoved her head underneath his chin. "That sometimes beds weren't necessary at all."

Michael's entire body went hard. Growling was the only way he could get the words out. "Is that right? So maybe, my carrying you might not be such a bad thing?"

Maggie trailed her nose along the column of his neck until her lips grazed against his earlobe. "You have no idea."

Michael turned his head to catch her mouth. The kiss was blistering and needy, sexy and carnal, but filled with promises of the hopeful and innocent. Maggie went to work on his vest and shirt, splaying them wide on his chest. She fell into him, kissing and licking his skin while Michael attempted to rearrange them against the wall. His hands shook as he hiked up her skirts and tended to his trousers. The moment his cock was free, she reached between them and held it in her hand.

These were the perks of loving a woman who didn't wait for permission.

Michael's head fell to her shoulder with a shudder. "What should I do?" she whispered, and even that innocent question made his balls tighten to an untenably delicious degree.

"Christ," he said, laughing. "Anything you want."

"No, show me."

Michael gathered his strength. He tucked one hand under her bottom and placed the other on top of hers. Then he did as she asked, starting with a steady rhythm that had them both panting. When the student had become the master, Michael went on his own journey. He reached the triangle between her thighs and rubbed her slit, bringing her to the same hysteria that he was battling.

Together they stared at their hands, watching the acts with open fascination and appetite. Maggie was as adventurous and curious as he was, and Michael wondered if there would ever be a day when she didn't surprise him. He doubted it.

He jerked her hand away and covered her mouth once more, flooding her with his tongue and passion. But Maggie refused to be passive. She guided his cock to her entrance. Michael didn't need an invitation. He drove into her in one surge, moaning along with her scream. He wanted to make it last, to make it romantic and gentle, but that would have to wait for another day.

They would have those. They would have many.

Michael pumped into Maggie and gritted his teeth at the heavenly pull she had on him, the squeeze and friction her body gifted him. She rode him, bucking with abandon, needing and wanting, taking and giving. She arched her back and cried out as she massaged his cock, pulsing and milking him until he was equally spent.

Michael's legs shook as he balanced them up against the wall. It was the only reason they were still standing.

He laughed, blowing Maggie's hair off her neck. "I think you might have to walk to the bed after all. My strength seems to have vanished."

She took his head in her hands and kissed his forehead. "So, is it true, then? Women really do weaken men's legs?"

Fuck. Michael could never let Tommy know. "I never thought so, but when it comes to you, yes."

Chapter Twenty

I
T ONLY TOOK two days for the families to begin flooding
Michael's doorstep. After the first few knocks, he couldn't
stand it anymore and forced Lady Alice and Maggie to come to
his home each day and facilitate the return of the animals. The
newspaper posting had done its job, and Michael spent most of
the hours in his study listening to sobbing pet owners being
reunited with their four-legged children.

Naturally, Maggie was in heaven being in the middle of the
happy gatherings, which only added to his contentment. He liked
hearing her throaty laughter, having her in his home taking
charge as if everything was hers. Which it was. She just didn't
know it yet.

On the third day after the newspaper announcement, Michael
was ready for one of his own.

Oddly enough, it was his father who spurred him to act. And
for once, Michael was ready to listen to him.

Late in the afternoon, Maggie peeked through the opening of
his study door and entered before he had a chance to tell her to
come in. He'd never seen her look lovelier. Half of her hair had
fallen from her bun and rained down her back. The other half was
barely holding on and hanging loose around her ears. Her face
was exultant and pink, her expression two parts proud and one

part miserable regret.

"They're all gone," she announced, coming to his side of the massive desk. Michael backed his chair away, hoping she might sit on his lap, but she chose to lean on the corner, her lips puckered in disappointment.

Michael trod lightly. When it came to dogs and Maggie, he was learning that that was always the best course. He'd even reached a détente with George. He hadn't teased the pet about its nonexistent hunting skills since the rescue, to spare Maggie's tender feelings—and the dog's.

"I thought you'd be happier…" He trailed off.

Maggie frowned, brushing hair off her forehead. "It's just so quiet without them. I suppose I'll have to go back to looking for a partner for George again. I think he liked having the others around."

Michael stole a glance at the lazy dog who was stretched out next to the window in a patch of waning sunlight. He didn't want to point out that the animal had spent most of the past three days with Michael, avoiding the racket and commotion in the rest of the house. If he could hazard a guess, it was that George enjoyed being an only child.

"Well, you have your cricket club," he pointed out.

"Yes," she sighed. "Practice will pick up again soon in time for the Matrons match at the end of the season. That will keep me busy."

"And you have me…"

Finally, a light broke through the clouds. Maggie laughed when Michael slid her backside across the polished wood to land on his lap. She hung her arms around his neck. "That's true, and you have your own special way of keeping me busy."

"Yes, it is special." *Though not busy enough.* Ever since the rescue, Maggie had insisted that Michael not come to her room at night. She said the animals would be too afraid to be left alone. He had disagreed—adamantly, since he had plenty of servants to keep them company—but lost the debate soundly.

Needless to say, holding her on his lap was both a luxury and a misery. But that could end now… with one little question.

Michael reached behind her and picked up a letter from a pile on his desk. He tapped it against the surface, searching for his voice. He'd thought this would be easier. But then, maybe easier wasn't better in this circumstance.

Maggie grinned, enjoying the frog in his throat. "What is it?"

"Um…" Michael smiled ruefully. "I received a letter from my father this morning."

"That's lovely."

"Yes, it was actually, for once."

"Well, what did he say?"

He grimaced over his smile, trying to contain the damned cheerful thing. "Would you like to read it?"

Maggie gave him a curious look. "If you want me to." Michael handed it to her and watched her eyes rove across the page and her mouth soundlessly read the words. He waited for the right moment. He would know it when he saw it. When her eyelashes flickered… when her lips stopped moving… when her eyes fell away from the lines …

But, as ever, Maggie did things at her own speed. She dropped the letter to her lap and her expression clouded with a question. She fixed her gaze on him, her eyes impossibly large. "Your father says that he's delighted by your decision. He says… he says that he couldn't ask for a better daughter-in-law. He can't possibly be writing about me."

"Who else would he be writing about? And he says more than that!" Michael said, snatching the paper. He pointed toward the middle of the letter. "He says you're a wonderful, beautiful, smart lady who will make a fine countess one day. Right there!" He smacked the letter with the back of his hand, but Maggie wasn't paying it any heed. She could only look at him.

"Did you tell your father that you were going to marry me?"

Why did she sound so surprised? Michael ducked his head, worrying that he'd done something wrong, been too heavy-handed. He traced the grain of wood on the desk with his thumb. "I might have mentioned it in a letter. We don't have to, if you don't want to," he said with a shrug. "We can keep going on as we have been…"

Her mouth twitched. "Would you want that?"

Michael exhaled, expelling all the breath in his body. "No, not particularly. I would like to be married before our son is born, but I'll leave it up to you. As I'm sure you're aware, my family is not immune to controversy."

Reflexively, Maggie flattened her hand over her belly. "Our son? I didn't know we were expecting one."

Michael nodded, gaining in confidence. "Oh, it's coming, sooner rather than later if I have my say."

Maggie's cheeks colored. She lowered her head, tapping her fingers lightly over her white day dress. "And… is that the only reason why you're asking me?"

Michael had had enough. How had this gone so badly so quickly? He rose from his chair, plopping Maggie on the desk, then ran a frustrated hand over his face before leaning forward to make their heads level. "Are you daft, woman? I've told you I love you. What more do you need?"

Maggie blinked. "I'm not sure. I'm just a little shocked, that's all. This seems rather sudden."

"Sudden! *Sudden?* There's nothing sudden about it!" Michael backed away from her, shaking out his hands before reclaiming his spot between her legs. "I want you to be my wife—not just my lover. And the mother of my children. So give me an answer—and by the way, I'm only accepting one, so don't think about saying the other." He threw up a hand when she opened her mouth. "And don't mention your parents. They are not us. I can love you and still be a fully functioning person. I will spoil our children rotten and never allow them to go to boarding school unless they truly desire it. I will let you have as many dogs as you want and not bat one eye if you play with them more than me. I will go to all your cricket games and not ridicule you over your swing. And, most importantly"—he dropped to his knees, clutching Maggie's hands between his own—"I will never, *ever* ask you to leave your children behind. Wherever we go, they will go. I will give you a family in every sense of the word. Just say yes, Maggie. Please tell me yes."

Tears were his only answer at first. One dropped from each of her eyes, slow rivers of light and hope that Michael clung to.

Then she squeezed his hands back, and he was finally able to release the breath that he had been holding. She smiled and pulled him in, wrapping her arms around him with laughter.

Michael had thought that would be enough, but he found that he needed more. He needed the words.

"Dearest, please answer me," he whispered into her neck. "Please tell me what you are thinking."

He held her at arm's length and watched as she wiped the tears from her round, charming face. "I'm thinking"—she hiccupped—"I'm thinking that this is truly something."

Michael grinned and cocked his head. "And?"

"And what you just said was the most beautiful thing I have ever heard."

"And?"

Maggie kissed him lightly on the lips. "And yes, I will marry you."

THE MOST AUSTERE butler Maggie had ever met led her and Aunt Alice somberly to the drawing room. The Countess of Waverly's townhouse was simple and elegant, not cluttered with bric-a-brac, but chiseled and honed with centuries of good breeding and taste. The ceilings were high and daunting; the walls were trimmed with exquisitely carved wood paneling. The scene was all the more alarming because one day, Maggie realized, it would all be hers.

Michael's mother placed her sewing aside and rose from her seat as the butler announced her guests. She was a petite woman, fine boned and delicate, like a piece of china. Maggie searched for signs of Michael in the woman, but with her pale, light-brown hair and restrained smile, his mother appeared to have been stingy with her polished features.

But as she clasped Maggie's hand tightly, the lady made her feel welcome, and that was all Maggie could ask for.

"I hear we have exciting news to discuss," the countess exclaimed, inviting the ladies to sit. Maggie followed the lead of Alice, who never looked out of place in a sumptuous house and always knew the right thing to say.

"Indeed," Alice replied. "We couldn't be happier, nor ask for a better pairing. Since the families have always been so close, it seems like it has always been destined to happen."

"I quite agree," the countess said. "I miss my friends, but they've always loved to travel. Where are your parents now?"

Maggie blinked when she realized the countess had directed the question at her. "Oh, um... Mother and Father are in Spain, I think, but they are on their way to India."

"India..." The countess smiled wistfully. "Yes, I could see them enjoying India—all the adventure, the vibrant colors. So, the wedding will wait for them to return? That sounds sensible."

Alice laughed casually, though Maggie detected nerves. "I'm afraid your son has different ideas." Maggie coughed, and Alice raised an eyebrow. "My niece does as well. A quicker marriage is their desire."

The countess's eyes narrowed sharply, though her pleasant smile stayed intact. "I hope there isn't any *particular* reason for a quicker marriage..."

Maggie coughed once more, understanding the countess's meaning perfectly.

"Not at all," Alice responded with confidence. "*Your son* seems to be the impatient type."

Maggie held her breath as she watched a silent conversation

flow between the two women. A battle of wills ensued, and Alice surprised Maggie with her steely front line.

The countess tapped her teeth together, breaking first. "Yes, I'm afraid Michael can be a bit bullish, although I never thought it would be over marriage, of all things. I thought he would drag his feet forever there."

Alice's smile was tight. "That was before Maggie. Men have a habit of jumping in line when they find exactly what they've been missing."

The countess angled her head. "You've never been married, isn't that right, Lady Alice? I suppose watching everyone else do it has given you a distinct perspective."

Sweat slowly dripped down Maggie's back as she waited for her aunt's response, hoping it would be more levelheaded than her own would be.

Alice reached for her teacup, giving the moment time to breathe. "You're right, my lady. I did develop a perspective while I watched all the happy marriages"—her gaze sharpened over the top of her cup—"and not-so-happy ones."

Maggie jumped in. The atmosphere had become much too sticky for her liking. "We wrote to my father. We hope to hear back from him soon to receive his blessing."

The countess's attention remained on Alice for an extra beat, but then found its way back to Maggie. "Oh, I'm not worried about his blessing. Your father has known my son since he was born and recognizes the man and earl he will be. No doubt he will be proud to call him his son, just as I will be so proud to call you daughter."

Maggie bowed her head. "Thank you. I cannot tell you how happy that makes me—"

"Although," the lady's voice lifted as she cut Maggie off, "things will have to change. You've always been a rather colorful girl… spirited. That will all have to be tempered when my son takes you to be his wife. Countesses can't go riding pigs in the mud."

Maggie flushed. "Rest assured I haven't ridden a pig in a very long time—"

"But you *have* taken a carriage to Whitechapel… by yourself, correct?" There was a distinct warning in the countess's tone, and Maggie realized that underneath the woman's fine bones and expensive fabrics was a wildcat just waiting to scratch. "Oh, don't worry, my dear. I have a way of hearing about things that others don't, and I won't hold it against you. We all make childish mistakes from time to time. Just as long as they don't happen after you marry my son. Do we understand each other?"

"We do."

"What was that?"

Maggie cleared her throat. "I do."

The lady's expression softened. "Excellent. Then I will rely on you to be a good, calming influence on my son. In fact, I'm relying on you to encourage him to set this boxing aside. I've heard he has a fight scheduled, against a man who has the potential to truly hurt him. I need you to speak sense to him and make him call it off. Enough is enough. Then we'll start making the wedding plans in earnest—after your father's letter arrives, of course."

Maggie could feel the color draining from her face. Had she just been given an ultimatum? She couldn't tell. The countess was back to wearing her placid expression, pure sweetness. Her words and her countenance were enough to give a person vertigo.

Maggie was at a loss. As always, she was an expert at knowing what she should say, though not so good at actually saying it.

Nevertheless, she was also good at loving Michael—Lord knew she'd been doing it long enough. And that love gave her the strength to face the countess head-on.

"I'm sorry, my lady, but I have no intention of asking Michael to stop boxing. He's worked too hard; he loves it too much."

The countess's eyelashes flickered as if she weren't used to differences of opinion. She pursed her lips, smothering her disappointment. "But he loves you, yes? So, he will choose you if you ask him to."

Maggie's resolve grew stronger. "I would never ask him to choose. He can have both."

"But he is a viscount, soon to be an earl."

Maggie shrugged. "He is also a boxer."

The countess chuckled and took her time placing her teacup back on the table. She regarded Maggie as if she were searching for the best way to get through to her, finding a common language that they both could understand.

"You think it's something now, this boxing," she began gently. "You only see the good because you can't see past your young infatuation. But mark my words, this boxing will embarrass you, embarrass the family. *If* you want to be a part of this family, you need to act in its best interest. Now."

If. Family. Maggie let the words sink in, and they cut her with their threatening implications. But in the end, they didn't matter, not as much as the life she and Michael were ready to share.

"Thank you again, my lady, for your hospitality today," Maggie said, rising from her seat. "We shouldn't take up any more of your time."

The countess nodded, barely disguising the annoyance at the topic being dismissed so fluidly. "I will ask you to think this through," she said as the butler returned to escort Maggie and Alice from the house. "You need to be sure of the man you're marrying. I tell you this as a friend—as a new mother—for your own benefit."

Maggie already had a mother. She mightn't be the most present one, but she mattered.

She turned to face the countess. "I am well aware of the man I am going to marry," she said. "I'm marrying him *because* he is that man."

Chapter Twenty-One

WITH MAGGIE AGREEING to be his wife, Michael's training took on a new level. He woke earlier each day and trained harder and longer. Beating Jack Harrison and becoming the new bare-knuckle boxing champion didn't seem like a dream anymore. It was within his reach. Michael's destiny was finally in his hands. Not only did Maggie make him feel like a whole man, he also felt more powerful than ever. Like he could do anything: live the life he wanted, love the woman he wanted, be the man he wanted.

The transformation astonished him. By giving himself up to his desires, Michael had found the way forward in claiming all of them. He didn't have to keep a part of himself hidden, as his father had advised. He didn't have to live a life in the dark and the light. With Maggie, his entire self was seen.

It made him want to do great things.

Tommy, on the other hand, took some convincing, but even he couldn't ignore the proof that Maggie made his fighter better. Every time Michael swung a fist, Tommy could hear imaginary ribs cracking.

Everything was running like a well-oiled machine. Everything was going to plan.

Until it wasn't.

A week before the Harrison fight, Michael was, yet again, the last man remaining in the gym. Tommy threw a towel in his sweat-drenched face. "You're done tonight, scrapper. Go home. Get some rest."

Michael tossed the towel on the floor. "Why don't we find someone else to spar with? I've got more left in me tonight."

Tommy groaned. He picked up the towel and placed it back on Michael's shoulder. "Do you see anyone here, Mike? Save it for that pretty lady of yours. You need to stop. Too much is no good; you know that. The last thing we need is for you to get hurt before the fight. You need to be fresh for Harrison."

Michael scowled. His blood was still pumping too fast. Tension gathered in his shoulders. But Tommy was right—especially about the Maggie part. He considered sneaking into her room but decided to go home first and bathe. Then he could get sweaty again.

"All right," he called out as the trainer was already heading out of the gym. Tommy tucked his cap low over his forehead before reaching for the door. The trainer was becoming something of a legend in the gym, now that he'd gotten Michael his prime fight. Every aspiring boxer hounded him to work with them, but Tommy wouldn't hear of it—he gave all his time and attention to one man. Michael wanted to win for himself, there was no doubt about that, but winning for Tommy was equally important. When no one else had taken him seriously, Tommy had given him his blood, sweat, and unmitigated belief. Michael would repay him with the championship.

He hurried to gather his things. Maggie liked to wait up for him after his late training sessions, but he didn't want her to if he could help it. Also, he simply missed her and didn't want to waste another second.

They still hadn't finalized a date for the wedding. Lady Alice had thought a Christmas wedding sounded like a rational plan. Six months was more than enough to make a tasteful, memorable event and give Maggie's parents time to return for the nuptials.

Michael hadn't minced words about what he thought of that ridiculous idea. He countered with six days and said he would write to Maggie's father and ask for forgiveness after the deed was done.

Lady Alice hadn't minced words either.

Currently, they were at a stalemate, which meant that Michael would have to continue acting like a thief in the night in the lady's home. At least George was behaving. Who would have thought that the dog would be his ally?

Michael spotted his carriage waiting for him. He'd lifted his hand to get the driver's attention when he heard someone clear his throat.

Rutherford came into view, showing off those crooked front teeth as he sauntered over to Michael. "I'm glad I caught you, Burlington. Do you have a minute?"

"No."

Rutherford laughed. "Quite right. No doubt anxious to see your fiancée after a long day in the gym. Congratulations on the engagement, by the way." He gestured to the dark purple bruise covering the side of his face. "I should have guessed."

"What do you want, Rutherford?"

Rutherford tapped his walking stick on the pavement a few times as if trying to gather his thoughts. The hair on the back of Michael's neck came to attention. Something was not right.

"Well, you see, Burlington, I have a bit of a problem, and I was hoping that you could help me fix it."

Michael's laughter was thin. "You're speaking to the wrong person."

"I'm afraid not," the man countered. "You see, I lost an awful lot of money the last time you boxed. Too much, really, and I desperately need to rectify that situation."

Michael sighed. *Of course.* "I have nothing to do with the odds."

"No," Rutherford said, leaning closer. His breath smelled like a bawdy house—and not one of the upscale ones. "But you have something to do with the outcome."

Michael stepped away, keeping his distance. "What are you asking me?"

Rutherford's mouth twitched into a toothless smile. "I'm not asking you anything. I'm telling you. You are going to go down exactly twenty minutes into the fight. And I am going to recoup my losses."

Michael almost laughed. "Are you drunk? When's the last time you've gone to your bed? Do you honestly think you can make me?"

Rutherford blinked and reached into his jacket pocket, taking out a small envelope. The smell hit Michael's first—its distinctive musky-floral scent was like a punch to the gut of his memory.

"What is that?" he asked.

"Oh, I think we both know what it is. Your father likes to write letters, doesn't he? He has such well-bred handwriting, and the smell"—Rutherford held it up to his nostrils—"well, quite distinctive. Would you believe that one of those fancy letters magically came into my possession? I didn't want to read it—but I couldn't help myself in the end." He made a face. "Quite graphic. It's old, but I hardly think that matters, do you? The newspapers will still be more than willing to print it. Oh, I know they'll hide the names, naturally, but they will offer enough innuendo. I hardly think it will take people long to discover the deviant who wrote the… colorfully descriptive words."

"How did you get it?" Michael gritted his teeth so hard that he was certain they would break.

Rutherford's vindictive façade dropped. "I have no idea. It just landed on my doorstep. Lucky me. I have a feeling I'm not the only person who wants to see your head hit the floor in the fight."

Michael closed his eyes, going through a million different ways to look at this situation. Nothing helped. "How much?" he asked. "How much for the letter?"

Rutherford tapped it against his smarmy lips before tucking it inside his coat. "Oh, you don't have enough. Besides, watching you lose also has its upside. So, I'll take both—your loss and the money I'll gain in the betting circles." He cocked his head, regarding Michael with animated curiosity. "So, do we have a deal? You go down and I'll give you the letter?"

Michael huffed. His imagination ran wild, and he could feel chains of powerlessness circling his wrists, yanking him to the ground. "How do I know you'll keep your word?"

The man blanched, placing a shocked hand onto his heart. "I am a *gentleman*. Something you could do well to remember about yourself. Come now, Burlington. You're going to be a family man soon. Will you really put that all in jeopardy for a little glory in the ring?" He chuckled. "Do you want your child to grow up without a father, like you did? Although—to be honest—you were probably better off away from that pervert—"

Michael punched him right in the nose. "Fuck!" he seethed, shaking his hand. He'd heard something crack, and desperately hoped it was Rutherford's nose and not one of his fingers.

Rutherford flopped to the ground, holding his face as he writhed like a panicky fish. He paused long enough to stare up at Michael. "So that's your decision, then? You're going to put your mother through all this embarrassment again? You're right. Maybe she's used to it by now…"

Michael went down on his knee. He picked Rutherford up by the collar and cocked his arm back for another strike.

Rutherford waved his hands. "But what about Maggie?"

"Don't you say her name!"

"But what about her? What will her family think? They're eccentric, but good *ton*. I hardly doubt they'll allow her to marry the likes of you. Oh… yes… you haven't thought about that, have you? That's a shame."

Michael changed tack. He began to rifle through Rutherford's clothes, searching for the letter. Sweet relief filled him when he detected the crip edges and yanked it from an inside pocket.

Only, that made Rutherford laugh harder.

"You didn't think I'd bring it with me, did you? It's safe in my home, where you will never find it. That's just the envelope. It's drenched in so much perfume I figured it would be enough."

Michael slumped as he lost himself in the paper he held. He recognized his father's writing, and nausea took over.

Rutherford staggered to standing, then straightened his jacket and sighed. "Just lose, Burlington. People do it all the time. What makes you think you're so special?"

➤➤➤➤❮❮❮❮

"I DON'T UNDERSTAND," Maggie said. "What do you mean you're going to lose on purpose?"

She studied Michael as he leaned against the opposite wall of her aunt's drawing room, his expression haggard, as if he were already preparing himself for defeat.

He'd surprised her this morning when he showed up at the townhouse. Maggie had assumed that he would be at the gym, like he was most days. However, he'd come inside and asked to speak with her, keeping his distance, giving himself no opportunity to touch her.

Michael locked his hands behind his back, and a blue vein pulsed in the middle of his forehead while he scowled at his floor. "I have to," he said. "I can't risk the letter getting out."

"But even Rutherford said the newspaper won't print names. No one will know."

"Everyone will know."

"But… but…" Maggie paced the room, searching for any way of changing his mind. "The letter is old. It's… not important. Does it matter?"

Michael gaze was as dead as his voice. "It will matter to my mother. She will be humiliated like before. I can't put her through that again. You don't know what it was like."

Maggie's heart shattered as she imagined the anguish he'd

shouldered in his youth. And she couldn't fix it. Her mind whirled, but she couldn't come up with any way to make this situation better. She couldn't dump a drink on herself or fall in a puddle of mud. Those were silly distractions. This was much bigger and beyond her control. Maggie was completely power-less.

And Michael had determined that he was the same.

She grasped at anything and everything. "We can offer him money—more money. There's got to be a number that will entice him."

His smile was bitter, lifeless. "Nothing more than seeing me lose."

Frustration raged inside her. "Did you ask?"

"Of course I asked!" Michael pushed himself from the wall. "Right before I beat him to a bloody pulp! I was so stupid!" His expression was like thunder, but Maggie didn't back away. She wasn't afraid.

Instead, she went to him, enveloping him in her arms, trying to send him all her strength. She ignored the fact that he kept his arms at his sides. "Please don't, my love. We need to stay calm. There has to be a way out of this. Remember? There are countless ways to look at something. We just have to find it."

He shuddered, but allowed her to hold him for a few more seconds before he pulled away. Michael's countenance was contained once more, his tone unbothered. "I have thought of everything, Maggie. And now I have to do what I have to do."

"You don't! All I ask is you talk to your mother. Beg her to understand."

He leveled her with a hard gaze. "Why can't you see this isn't only about her? I'm doing this for you. For us. I won't allow you to enter a marriage with me being the topic of jokes, having whispers and odd stares follow you in every drawing room in London."

"I'm quite used to people looking at me and not knowing who I truly am."

"Maggie." Michael sighed out her name like she was a child who couldn't keep up with the lesson. But she was beginning to understand—all too well.

He reached for her, holding her head in his hands, but it wasn't like before. There was no tenderness in his fingertips, no subtle passion in his embrace. Only patronization and pity. "My love, you were always left alone when you were a child, left to your wild whims. You don't know what it's like to have to have a family rely on you… ask you to keep its secrets safe."

Maggie jerked from his hold, her chest tightening with indignation. "I have a family, Michael. I have parents that love me in the best way they can. I had a grandmother who taught me to never be afraid. I have brothers who are always excited to see me. I have an aunt who accepts me—who *loves* me for my differences. Just because I didn't grow up like you, doesn't make my family any less a family—"

"I know, I'm sorry," he rasped, running his hand through his hair. "I'm not explaining myself well. I'm just trying to make you see—"

"Oh, I see. I see everything clearly." Maggie bit her lip, attempting to keep her voice stable. She couldn't allow any cracks in the veneer now, not with what she had to say. "You're doing this because you're afraid—"

"I am not—"

"You're afraid of being laughed at again, of being the little boy who couldn't control what others said about him."

The vein in his forehead throbbed even more. He averted his gaze to her chin, as if he didn't trust himself to look at her. But she wanted that anger. She invited it.

"Stop it, Maggie," he said. "Don't say another word."

"I will because you need to hear it," she replied.

"Goddammit, I said that's *enough*."

She shook her head. "No. Not until you realize that none of that matters—those boys, the opinion of the *ton*, your father's infidelities and indiscretions. All that matters is us. I have loved you for most of my life."

"You said you loved the sad little boy."

"Yes," she replied. "I loved the sad little boy at first. But I fell in love with the man who dared to be different. He chose to do what felt right and good. To do what he loved. I'm asking you to continue being that man." She took small steps toward him, reaching out until her hand rested on his heart. It beat hard and fast.

With a ragged exhale, Michael placed a hand on top of hers. For a moment, Maggie thought that she had broken through, but then he lifted his head. He tried to smile, but it only made her feel worse. "I am that man. But I'm a viscount, remember? And I can't let this happen to my family. I won't."

A pressure that Maggie had never felt before squeezed her heart. It collapsed her lungs, making her next words breathless and forsaken. "I thought you were a bare-knuckle boxer *and* a viscount."

Michael tucked a lock of hair behind her ear and then dropped his arm to his side. "I'm not."

Chapter Twenty-Two

MAGGIE CONSIDERED SPENDING the rest of the day crying in her bedroom. She tried it for a few minutes, but George refused to leave her be. The animal was restless, barking continuously at her window at the comings and goings on the street.

So much for his lessons with Michael, she thought with irritation.

Maggie smashed a pillow over her ear as she lay on the bed. Everything needed to be kept at bay. Everything offended her, from the bright sunshine streaking through the glass to the ordinary conversations that could be heard outside from people who thought this was an ordinary day and not one of the worst of her life. It was no consolation that her beloved pet didn't enjoy all the casual chitchat either.

"George, enough!" Maggie cried. But the dog wouldn't listen. When he wasn't yipping at the lively scene outdoors, he bounced around the room, squeezing himself through every nook and cranny, searching for something she couldn't comprehend.

Maggie watched him, a smile forming on her face. "I don't care what Michael says, George," she grumbled. "You *are* a hunting dog. You bark so much because you shouldn't be cooped up in this house. You need adventure, and the open field—you need space. You misbehave here because it's in your nature, pure and simple…"

Her words trailed off. Maggie was acting equally as incorrigible while she lolled around and felt sorry for herself, she realized.

Because it wasn't her nature. Maggie needed to act. She needed to try. She wasn't the type of girl who sat around waiting for someone to fix everything for her. Besides, no one was coming—that was evident enough.

George continued to bounce off the walls.

Space. They both needed space.

And Maggie had a good idea of where to find it.

THE EARL OF Waverly's pen scratched to a halt on his page when the butler announced Maggie into his study. She hadn't seen Lord Arthur since she was a child; nevertheless, she could never forget his pleasing, handsome features because they were almost exactly like Michael's. With his dark brown hair and the wide smile he turned on her as he stood to bow, the earl was an older, more weathered version of her fiancé.

Maggie desperately wished he would be wiser as well. She contained her apprehension as she walked into the decadent room, eyeing the man who she hoped would be the missing answer to the riddle of her life.

"Lady Maggie. How lovely to see you. It's been too long." The earl greeted her warmly with arms outstretched. He clasped her shoulders and kissed both of her cheeks as if she were a long-lost daughter. "I cannot tell you how delighted I am by the engagement. Did Michael inform you that I wrote to him?" He glanced over her shoulder. "Is he here with you?"

One couldn't miss the anxiousness—the longing—in his tone when he mentioned his son.

"No, my lord," Maggie replied, her nervousness beginning to

grate. "I came with my aunt. I hope you don't mind, but I needed to speak with you."

A shadow of disappointment passed over his face, though he did a decent job of recovering. "Of course, my dear. Of course." He nodded toward the door. "I was just ready to go on a walk. It's such a fine day. Would you care to accompany me?"

Maggie nodded, allowing the earl to lead her through the back of the house, out to the expansive and lively lawns. When she was a child, Maggie had thought the earl's estate to be one of the grandest she'd ever visited, probably only second to the late king's. Age had not diminished its shine in her eyes. Stepping out into Lord Arthur's oasis was like entering another world, one of abundance and unlimited color. The earl wasn't a fan of the typical manufactured garden with rows of perfectly cut hedges and order. Paths meandered. Flowers stretched out their fat leaves and curly stems for attention and appreciation. It was a hodgepodge of decadence that was still incredibly pleasing to the eye.

"Now, tell me, my dear," Lord Arthur started, pausing to pluck a purple bellflower and tuck it in his jacket pocket, "what was on your mind that you had to come all the way to Leicester? I'm sure your aunt told you that you could write."

"She did, my lord, but I don't have the time for letters. And, I suppose, I'm not good at waiting. I wanted to speak about this in person."

The earl nodded, locking his hands behind his back, breaking into a smooth, lackadaisical stroll. "It's not my wife, is it?" He chuckled in a halfhearted manner. "She is protective of Michael. If she's hard on you at first, don't take it too personally. She'll come around. She's a good woman."

"No, no, you misunderstand," Maggie replied, although she had to admit that the man was right about his wife. She was *rather* hard. "The countess has been incredibly… polite."

"Ha! Very good. She is polite, that is true."

Maggie went on. If she didn't get it out now, she wondered if she ever would. "It's your son, my lord. It's Michael."

The earl's easy pace faltered. "Michael?"

"Yes..." Maggie closed her eyes, finding it difficult to look while she said what needed to be said. "He's been training for a fight against the champion. I'm sure you've heard of it. It's a dream come true for him."

"Yes, I'm well aware of my son's dreams."

"But something happened and someone—a cretin—is blackmailing him, saying if he doesn't lose the fight then the cretin will release a certain letter to the newspapers."

She tried not to squirm while the earl studied her. "A letter, you say?"

She nodded.

"Let me guess. This letter has to do with me?"

"Lord Rutherford claimed that someone had left it at his home. Michael said it... Well, it contained..."

The earl's voice hardened. "I'm sure I know what it contained."

"Yes, well. I understand that the correspondence is old, but Michael still believes it has the power to harm you and the family. He believes it so strongly that he's willing to do what Rutherford says—to lose."

"How old?"

"What?"

The forcefulness of the earl's tone struck her. "The letter. How old is it?"

Maggie shrugged. "I'm not sure. I'm sorry, I don't know the particulars. I just know that Michael won't listen to me." She frowned, wringing her hands as if trying to squeeze an answer out of them. "He won't... try."

The earl huffed. "And you think he'll listen to me?" He resumed his walk, but the pace was faster now, marching rather than strolling. "That's what you came here for? To ask him to disregard it. He won't do that, my dear, not if the letter has the potential to embarrass his mother—and you."

Maggie paused, allowing Michael's father to walk ahead of her. "That's not why I came here."

The earl glanced over his shoulder, frowning when he noticed Maggie had fallen behind. "So why did you?"

She stretched and clenched her fist as she had seen Michael do many times before, digging deep for courage. "I want to know… did you send the letter? Your wife has made it no secret that she wishes Michael to stop boxing. He told me that you feel the same. So, I apologize for offending you. I apologize for speaking out of turn. But it's who I am, I'm afraid. And I love your son. And I'm strong, but the thought of his giving up on something when he's so close breaks me in ways I never knew I could break."

The earl didn't blink. Not once. He let the seconds drag on, remaining inscrutable. "Yes," he finally replied. "I believe you are strong." He raised his hands defensively. "But I'm afraid you've got the wrong man."

Maggie's stomach lurched. "What?"

"You're right, little Maggie," he said, retracing his steps back to her. "I hate my son boxing. I don't know why he does it, but he does. However, I have always held the belief that it's never a good thing to get in the way of people and their passions."

Maggie shook her head. Desperation pounded against her temples as she feebly attempted to make sense of what he was telling her. She caught sight of a lone figure near the back of the house—a man who seemed very interested in the conversation. She stared at the figure for a beat too long. "Then who could it be?"

"It's not him," the earl replied instantly. "Maxwell would never betray me like that." His words were gentle, but they were laced with something Maggie had heard in Michael's voice, a possessiveness that went beyond the ordinary.

She lowered her head. "I'm sorry. I didn't mean to come here and…" Her words trailed off as hopelessness gripped her in its iron vise. She'd been so sure that the earl had been behind the letter and that he could get it back. Maggie had no more plays.

That was it.

Until the earl laughed.

"You didn't mean to come to my house and insult me? Yes, that's quite all right. You were wrong, my dear, but you weren't wrong about everything."

"About everything?" she asked.

Lord Arthur's smile showed no teeth. "Do you know why I moved here?"

"I think I do."

"People in Town like to believe they do also. But they don't. You see, I got in a bit of trouble one night. I went to a club with friends"—he lowered his voice—"people like me who are different than others. Police became involved and I managed to stay out of the papers—and handcuffs." He smiled wryly. "One of the perks of being a lord, and I didn't hesitate to take advantage of it."

"And that's when you moved here?"

"No. That came later. A whole year later." He thrust his hands into his pockets. "My wife belongs to a very old family, practically came over with the conqueror. She'd never be so gauche as to ask me to leave over a bit of fun." His lips curved down with the memory. "But love, on the other hand, proved to be something she couldn't overlook. You know... I prided myself on trying to be a good husband. I never flaunted my liaisons like so many others did. However, inevitably, I became sloppy and arrogant, and she found a letter that I'd written and hadn't sent yet. It... it caused her great pain. You see, she could almost understand lust between..." His face colored. "But love was a step too far. She could never forgive that. So she asked me to leave. And I did. I didn't want to live so far away from my son. But I wanted to do what was right for my wife. I couldn't give her love—not the kind she desired—so I gave her the next best thing. Absence—and space."

Rough, jagged pain pummeled Maggie as she listened to the earl's story. Some of it she knew, but it was vastly different hearing it from his mournful lips.

But he wasn't just telling her a tale. He was giving her an answer.

"I'm sorry to dig up this past, my lord," she began, "but I don't understand—"

"I'm saying," he cut in impatiently, "that there is one letter out in the world, and I know the person who had it last."

Oh!

"The countess?" she shrieked. "Would she do that?" A million thoughts clamored inside Maggie's brain, fighting for purchase. "But why would she give it to Rutherford… risk it getting out?"

The earl rolled his eyes. "Because she knows it won't. Michael would do anything to save her heartache. I don't blame him. Hell, I don't blame her. Sons may grow up, but they are always their mother's children. A mother would risk almost anything to keep them safe."

Maggie's mind went directly to George and Whitechapel. Yes, she knew it wasn't a perfect comparison, one that most mothers would scoff at, but George was the closest thing she had to a child, and she'd acted without thinking that fearful night. She couldn't imagine what she would feel compelled to do when she had her own baby. Furtively, she slid her hands over her stomach. Could Michael be right? Could she be with child right now?

"Do you think we can talk to her?" she asked. "Do you think she might listen to us?"

Lord Arthur huffed. "You? No. Me? Definitely not." He started back toward the house. Maggie had to run to keep up with him. "We have to steal the letter back."

"Steal it?" she panted. "How can we do that? Rutherford said he keeps it in his home. How would we know where to look?"

"We'll worry about that when we get there. Let's get to Town first."

"Wait." She lurched for Lord Arthur's arm, pulling him to a stop. He stared at her hand and then regarded her with admiration—and annoyance. "You're coming with me? To London?

You'll help me find the letter?"

"Of course. You can't do this on your own."

That stung her pride. "Yes, I can."

"All right, you probably can," the earl allowed. "But you're going to let me come along and help anyway."

"Why?"

Lord Arthur smirked, pride sparkling from his eyes. "Because I've missed too many things in my son's life. Now, you tell me he's going to be the next bare-knuckle boxing champion. I'm going to be there to see it."

Chapter Twenty-Three

MOST NIGHTS BEFORE his fights, Michael craved being alone. He would sit in his study and close his eyes, imagining how the boxing match would play out. Punches would be traded, blood would be unleashed, power would be exchanged. And Michael would ultimately be the last one standing.

But, for unfortunate, obvious reasons, this night was different.

It didn't help that Tommy had barely talked to him that day, only sending the odd grunt in his direction. The trainer didn't know what his fighter planned to do against Harrison, but he could sense something was wrong. Tommy's job was to see things, and even though Michael's strength hadn't diminished, nor had his training been half-hearted, he could tell that Michael's heart was lost.

A lucky man could win a fight on no sleep, with no food in his belly, no technique, and no hope. But he couldn't win without heart.

And Michael hadn't felt his in days, not since his fight with Maggie.

He'd assumed that she would come to him when she realized how unfairly she'd treated him. Did she actually believe he wanted to lose on purpose? Did she think that he wanted his big—and maybe only—chance to end in this deplorable way?

But his father had been right all along. The world had decided what Michael would be the moment he was born into it. And that was a viscount. One day, an earl. And that came with responsibilities. A calamitous juxtaposition of power and helplessness.

Michael would yield now. His body would hit the ground and not come back up. And his mother would be safe. His father would continue to live quietly in the country. Maggie and he would start a life together fresh, without gossip or innuendo. It was the best way forward. The *only* way forward.

She'd been wrong when she told him that he was doing this because he didn't want to be the little boy all the others laughed at again. Michael could take it. In her confusion and disappointment, Maggie couldn't see that the tables had turned. It was his time to grasp the world's attention in order to save the people he loved.

He would do it without complaint. Without bitterness.

He only asked for her.

So, if Maggie wouldn't come, he would go to her. Because he wasn't leaving her. Ever.

As usual, George was the first one to greet Michael. The enthusiastic animal met him at the top of the staircase as Michael made his way to Maggie's bedroom. It had become their routine. After sneaking into Lady Alice's townhouse, he would spend a few minutes in the hallway playing with the excitable pet, rough-housing and emptying his pocket of treats until the animal was satisfied and exhausted. Michael had initially done it to wear the dog down so George wouldn't think to bark or alert the house of his nocturnal plans. Now he did it because he liked it. George was his friend. If Maggie held his heart, George also had a piece.

The light was on in the bedroom. Michael didn't think to knock, and when he entered, he found Maggie standing next to the window peering out into the street. Her spine was straight, her shoulders were wide; even now, Maggie was not a beaten woman.

He could practically see the gears spinning in her head. She wore a thin robe over her even thinner chemise. Michael gave in to the moment and appreciated the way her bottom curved beneath the pale-yellow silk. Her thick hair was plaited in a long braid down her back, something she didn't usually do, since she knew how much he enjoyed running his fingers through it as they lay together. Either she was still angry with him or wasn't expecting him. Michael hated both of those options.

Her laughter drew his attention, and Michael watched as her breath fogged up the window glass. "I never have to look to know you're here," she said. Her placid voice gave no indication of her mood. "I only have to smell the dried meat."

Michael shut the door behind him and entered the space that had felt as much like a home as his own. Now, he couldn't shake the notion that he was an intruder. Why had he let their argument go on this long? It had been close to a week, and it seemed more like a lifetime.

He waited for Maggie to turn to him before he spoke. Her eyes were questioning, but not damning, and that gave him the push he needed to go on. "George and I have an understanding."

"And what's that?"

Michael opened his jacket wide on both sides. "I give him everything I have, and he accepts it willingly." Maggie laughed again, only this time it was real and not forced. He fought to keep the smile on her lovely face. "I thought that was our understanding as well."

She moved away from the window, hugging herself against the night's chill. The moon streaked through the glass, giving her an ethereal, otherworldly quality. She was his Lady in the Lake. And Michael had come to ask her for what only she could give.

"Did we have an understanding?" she asked quietly.

"Oh yes." Michael nodded, taking small steps toward her, desperately hoping he wouldn't scare her off. "I gave you my heart, remember? I gave you all of me and asked you to watch over it. You said you would never give it back."

"And I won't."

"Then why have you not come to me? Are you trying to teach me a lesson? If so, I'm afraid I'm not smart enough. Too many punches to the head, remember?"

"I was giving you space."

"Take it back. I don't want it."

Her smile was tired. "I was angry—"

"I know."

"I shouldn't have been."

Michael resisted replying. He was unbalanced, unmoored, on the edge of a mountain without any support or notion of how to get down.

Maggie flinched. She clearly thought to come to him but stopped herself. That indecision nearly cut him in two. When she spoke, it was stilted and choppy, as if each word deserved all of her concentration. "You know… long ago I told some people that I wanted you to feel as powerless as I do at times—like most women do. And now that it's here, now that it's happened, I only want to spare you."

She was so close. Michael could reach out and take her in his arms, but he held back. Maggie wasn't ready. Besides, the moment he captured her, she would no longer be able to speak.

"I'm not powerless, my love," he told her. "I have you, and you only give me strength."

"But the match—"

"I don't care about the match!" he growled. "I only want to be the man you love, the man you want. Can I still be that man even if I'm no longer in the ring? Will you still love me if I'm no longer a boxer?"

"How can you ask me that?" Maggie cried, her voice breaking. She launched herself into his arms. Michael squeezed her with ferocious need. "It doesn't matter what you call yourself or what the world thinks you are. I know." She raised her head, haunting him with the depths of her gaze. "I've always known who you are. You're beautiful and strong and demanding and loyal and—"

"Yours. Maggie, I'm yours. That's all I need to hear right now. That's all I ever want you to think. If the history books ever write anything about me, I will just ask them to write one simple description after my name: Lord William Conroy, eighth Earl of Waverly, is Maggie's husband."

Maggie's eyes sparkled with mist. "And you can handle that? You can live with that kind of notoriety?"

They swayed together as he chuckled, resting his chin on top of her head. "I've told you before, my family is no stranger to controversy. I should have always known that you were destined to be my countess."

"When you saw me covered in filth in front of everyone?"

He kissed her forehead, holding her face in his trembling hands. "No. When I saw the way you looked at everyone. Like you were exactly where you were supposed to be, doing exactly what you were supposed to be doing. Always comfortable in your own skin. How I envied you. And adored you. Even then."

Maggie stepped back, and Michael had to force himself to release her from his grip.

"I am comfortable in my skin," she said. She pulled her shoulders back and allowed her robe to fall off her narrow frame and land on the floor with a *whoosh*. Michael worried his breath made the same sound as it fled his body. Maggie stood before him like the perfect mixture of angel and demon, life-giving but terrifying. Her nipples poked through the delicate, virginal fabric of her chemise. What was left of Michael's heart thundered against his ribcage.

Even with all her self-assuredness, Maggie couldn't stop her smile from turning shy. She clutched at the dainty neckline and pushed it over the edge of her shoulders, to the floor.

Michael's jaw clenched. His balls tightened. His axis tilted.

"Please, don't tell me you don't know what to do with me again," she teased.

Michael shook his head. He tried to speak, might have even opened his mouth, but nothing came out. Maybe a grunt.

Finally, she took mercy on him and held out her arms.

"Come here, my love. Let me show you how comfortable my skin is."

Michael sheathed himself in her embrace, surrendering to the powerful spell she cast over him. He was lost to madness, and he kissed Maggie with all the love and devotion that she'd uncovered in him. And soon enough, thinking was no longer an option.

As always, his body took over, becoming his guide. How he managed to get Maggie to the bed would always be a mystery to him. Her hands wouldn't stop grasping, untying, unbuttoning while he made the short walk across the room. By the time he laid her on the mattress, Michael's clothes were hanging off him. He made short work of the rest.

When he climbed on top of Maggie, she was more than ready, wearing the expression of a well-loved woman who knew what to expect and gladly awaited it. But Michael didn't want her to be the only one with all the surprises that night.

He captured a breast in his hot mouth, running a hand down the side of her body as she arched dreamily, like a cat. Michael couldn't stop with the one, and gave the opposite mound the care and awareness it deserved. Maggie clawed at his shoulders, urging him to settle between her thighs, but he had other ideas.

He slid off her, catching the disappointment on her face before he flipped her over on her front. Maggie squeaked as he lifted her arse high in the air, massaging the succulent globes with veneration and tenderness. He bent over to place light kisses and bites on the delicate skin, holding Maggie's hips while she swayed and jerked from the unabashed attention.

"Michael!" she said, giggling. "What are you—"

Her mouth clamped shut as he fitted his cock at her entrance. She jerked away reflexively.

"Michael?"

"Let me, my love," he panted. Just covering his tip with her wetness was enough to make his chest constrict in lethal ways. "Take me this way. Feel how deep I can touch you."

She nodded, but her body remained tense. Michael eased into

her, inch by inch as Maggie became reacquainted with his length. He slid over her, covering her back with his chest as he encased himself completely inside her.

"You were right, Maggie." His lips grazed her earlobes as he whispered, "This is very comfortable."

She twisted her neck to find him, closing off more words with a savage kiss that invited Michael to go faster. He pulled out and surged again, this time rocking her so hard that Maggie had to throw her arms out to brace herself on the bed.

"Is this too much?" he asked, panic gripping his stomach.

"More," was all she replied, and he felt her bottom jerk back against his cock, urging it on.

Michael didn't need to be told twice. He swept an arm under her torso, grasping her breast as he took himself off his leash. Pinching and playing with her nipple, he pumped into her taut body, reveling in his woman who gave as good as she got. Never were there half-measures. Maggie always met him on the line, encouraging, demanding more.

He wanted it to last all night. Hell, he wanted it to last forever. But Michael was only a man. When her slick walls began to narrow and pulse against his rod and her breath came hard and fast, he thrust one more toe-curling time, spilling into her gracelessly, frantically. Wholly.

Michael collapsed to her side. Though it took a few minutes, Maggie eventually roused herself to face him. Her skin was bright and sweaty. Her eyes were as clear as a lake, untouched by man. With a sleepy, contented smile she brushed the hair from his forehead, smoothing it behind his ears. "Where would I be without you?" she asked, her voice full of wonder.

Michael caught her hand and kissed her palm. He answered with a wry smile. "You'd be fine," he said, echoing words she'd used on him once before.

Maggie nodded, as he knew she would. But then she said, "You're right. I would be fine. But I would never be the person I am when I'm with you."

Chapter Twenty-Four

MAGGIE WOKE UP the next morning with a warm, large, eager body next to her. Michael's heavy arm was draped across her front like a sash. Weak light peeked through the window, and she could hear the household beginning to stir. Soon, George would start scratching at her door asking for cuddles.

She'd never believed this thought would ever enter her mind, but Michael had to leave—now. Maggie was expecting a note from his father any minute. She and the earl hadn't had much contact since they'd returned to the city together. However, the day before he'd sent a messenger telling her that news would come in the morning and that she should be ready at a moment's notice.

Maggie frowned at Michael's tousled hair. Hard to do that when a fourteen-stone man who battled giants for a living was using her for a pillow.

Michael's fingers twitched and his hand began to wander, following a trail under the swell of her breast, down her ribcage, coming to rest on her lower stomach. "Go back to sleep," he murmured, his breath tickling the soft skin behind her ear.

When his hand started to rove lower on her body, under the cover, Maggie placed her own on top of it, intertwining their fingers. "You have to go."

Michael shook his head against her shoulder. This was so unlike him. Usually, he was the one waking her up... in most imaginative ways. She knew avoidance when she saw it. The poor man didn't want to start the day. He thought he already knew how it was going to end.

Maggie wasn't so sure.

She slid out from under his arm and watched him from her side. He kept his eyes closed, fighting the morning. With the tip of her finger, Maggie traced the gentle slope down his nose all the way to the cleft in his chin. His face had finally healed from the O'Shaughnessy match. The purples and yellows and blues had faded into nothing, leaving only the light pink of his lips. It was a shame that they would all be back tomorrow.

Maggie leaned forward and kissed those lips. It was how he woke her most mornings, and she knew it to be effective. Michael's hand escaped from hers and wound its way up to the back of her neck. When he started to apply more pressure—and the kiss turned hotter—Maggie broke free.

"You have to go," she repeated, softening the command with a smile.

Finally, Michael opened his eyes. He reached for her once more, but Maggie wiggled out of reach. "My aunt can't find you here," she explained.

He sighed. "I know that. I just..." He rolled onto his back and stared at the ceiling. His profile was so beautiful to Maggie—his nose so regal and straight. She would never consider herself a shallow woman; however, she would hate for Harrison to cause it any damage tonight.

She rested her head in her hand. Her heart ached. She wanted to comfort him; she yearned to touch him. But she needed him to leave more. For his own benefit.

Maggie wasn't sure what would happen if the earl's note came while Michael was still there, though she doubted it would be good. He'd told her that everything was set, how the fight was going to play out, and she'd seemingly accepted it. Would finding out that she was working with his father be considered a betrayal? Maggie didn't know the answer. And she didn't want to learn it before she had time to splash water on her face and change into fresh clothes.

"Michael. Whatever happens tonight… just know that I love you."

He could only come up with a half-smile. "Only one thing is going to happen tonight." He lowered his gaze. "Will you be there? I understand that I shouldn't ask this of you…"

"There is no place I would rather be."

Michael nodded, and she could see that her answer had pleased him. "I'll send a carriage for you—"

"Oh, no need. I have plans."

He groaned and covered his face with his palm. "God, Maggie, tell me you're going with *him*," he said, muffled by his fingers.

Maggie grinned. She was certainly not arriving at the Oyster Inn on Lord Oliver's arm that night, but it wouldn't hurt for Michael to think so. "Whyever not? I'm more than safe in his company, and his boxing knowledge is exemplary. He's a perfect companion."

Michael groaned again. "Please don't use the word *companion* when you mention the duke."

She tore his hand off his face and smiled. Michael rewarded her with a begrudging one of his own. Then he moved like a flash, flinging himself over Maggie before she knew what was happening.

"Michael," she said, pushing against his shoulders… though not as hard as she should have.

"I know. I know." He dipped his head and captured her lips in a sweet, chaste kiss that Maggie was sure she would be sighing about for days. "I'm just not in the mood to leave just yet."

Maggie rolled her eyes as he traced her collarbone with his tongue. She could feel his desire pulse and burn against the triangle of her thighs. Her resistance was weak before; it was nonexistent now.

Michael lifted his head and waited. Maggie had no doubt what he was waiting for.

She didn't have the heart to refuse him. It would be like cutting off her nose to spite her face. "What are you in the mood for, my lord?" she asked in a mocking tone.

Michael lowered his mouth to the valley of her breasts. "Well, my love… I'm so glad you asked."

⇒⟫⟪⟸

LORD ARTHUR SHOT out of his seat as Maggie hurried into the drawing room. "Where have you been?" he cried, ripping his watch from his jacket pocket. "I have been waiting *forever* for you, woman. I told you to be ready!"

"You told me you were sending a note!"

"Well, I sent myself instead. I'm so very sorry for the inconvenience."

Maggie caught her breath. Dealing with two Conroy men back to back wasn't for the faint of heart. "I'm sorry, Lord Arthur. Truly. I just…" Her face burned. "I had to take care of a few unexpected things this morning, that's all. But I'm here now. I'm ready now."

The earl *humphed*. Despite his intentions, Michael's distractions hadn't put her *that* behind schedule. He'd escaped out the back door minutes before his father's carriage pulled up to the townhouse.

Lord Arthur's gaze narrowed as he continued to scrutinize her. Could he smell his son on her skin? That was the main reason she'd been so late. She'd scrubbed herself raw during her extra-long bath. She didn't ordinarily bathe in the morning, but considering her nighttime companion—and present company— she thought it for the best.

Maggie couldn't tell the disgruntled earl that, though. She tried to recall what people said about the road to hell and good intentions.

"Well, you're here now," Lord Arthur replied, slightly mollified. "And we've got work to do."

She took a seat across from the earl, giving him her undivided attention as he filled her in on all that he had uncovered over the last few days. Maggie learned quickly that the man might have been living in exile for the better part of a decade, but the Earl of Waverly still commanded respect—and had a more-than-decent ear for gossip.

"I've been watching him like a hawk," he said. "Rutherford doesn't keep hours like a gentleman. He lives by a bachelor's schedule that can be erratic at times. Some mornings he sleeps until midday. I must be getting old if I'm no longer jealous of a rake's life."

"But you said you found something... something that can help us?"

The earl's eyes lit up. "Oh, yes. I found out he had a mistress, and, with a little monetary persuasion, she informed me that he usually arrives every Tuesday, late in the afternoon so he can still squeeze in a decent dinner party," he explained. "He never misses. Every Tuesday he is there. Which is wonderful news for us. We'll have a sliver of time to search for the letter and, hopefully, get it to the match before Michael's on the floor."

Maggie felt like a cannonball had lodged itself in her stomach. "But that doesn't leave us with much time. What if we can't find it? What if we're late?"

The earl hooked a leg over a knee and regarded her coolly. "Then we lose."

"I don't like losing!"

"Yes, I can see that," he noted dryly. "But it's the best we have. I've already asked an investigative friend to help us. He has a nose for these things. He's a decent hunter and should be able to flush out the letter."

An odd idea came to her, and as if on cue, George scrambled into the drawing room, making a beeline for the stranger daring to speak to Maggie without his consent.

The earl hopped to his feet, but instead of being annoyed by the noisy animal, he smiled. "Good Lord, is that a dachshund? I rarely get to see one of these little beauties!"

He fell to the floor like a child rounding up presents on Christmas Day. George's wariness lasted for approximately two seconds and then he was mauling the earl, wiping the peer's face clean with his long, rough tongue.

Maggie was stunned. "You... you like dachshunds?" she asked.

Lord Arthur refused to stop kissing the dog's belly, so his voice came out muffled. "Like them? I adore them. Not many people use them for hunting, even though they should. Damn fine tracking dogs. I've been searching for one for ages. I've had a badger problem of late." The earl climbed to his feet and brushed the little black hairs from his coat. "Did Michael tell you that I like to hunt? No, he probably didn't, but it's a passion of mine. I always wanted Michael to do it with me, but he never showed much interest—probably because I loved it so much."

He smoothed his loose locks back over his forehead, his color high and glowing. "You know, I think I have a neighbor who used to have one. Maybe still does. Would you be interested in breeding this adorable beast?" The earl bent over and scratched George's ear until the dog's back leg thumped so wildly that he lost his balance and tipped over. "This beautiful, lean specimen would make a gorgeous sire. I would never mention it to my current hunting dogs, but they are getting a little long in the tooth. Noses aren't what they used to be. But they were the best dogs a man could ask for." He stared up at the ceiling, lost in his sweet memory. "It didn't matter what scent I gave them; they'd be able to track it for days. Maxwell and I"—he sobered—"well, we spent many happy afternoons with those dogs. Many happy afternoons."

There were so many questions fighting for the head of the queue in Maggie's head. She landed on the one most important to her. "You don't think George is too fat?"

"Fat!" the earl sneered, giving George a closer look. He scrunched his nose. "He needs more exercise, that's true, but he's not fat. He's well rested."

Tears built behind Maggie's eyes. She'd never found such a kindred spirit before—had given up hope that they even existed. But without a shadow of a doubt, she considered that the earl could be hers—when it came to dogs.

"Yes," she said, choking on her flailing emotions. "Yes, I would like to breed George. He is a champion."

"A king among princes!"

Maggie flew into his arms, hugging the earl with all her might before kissing both his cheeks. "Thank you, my lord. I've been waiting a long time to hear someone say that."

The earl flushed as his eyes darted around awkwardly. "Of course, my dear. Of course. Now, what do you say about the plan for my son? Do you think we can make it work?"

Maggie had never felt so right about anything in her life. "Yes, my lord. I do. I just have one suggestion."

"What is it, my dear?"

She picked up George and settled him in her arms. "You said you have a man to help. But I think mine will get the job done faster."

⊱⊰

LATER THAT AFTERNOON, the Earl of Waverly, his investigator, Maggie, and her dachshund waited impatiently for Lord Rutherford to exit his townhouse. Their tenacity was rewarded when just after five, the front door opened, and Rutherford emerged with a shiny top hat on his head and a distinct dance in his step. He climbed into his conveyance and set out along the road without noticing the carriage that had been sitting idly outside his home for over an hour.

Short minutes later, the foursome was standing in Rutherford's foyer after the earl had promised the butler an exorbitant amount of money for entrance… and his silence.

The investigator looked at Lord Arthur.

Lord Arthur looked at Maggie.

Maggie looked at George and placed him on the ground.

The earl dug out an old necktie from his pocket and showed it to the dog. George thrust his nose into the fabric, taking in the earl's distinctive, musky perfume.

When the earl deemed that time was up, he stuffed the necktie back in his pocket and looked at Maggie once more.

She smiled and looked at her pet.

"All right George," she said. "It's time to show everyone what you're made of."

Chapter Twenty-Five

THE JOURNEY TO the Oyster Inn seemed interminable. By the time their carriage pulled up to the site of the boxing match, Maggie was at her wits' end, checking Lord Arthur's pocket watch every few seconds.

George had been a revelation. He sniffed out the letter in ten minutes, giving the group ample time to reach the match, but traffic proved to be an unexpected issue. The earl had lived away from London for too long, and Maggie had never experienced a boxing match of this magnitude. Even though it was taking place outside the busy city, the road still became jammed with wagons and carriages the closer they came to the inn. The last mile felt like they were traversing all of Russia.

Maggie barely waited for the carriage to stop before she pushed open the door. "Hurry, I think they might have started early," she cried, hopping down into the dark field. She could make out the match on the other side of the lot where torches and gas lamps surrounded the ring, giving the event a shadowy, dreamlike quality. But it was real enough. And Michael was still on his feet, which meant they weren't late—yet.

Maggie twisted back to the door. She was about to bark another command at the earl when she noticed he hadn't moved from his seat. He continued to sit there with his hands placed calmly on his thighs, his expression bordering on sheepish.

"What are you waiting for?" she asked, flashing him the crumpled letter that George may or may not have taken a bite out of. "We have to go!"

"You go," he said, straightening his hat on his head as if that were his chief concern. "I have a feeling your legs are much faster than mine."

Maggie blinked in disbelief. "What do you mean? You came all the way here. You can't hold back now."

"It's for the best."

"But he'll want to see you. He'll want you to be a part of this."

The earl's mouth curved up slightly, but his eyes remained strained. "You're a sweet girl and I appreciate what you're trying to do, but I know my son. I'll watch, don't worry about that, but I'll do so from a distance."

Maggie glanced at the letter, suddenly feeling completely adrift. "I don't want to do this on my own."

The earl's expression was kind. He nodded toward the crowd of people. "You're not. Now go to Michael. Tell them to give the people the fight they came for."

IT HADN'T RAINED in days, but the soft field still tried to eat Maggie's boots with every step. Without Lord Oliver with her, it was difficult elbowing through the excitable horde, trying to carve a path toward the front. A few times she stood on tiptoes and managed to spot Michael, but calling out to him didn't work. The atmosphere was too charged; everyone seemed to be yelling or arguing at the top of their lungs.

Getting to Michael was like climbing a mountain that kept falling out from underneath her feet. One step forward, two steps back.

But Maggie told herself to keep going. She was making headway, however small. Five minutes into the struggle and her calves began to burn from the effort. Nevertheless, the smells buoyed her. The more she trudged through the bodies, the more pungent the tobacco and sweat-stained men became, which could only mean one thing—she was within reach.

But then the entire throng erupted in cheers as Maggie heard a decisive *thud*.

"No!" she screamed. It couldn't be over. That couldn't be Michael's body hitting the ground. She still had time. Didn't she?

She craned her neck, but it was useless. Everyone else was doing the same thing to see if the fallen boxer would make it back to his feet.

"Who was it?" Maggie asked anyone around her. "Who got knocked down?"

But the only answer she received was a harsh and guttural "Fuck!"

Maggie felt an insistent hand on her arm, and she twirled around to find Lord Oliver towering over her with an expression that could frighten the dead.

"What are you going here—alone?" he yelled over the clamor.

Maggie squirmed out of his hold. She couldn't stand anyone touching her right now. Nothing could be contained, not her disappointment nor her failure. "Who was it?" she pleaded. "Who went down?"

Lord Oliver returned a curious stare. "It was Harrison," he answered. "Michael connected cleanly with his jaw. It was gorgeous."

Relief washed over her. "Pick me up. Pick me up," she said, slapping the duke in the chest until he did as she asked. Holding on to her waist, he lifted her until she had the ring in her sights. Oliver had been right, though Harrison was no longer on the ground. He was limping over to his corner, where he would be given thirty seconds to contain himself before needing to meet

Michael at the line for the next round.

Oliver's voice floated up to her. "I would have expected Michael to show a little more emotion after that hit," he said.

Maggie's gaze shifted to Michael. He waited in his corner next to Tommy without any sign that he'd just put the champion on the mat. "He doesn't think he's going to win," she whispered to herself.

"Then he's a fool," Oliver spat, setting her back on the ground. "You shouldn't take a fight if you don't believe you can win. It's no fun for the rest of us. What's that?"

Maggie shook her head, noticing the duke's interest in the letter she still clutched in her hand. "Nothing. I have to go."

"Don't go," he whined, pulling her back to his side. "I'm all alone. Stay and talk to me."

Maggie rolled her eyes, wriggling out of his hold. "Where are your paid companions?"

He returned a sulk. "They're *companioning* other people tonight. It's my fault. I haven't been particularly good company lately."

"I'm sorry for that, Your Grace," she replied, tunneling into the crowd with more vigor. "But I really must go."

"How rude you are! Aren't you going to ask me *why* I haven't been good company?"

Maggie threw him a beseeching look over her shoulder. "Later, Oliver. I'll ask you later, I promise."

He threw up his hands. "When?"

"After Michael wins!"

Maggie was almost there. Tommy was only a few feet away, his back to her as he yelled at his fighter. "For God's sake, Mike! Use your feet. Are you trying to let him hit you?"

She watched his shoulders slump. It had only been a few minutes since Michael had knocked Harrison down, but it felt like the entire match had changed. The air was different, as was the mood of the crowd. No one expected Michael to win, and when Harrison fell, it seemed like an upset might occur. Now, with Michael taking punch after punch and wobbling on his toes, the inevitable was happening. He didn't have long.

Maggie stretched out her arm. She was just about to grab Tommy's shoulder when she heard that fateful thud again, and this time she instantly saw who was on the floor.

"Stay down, fancy lad," a man next to her yelled, waving a newspaper high above his head. Others piled on, echoing the words, proverbially kicking Michael while his body lay beaten and prone in the ring.

Tommy, to his credit, would never give up so easily. "Get up, scrapper!" he cried, hanging on to the ropes. "Get up!"

Maggie reached his side, slamming into him. Tommy gave her one bewildered stare before going back to his work. But Michael wasn't listening to him anymore.

His eyes were fixed on Maggie.

She had to fight to contain herself. Half of Michael's face was covered in blood; the other was shiny and swollen. One eye still worked, but the other was so puffy that she doubted it was of any use. He lifted his hand off the mat, and when he opened his mouth, blood trickled out. "Get out of here," he yelled.

Maggie stood her ground. "I'm not leaving," she said with unwavering intensity. "Get up, Michael. Get up. You can do it."

He shook his head against the ground. The whole scene seemed to slow, as if the ring were underwater. Maggie watched the anguish tear at him as he considered getting to his feet, fighting on. His body wasn't made to quit, and that realization may have chained him to the ground more than Harrison's left jab.

"Please, Michael," she begged. "I need you to get up. Now." She beckoned him to her. "You need to hear something very important."

Maggie flashed the letter, but Michael only squinted at it. However, something had clearly worked, because he started to move. Bit by bit his body snapped back together, and, to the crowd's thunderous applause, he made it back to his feet and stumbled to his corner.

"Goddammit, Maggie," he shouted, leaning against Tommy

for support. "You shouldn't see this. Wait for me inside the inn. I'll be there soon."

"No," she cried. "I have to show you something."

"It can wait."

"It can't! Just listen to me!" Maggie flung the letter at his bruised chest. "Some people can look at something one thousand different ways and not understand it, not find what they're looking for. I tried and I failed—"

His expression crumpled in despair. "Stop, Maggie. It's over. Just let me—"

She cupped his chin in her palm, raising his head. "But I'm not George."

"What?"

She smiled proudly. "George only needed one try." She nodded at the letter in his hands.

Michael stared at it for a few seconds, though comprehension was slow to come. But Maggie noticed an important clue right away—his voice got stronger. "What is this? What are you saying? Is this what I think it is?"

"I'm saying you owe my dog and me an apology. And maybe some sausages."

His swollen eye fell on her, and Maggie bit her lip to keep from crying. She saw suffering and carnage in that eye, but she also saw hope. "I don't have any on me," he said.

"Then why don't you win, and we'll call it even."

Michael's hands dropped to his sides. She grabbed the letter back for safekeeping.

"I don't... I don't understand."

Maggie took his head in her hands and rested his forehead against hers. "I'm telling you to win, scrapper. Don't be the man you were born to be. Be the man you are. Do you think you can do that for me?"

Michael leaned back, and this time when he opened his mouth, the blood on his teeth didn't make her wince. Because he gave her a smile.

"I can do that, Maggie. I can do that."

Chapter Twenty-Six

THE DUKE OF Winchester poured so much brandy in Michael's glass that it spilled out over the top.

"Enough, enough," Michael said, taking his drink back. "I can't possibly have any more!"

Lord Oliver gave him a disgusted look. "Yes, you can. I've never drunk with a bare-knuckle champion before, so you are going to indulge me."

Michael watched as Maggie rolled her eyes heavenward, a small smile peeking through as she continued to work on his face. Just like after the O'Shaughnessy match, Maggie had met him in the little room at the Oyster Inn and grabbed the clean linen on the bureau. Unlike after that match, she wasn't alone for long.

The duke had forced his way in just as Michael was tearing the linen out of Maggie's hand and leading her to the bed. Never one to be left out, Tommy followed on his heels. Apparently, everyone decided that Michael would celebrate that night, whether he liked it or not.

In all honesty, he didn't mind it all that much.

"Top me up, Your Grace," Tommy said, holding his empty glass out to the duke, who didn't hesitate to fulfill the order.

Maggie giggled, leaning over Michael's left side, inspecting his puffy eye. He had thought O'Shaughnessy had ham hocks for fists, but Harrison was in a league all his own. But he was the champion.

No. Not anymore, he isn't, Michael reminded himself. *He* was the new bare-knuckle champion.

Tommy tossed his drink back and wiped his mouth on the back of his hand. His eyes shone like those of a man who'd just seen the divine, or better—a man whose hard work had just paid off. "I can't wait to read the headline: *Fancy Lad Takes Down Champion.*" He hugged himself like a giddy, *drunk* child. "I don't think I've ever been this happy in my life!" His excitement plummeted, and he looked at Michael with alarm. "Mike, what do we do now?"

"You win," Oliver answered drolly, refilling Tommy's drink. "And then you do it again and again." He lifted his glass in a toast. "And maybe one of those times, I might even bet on you."

Maggie's hand paused over Michael's eye, and her skirts twirled as she faced the duke. Michael was in too good a mood to listen to their arguing or care about the familiar way they spoke to one another. His one good eye was planted on Maggie's lovely hips as she unleashed her ire on the duke. A river of hair had fallen out of her bun, and it mesmerized him as it waved over her back. Michael couldn't wait for the well-meaning bastards to leave. He needed to lie down, and he knew exactly where he wanted his head to go.

He thought it best to make Lord Oliver aware that Maggie would not be driving home with him that night.

Michael stood up, wrapping his arm around Maggie's waist, pulling her to his side. She was in mid-rant, but she stopped instantly when he gave her a little squeeze. "I will take Maggie home tonight, so you needn't wait for her if you want to leave," he said, hoping his hint wasn't that obvious.

Turned out it wasn't. Lord Oliver lifted his shoulders, clearly bewildered. "Why would I want to leave? And why would I be waiting for Maggie?"

Maggie tensed. Michael eyed her curiously. "I thought you

came with her?"

The duke scoffed. "I am not that woman's keeper." He took another sip. "God help the man who is."

"I am," Michael stated a little too possessively. "I am her keeper." He slid Maggie in front of him, blocking the duke from view. "Maggie?" he said, waiting for her gaze to meet his. It took longer than he would have liked. "Who brought you here today? And now that we're on the subject, I think it's time you told me how you came to have that letter."

Maggie's shoulders bunched up toward her ears. "Does it *really* matter?" she asked. "Isn't it enough to know that we have it and we're safe?"

"No."

Maggie frowned. She played with the buttons of his shirt, and it felt so damned good that Michael was certain she was trying to distract him.

"Maggie," he prodded, "do you have something you want to tell me?"

"Michael, I have *so* many things I want to tell you," she exclaimed, wrapping her arms around his neck. Despite their audience, she rose on her tiptoes and covered his mouth with hers in a savagely sweet kiss that Michael felt all the way down to his toes. She pulled away, gifting him with that sultry smile that he craved so much. "How can you expect me to settle on one? Do you want to know how much I love you? That I'm proud of you? That I can't wait to be your wife and the mother of your children? Because I do, and I am, and I can't. Will that do?"

Yes, that would do just fine. But she was missing something. "What else?" he asked.

Her eyes widened. "Oh, yes. That you're mine. Always and forever. Mine."

Yes. That was it. Being champion was a good thing, there was no arguing with that. But being Maggie's was infinitely more satisfying. He could be that for the rest of his life.

Michael seized her again, laying claim to her mouth, dying

little deaths over and over again as her tongue mingled with his. It wasn't until Lord Oliver coughed that Michael remembered they weren't alone in the room and that he'd asked Maggie a once-important question that had completely slipped his mind.

He sniffed her neck to fill his lungs with the floral notes of her soap, but only came back with his father's scent. The damned man practically soaked his letters in his perfume, and Maggie had clung to one for most of the night.

However, that hardly made sense. After all these years, the perfume on the letter couldn't be *that* strong. Maggie smelled like she'd been in her father's company... but how was that possible?

She was here with him, and his father was... his father was...

Standing in the doorway of Michael's room at the Oyster Inn, staring right at him.

The Earl of Waverly coughed lightly and locked his hands behind his back. "I apologize if I'm interrupting..."

Maggie moved at once. She went to Michael's father and kissed both of his cheeks. *Christ,* Michael thought, *is the old man actually blushing?*

She hooked her arm through the earl's and towed him into the room, introducing him to Tommy and Oliver.

"It's been a long time, Your Grace," the earl told Oliver warmly. Perhaps his suavity sparked something in the duke, because he managed to straighten his spine and act like a gentleman for longer than a couple of minutes as the two chatted over their estates. Apparently, the earl's had a badger problem.

When Oliver asked about the current state of the earl's farms, Michael couldn't take it any longer.

"What are you doing here?"

The duke raised his brow and slinked away from the conversation, joining Tommy by the brandy bottle. Maggie took his place by the earl's side.

She raised her chin. "I asked him to come. He helped me find the letter."

Michael nodded, keeping his focus on his father. "Is that

true?"

The earl nodded in the exact same way. Once again, Michael was struck by their resemblance. "Maggie asked me for help, and I gave it."

Michael glanced between them. "Maggie doesn't like to ask for help."

His father chuckled. "She doesn't like to give up, either. And she didn't. Not on you."

Michael reached for his ribs. Harrison hadn't broken anything, but he'd been close. And every time Michael took a deep breath, he paid for it.

His father watched him wince. He glanced at Maggie and forced a smile. "I think I should go. It's a long way back to Leicester. I just wanted to say congratulations."

"No, stay!" Maggie said, gripping his arm, but the earl merely gave her a kiss on the cheek and unwrapped himself from her hold.

"I'm glad I came. Thank you for giving me a chance to be a part of my son's life. I will never forget it."

Lord Oliver and Tommy nodded at the older man, raising their glasses as he took his leave.

Maggie whipped back to Michael, and he wanted to tell her to stop scowling at him, but it had been a long day. His muscles ached; his heart was bursting; his life was full. He only had the energy to ask his father one question, because it was the only one that mattered to him.

"Father… are you glad I won?"

The Earl of Waverly turned back to Michael with cloudy, loving eyes. "Oh, my son," he said. "You have no idea."

Epilogue

W ITH MICHAEL BEING so adamant on a quick wedding, it surprised Maggie when he eventually relented and gifted Aunt Alice a full eight weeks to plan the event. She'd been grateful, to say the least.

He'd told Maggie that he wanted his bruises to heal before he met her at the end of the altar, and Maggie had taken him at his vainglorious word.

She shouldn't have.

When her parents hurried into Aunt Alice's townhome the day before the wedding and crushed her in their arms, Maggie realized that Michael had postponed the event for her benefit. Somewhere, somehow, he'd understood how important it was for her parents to be a part of the wedding.

In the drawing room, sandwiched between her lively little brothers, Maggie spent the last day of her singledom listening to her parents' stories, soaking up their far-off tales of intrigue and gossip. She reveled in their excitement and their limitless zest for life and adventure. And she felt complete.

Not home. But complete. Able to move forward in her life.

Home, Maggie now concluded, was wherever Michael was. The lovely man had believed that he was giving Maggie her family for her wedding day, but it was more than that. In the long, joyous hours she spent with her parents, she was reminded of who they were—who they would always be. And Maggie would never be able to change them. The marquis and his wife loved their children in their own way. And Maggie had to accept that. It wasn't the way that she would experience a family with Michael, but it had been *their* way. And, perhaps, if they hadn't been that way, Maggie might not have become the woman she had. The woman that loved Michael. The woman that he loved.

So, she sat there with her siblings and lost herself in the familial moment, not wondering about what could have or might have been. Maggie only felt love for the family that she had, and was determined to keep that feeling with her forever.

The following day, when Lady Maggie married Lord Michael, they were surrounded by family, and the friends who were just as important as family.

And they only had eyes for one another.

Their house was a place of love. Their doors were always open to any and all who wanted to be a part of it.

Michael's relationship with his father took time, but that too reached an acceptance that neither man had dared hope for.

And new life was the balm that smoothed over the old scars, hiding them away until no one could even tell where they'd once smarted.

The labor had been long. Michael was routinely informed that first babies usually went like this, but that didn't stop the tortured man from ruining his carpet with all his pacing back and forth. For two days, he waited in anguish, listening to Maggie's wails and heavy, laborious breathing from behind thin walls and (when the midwife banned him from the corridor) down winding staircases.

Tommy, knowing a thing or two about settling a fighter's nerves, was the one to take the matter in hand and thrust a full bottle of gin in Michael's. If the trainer couldn't stop Michael from fixating on every scream, then he would get him so soused that he wouldn't be able to hear anything over the ringing in his ears.

And that worked, to the thanks of everyone in the home—especially Maggie, who was too busy at the moment to worry about her husband's nerves.

When Michael first laid eyes on his beautiful, tiny, healthy daughter, he didn't trust himself to hold her; however, when Maggie offered Lady Jeanne with a proud, tired smile, he couldn't resist. The lethal hands that fought for a living, that pummeled men to the ground, that had saved him from a childhood of fear and sadness, shook like crisp leaves when he accepted his daughter in her tight, swaddled bundle. And he had never been more grateful for such an unearthly gift, nor had he ever realized how unworthy he was of it.

He turned to Maggie, leaning over to kiss her forehead, but she had already fallen asleep with that same proud smile on her pale face.

"The real fighter in the family needs her rest," Michael whispered to the newborn. He backed away from the bed, taking his daughter to the nearest window, where dawn was finally breaking over the terrifying, otherworldly night. His body swayed in a natural rhythm as his daughter fit perfectly in the crux of his elbow, as if God had known and designed Michael just this way for the comfort of his firstborn child.

He kissed her fuzzy head, grinning at the way her entire body squirmed before settling back into its deep sleep. Being born must be an exhausting endeavor, Michael thought. And his daughter had done it like a champion. There was so much more to come.

And right there, in the beginning of a new day, with the nascent sun's rays shining upon his daughter's closed eyes, Michael was filled with peace. Because he knew this little girl would be able to handle anything that life threw at her. She was her mother's daughter, after all.

THAT WASN'T TO say that Michael wouldn't do his damnedest protecting the independent women in his life. As he would always say, someone had to save them from themselves.

Which was why no one was allowed to visit his daughter for the first two months. Maggie laughed at her husband, calling him overly protective—and he was—but the truth was that he merely wanted them to himself. Perfect moments in time were fleeting. Michael would string out these short days with his wife and child for as long as he could, knowing full well that doors would have to be opened sooner or later. The outside would always yearn to come in—especially when a viscountess gave birth to the most beautiful and intelligent baby in the history of babies. Maggie *did* agree with Michael on that part.

Maggie's parents were the first to arrive. Blessedly, they were in between travels, and had halted further plans until the birth. Although Michael could not fully understand the couple and their meandering ways, he'd come to enjoy their company and appreciate the joy they gave his wife when they were in town. They fawned over their granddaughter, which, to Michael's eyes, also showed good and sound judgment.

His mother came next. The Countess of Waverly's staid composure was never going to match the Amesburys' zeal, but she doted on the child in her own austere manner. Michael had been touched when he saw her wipe away a tear from her cheek as she held the baby, thinking that no one was watching.

He hadn't anticipated that.

Nor had he expected the countess to come every day after, stopping in at the house, saying it was on her way to this event or that. Maggie, always hoping to foster a kinship with his mother, delighted at the time spent together, and Michael wouldn't complain while they left him out of most of their conversations.

His father was the last to come. Maggie had just finished feeding the baby when the butler announced the arrival of the Earl of Waverly. He swallowed up the doorway minutes later.

And he wasn't alone.

A gentleman joined him. Michael knew him at once. Over the past year, he had done better, visiting his father at his estate, and Arthur had slowly introduced him to the man he shared his life with. Hardly all at once, it was like a slow drip. Maxwell no longer fled a room once Michael entered it. They three men had shared drinks together, gone on rides. Conversations weren't long or particularly intimate. But for the time being, it had been enough. It made Arthur happy. And Michael realized that he wanted his father to be happy. Just as he was.

"Oh, my darling girl, I knew you could do it!" the earl cried, charging into the room like a conquering father. He claimed Jeanne at once, holding her to his chest like a man who had done it countless times before. Michael's heart thumped oddly as he watched his father turn to utter mush around his daughter, cooing nonsensical words, making ridiculous noises in an effort to get Jeanne to smile and laugh.

Which she did. Instantly.

The earl held the tiny baby up in front of him, and the two stared at one another with the same ice-blue eyes, studying this new person who was now such an integral part of their life. "She's perfect," the earl announced. "Absolutely perfect." He tucked the baby into his chest once more and turned to his son. "I knew Maggie could do it; I had no doubt... but you, sir—I didn't know you had it in you to create such magnificence. But then again, you are half me."

Michael laughed... because he didn't know what else to do and because he was determined to never be annoyed or angry or anything other than mild-mannered around his daughter. "Thank you... I suppose."

"You're welcome!" the earl chirped, his entire focus still on Jeanne, who yawned widely. "So lovely," he whispered before looking to Maxwell, who'd stayed near the door. "Max! Get over here at once. Have you ever seen a baby as beautiful and perfect as this? I'll answer for you, no you haven't. What are you doing over there? Come here. Hold her! You have to smell her." The earl tucked his nose under Jeanne's chin and inhaled with closed eyes. "She smells like *new*. Did you know that new could have a smell? It does. It's her. It's perfectly her."

Maxwell shook his head, smiling shyly at the floor. "It's fine, Arthur. I like watching you hold your granddaughter."

Arthur stared at the man, disappointment evident in his expression. An unspoken conversation seemed to flow between them, and, resigned, Arthur eventually returned his attention to the baby.

"Please?" Maggie said softly from her chair. It took Michael a beat to realize she was speaking to Maxwell. "She's such a sweet baby. She won't cry, if that's what you're worried about. You can hold her. I'm sure she would love that."

Arthur's face lit up again, and he knew he'd won. He walked the baby to Maxwell, who had stepped a few inches inside the room. He extended his arms, mirroring the way Arthur held his.

"There now," Arthur said, handing the baby over. "Good. Just like that. Mind her head. Yes. Exactly. Look at you!"

Michael was transfixed by the pair. Arthur hugged Maxwell's side as they regarded the baby together. Were *his* eyes glassy? Or were Michael's?

He heard the chair squeak, and Maggie came up beside him. She wrapped her arm around Michael's waist and held him close. Maggie had known what to do. She always did.

Maxwell laughed softly, pulling Michael's attention from his wife. "She's so small."

"Babies usually are," Arthur quipped. The earl looked up from the child and caught his son's eye. So much was said in that one, short moment. "Thank you."

Michael nodded.

Arthur dashed a tear from his eye, not bothering to hide the emotion. "All right now, you can't be the only one to hold the baby. Give me back my grandchild," he ordered Maxwell jovially, accepting Jeanne back in his arms. Maxwell appeared a little relieved—and wistful—after the exchange was made.

"What is it?" Maggie asked him.

Maxwell blanched, caught off guard by the attention. "Ah, it's nothing," he replied, swiping a hand through the thin brown strands left on top of his head. "I just didn't think it was possible to love something so quickly. It's overwhelming." He blinked and jerked back as if realizing that he'd just said the words out loud. "I'm sorry, my lord," he told Michael. "I didn't mean to... I shouldn't have said—"

Michael waved a hand in the air. "No harm. I know exactly what you mean. And you're right." He wrapped his arm around his wife's middle, gazing down at her bright, smiling face. "Overwhelming is the perfect word for this."

For all of this. For this new baby. This new world. This new family. It would take time. But they would forge forward.

Together.

ABOUT THE AUTHOR

I'm a lifelong reader of romance novels. Some of my earliest memories are of sneaking into my mom's room at night and stealing any books I could find.

After moving around quite a bit, I've finally put down roots in New England with my two sons and husband. I've always been a writer, starting out in newspapers, but it wasn't until my sons began going to school full-time that I began working toward my dream of becoming a romance author.

I enjoy crocheting toys for my kids, hiking with my Saint Bernard, and watching Real Housewives on the couch with my very old and very fat pugs.